SECOND TIME AROUND

"You must have loved her very much," Hannah said in an empathetic voice.

"My family arranged my marriage, Hannah," Max admitted. "Love I did not expect, but it grows from a strong bond of friendship that comes slowly with respect and regard . . ."

Hannah listened with fascination. He was loyal and steadfast, a man who made a commitment and honored it.

Hannah placed a gentle, reassuring hand on Max's arm in understanding of the ordeal this man had suffered as he sought so valiantly to hold his family together.

"I would never marry again without love," Hannah said.

To her surprise, he covered her hand with his work-roughened one. "Love is that important to you?"

"I didn't think so once, but yes, now it is that important."

"I see," was all he said. They gazed into each other's eyes for moments, for she had no right to hope, although if truth be known, she had begun to.

Unable to tolerate the burgeoning tension filling the room any longer, Hannah tried to retrieve her hand and rise, but he held her tight.

"No. Do not go this time."

He was so near that she could feel his warm, moist breath caress her neck, his eyes silently devour her lips, his fingers memorizing the contours of her hand, mesmerizing and heightening her senses until she leaned toward him and closed her eyes . . .

Taylor—made Romance From Zebra Books

WHISPERED KISSES   (3830, $4.99/5.99)
Beautiful Texas heiress Laura Leigh Webster never imagined that her biggest worry on her African safari would be the handsome Jace Elliot, her tour guide. Laura's guardian, Lord Chadwick Hamilton, warns her of Jace's dangerous past; she simply cannot resist the lure of his strong arms and the passion of his *Whispered Kisses*.

KISS OF THE NIGHT WIND   (3831, $4.99/$5.99)
Carrie Sue Strover thought she was leaving trouble behind her when she deserted her brother's outlaw gang to live her life as schoolmarm Carolyn Starns. On her journey, her stagecoach was attacked and she was rescued by handsome T.J. Rogue. T.J. plots to have Carrie lead him to her brother's cohorts who murdered his family. T.J., however, soon succumbs to the beautiful runaway's charms and loving caresses.

FORTUNE'S FLAMES   (3825, $4.99/$5.99)
Impatient to begin her journey back home to New Orleans, beautiful Maren James was furious when Captain Hawk delayed the voyage by searching for stowaways. Impatience gave way to uncontrollable desire once the handsome captain searched *her* cabin. He was looking for illegal passengers; what he found was wild passion with a woman he knew was unlike all those he had known before!

PASSIONS WILD AND FREE   (3828, $4.99/$5.99)
After seeing her family and home destroyed by the cruel and hateful Epson gang, Randee Hollis swore revenge. She knew she found the perfect man to help her—gunslinger Marsh Logan. Not only strong and brave, Marsh had the ebony hair and light blue eyes to make Randee forget her hate and seek the love and passion that only he could give her.

Available wherever paperbacks are sold, or order direct from the Publisher. Send cover price plus 50¢ per copy for mailing and handling to Penguin USA, P.O. Box 999, c/o Dept. 17109, Bergenfield, NJ 07621. Residents of New York and Tennessee must include sales tax. DO NOT SEND CASH.

GWEN CLEARY
TENDER HEART

ZEBRA BOOKS
KENSINGTON PUBLISHING CORP.

To Samantha,
the greatest joy of my life.

From a duckling
herein
Emerges a swan,
and
This
It is my song . . .
—*Gwen*

ZEBRA BOOKS are published by

Kensington Publishing Corp.
850 Third Avenue
New York, NY 10022

Zebra and the Z logo Reg. U.S. Pat. & TM Off. The Lovegram logo is a trademark of Kensington Publishing Corp.

First Printing: August, 1994

Printed in the United States of America

Prologue

"You make your bed, you lie in it. That's what I always say, Hannah, as did your grandmother before me. Believe you me, it's a sound maxim." A triumphant expression on her etched face, the white-haired woman swung out a bony arm. "Just look around at how well it has served you for the last five years. Never let it slip from your mind, Hannah. Never."

"No, Mother, I shan't." Her mother's favorite adage stung Hannah Turner. Tennyson's words echoed in her mind. *With a little hoard of maxims preaching down a daughter's heart.*

Directing her attention out the window at the rain drenching the sprawling estate, Hannah gingerly touched the tender bruises hidden beneath the fine watered-silk at her collarbone to remind herself of the decision she'd reached. Tonight she was going to tell the biggest lie of her life.

For an instant Hannah wondered if her mother had a favorite old cliché for that too.

"Hannah, don't stand at the window, fidgeting with your fingers as if you're hiding some earth-shattering secret."

Hannah's palm dropped to her midriff, and despite the knot that usually formed in her throat when her mother began another lecture, her courage impulsively returned. "Mother, what do you think Emmett would say if I were pregnant?"

"Don't be silly. You know how he feels about children." Mildred glanced up at her daughter. There was an unmistakable glow in her daughter's eyes, which caused her heart to sink.

"Oh, my God," Mildred huffed out, "you didn't dare go against your husband this time, did you?" The older woman waited, praying without hope for her daughter's denial. When it was not forthcoming, she sighed. "You foolish little idiot. Does he know?"

"No." Hannah lowered her eyes under the oppressive intensity of her mother's disappointment in her. For as long as she could remember, Hannah had felt it. It was always there. No matter what she did she had somehow managed to come up lacking in her mother's eyes.

"Good," Mildred sighed in relief. There was still time to rectify Hannah's stupidity. "I'll arrange for you to pay a visit to that woman down by the river who takes care of such mistakes."

Hannah raised her head and opened her mouth to proclaim that it was not a mistake, but her mother waved her off.

"Until I make the necessary arrangements, you are to keep your mouth shut and run Emmett's estate in accordance with the written instructions he leaves for you daily."

Horrified by the very lengths to which her mother planned to stoop in order to placate Emmett, Hannah self-consciously tucked an errant chestnut curl behind her ear and swallowed all further thoughts of protesting. Her mother was too blinded by Emmett's enormous wealth to listen to reason.

"You are so fortunate to live among all these exquisite treasures, and I'll not see you lose a one of them due to your momentary lunacy. How many other plump, mousy-haired spinsters have been given the same opportunities that Emmett has given you?" Mildred snorted, gazing around at the sheer opulence of the gilded room. "So fortunate."

"Yes, fortunate, Mother." Hannah forced a tight smile and bit her tongue to keep from retorting that she had no intention of giving up her unborn child.

Hannah desperately wanted this baby. She knew she had been a mistake, which her mother had futilely tried to rectify, and never let her forget it. But there was no point initiating another fruitless argument with her mother.

Hannah stared at the rumpled bed. *It is my bed and I have lain in it. And now I am about to lie because of it.*

Her stomach churning over what she was about to do, Hannah fought the rising waves of nausea the rest of the afternoon.

Sitting at her dressing table, Hannah closed the last lace-covered button at her throat and pinned a heart-shaped diamond heirloom brooch at her shoulder. Praying that Emmett would soften his stance once she had time to prepare him for the joys of fatherhood, Hannah took a buoying breath and headed down the stairs to face Emmett.

Wind and rain howled into the foyer as Emmett thrust open the door and staggered inside, causing Hannah to halt at the bottom of the winding marble staircase.

Despite her uneasiness at the possibility that Emmett had been drinking again, Hannah tried to focus her attention on what had originally drawn her to him. Her fingers used to curl in those thick blond waves. Dimples used to punctuate his fine patrician features when he smiled. And with his love he had promised her the world.

But when she glanced into cold, glaring blue eyes shot with red, her heart began to pound with the reality of those empty promises, now riddled with cruelty. It was embedded there, that same brutal intensity she had witnessed all too many times during the past few years.

She forced a smile. "I had the cook personally

prepare your favorite supper, Emmett. Why don't we go directly into the dining room tonight?"

"What's the hurry? I haven't had a glass of wine yet." Emmett tried to focus his bleary vision on his wife's buxom form. She looked almost radiant tonight. Too radiant with his grandmother's diamond heirloom brooch winking at her shoulder.

"What are you standing there for? Go fix me a drink," he hissed. "Then I want to know about your secret little visit to the damned doctor right after I left this morning."

For an instant she wondered how he knew. But the word *secret* caused her hand to slide down over her flat belly and a trembling smile hovered around her lips.

This morning the doctor had validated her suspicions: she was pregnant. She had been filled with joy at the news, then her conscience assailed her. She had done the unprecedented, the inconceivable, the unforgivable. She had ignored her husband's wishes and deliberately disobeyed him.

Now she was about to add to her sins. She was going to tell an outright lie. After she deliberately lied to her husband about her condition until it was too late for him to demand that she rid herself of the child she carried, their lives would be forever changed.

"Well, what are you standing there for? Answer me," he demanded, breaking into her moment of reverie. "What the hell were you doing paying a secret visit to that doctor?"

Hannah's breath caught at the force of the accusation in his voice. "I did not feel well," she offered in a choked whisper.

There it was—The Lie.

It was out, standing like a mighty sentry of doom between them. There was no retrieving it now, no calling it back. "I thought perhaps the doctor could provide me with a tonic or something. I am sorry. I should have sought your advice first."

A heartless smile stretched Emmett's thin lips. "Don't you think I know what you're up to when I am not here?"

Hannah lowered her eyes and hurried to pour his favorite libation. When he was in one of his moods it was wise not to try to reason with him. As she passed him, he grabbed her arm in a hurtful grip.

"If you think that when I'm away you can use those sparkling green eyes"—he squeezed her chin with his other hand and forced her to look into his dark face—"and those luscious full lips to seduce some pathetic doctor, you're wrong!"

"Emmett, please, you're hurting me."

His fingers dug deeper into her arm. "I'll do more than that if you don't tell me the truth. Now, *exactly what* are you up to with that medical quack? The truth, Hannah."

She opened her mouth to embellish on the lie

she had rehearsed, but he cut her off. "Do not try to plead the vapors or some other such silly female ailment. I know better. The detective's report indicated you were in the man's office for over an hour," he said, the accusation in his voice rising in concert with his ire.

Frightened by his latest unfounded allegation, Hannah wrenched her arm out of his grasp and took a step backward. "You've had a detective following me?" she cried in disbelief. "How could you!"

"I picked you and your mother out of a gutter. You think I don't know about your kind? I have seen the way men look at you when they think I'm not aware. I know what's on their minds, and I'll not have my wife whoring behind my back," he shouted. "You hear me?"

His hand shot out to strike Hannah, but the door he had left ajar was blown open by a gale-force wind gust. In that instant Hannah's five-pound, foxlike black pup scurried in snarling and sank bared teeth into Emmett's ankle.

"Yeow!" Emmett howled. Thrown off balance, he broke his fall by grabbing at Hannah, which sent her smashing headfirst against the wall.

Hannah's palm flew to her stinging cheek in horror and fear. Emmett's rage was already out of control, and now her tiny, pointy-eared pup would suffer his wrath as well.

"I'll teach you!" Emmett roared, and raised the back of his hand, stumbling toward her.

"No! Never again!" Hannah grabbed a nearby umbrella to ward him off and then scrambled out into the soaking rain, the pup barking and racing after her.

Warm yellow light surrounding Emmett's dark shadow spilled out the door after her. He bellowed obscenities. "If you don't come back this minute, I swear I'll divorce you before that expensive gown I bought and paid for dries. You cannot hide from me. No matter where you go I'll find you, and then send you back to that shack down by the river penniless. You hear me?"

He continued shouting threats, but Hannah did not stop. She ran, knowing only that she had an unborn child to protect now; she had to get as far away as was humanly possible from the monster Emmett had become.

One

Hannah peered out the train window as miles and miles of prairie rolled by. Other than heading west, she did not know or care where she was going. She had no doubt that now she was a disgraced and divorced woman, unheard of in Emmett's social circle. But rather than be exhausted by two days of noise, dust, and hard benches in the hot train car, Hannah experienced a great sense of relief. She had finally regained the courage to take control of her life, and was never going to relinquish it again.

"Mind if I join you?"

Disturbed from her musings, Hannah glanced up and stared, open-mouthed. Standing over her was the largest middle-aged woman Hannah had ever seen. Beneath a hideous plumed hat, the woman's gray-streaked hair was pulled back into a severe knot, accentuating her reptilian features. Her hands grasping a huge bag in front of her were so rough, they appeared scaly.

The woman plopped down and straightened a gray-green gingham dress, which gave further credence to her lizardlike appearance. "Name's Timm. Wilma Timm."

"Hannah Turner." Hannah forced a smile while the giant of a woman pumped her hand as if she were cranking an obstinate siphon.

"Your man allow you to dress like that?" Wilma questioned of the lavish lacy lavender dress and looked around. "Where is he? You ain't travelin' alone, now, are you?"

"I don't have a man and I don't need one," Hannah said with conviction, causing the Timm woman to narrow sly, disbelieving eyes toward her while Hannah self-consciously straightened the skirt of the only dress she now owned.

Wilma crowed, "I've buried three husbands myself, and I'm aimin' to catch me number four. Why, any woman in her right mind needs a man to look after—"

"She's got me to look after her," a thin, scruffy youngster announced from the bench behind Hannah and promptly popped up, stunning Hannah before she could refute the woman's smug proclamation. "Why you askin' so many nosy questions?"

"Just makin' talk." Wilma's lips went tight when she glanced up. "You!"

"Yeah, me. Somethin' wrong with that?" the child said.

"If I could prove that you were the one who stole my train ticket, makin' me have to pay an additional fare, there would be."

The child smirked. "But you can't, can you?"

"Who are you?" Against her better judgment, Wilma restrained herself from rehashing the earlier confrontation she'd had with the conductor over the foul-mouthed moppet with that filthy cap drawn low over glaring brown eyes. The overdressed woman remained mute, and Wilma wondered if the pair of them could be in cahoots.

"Franc." The youngster glared at the big woman. The child clipped filthy fingers around the top of equally filthy denim overalls.

Wilma looked the youngun up and down, determined to ferret out the truth about her ticket. "Franc? That ain't no lad's hand, youngun. And unless I miss my guess, you ain't no boy, even though you're suited out like one of them grubby little beggars. What did you say your name was?"

Although Hannah wanted to maintain a low profile and not draw attention to herself, she felt an overwhelming urge to come to the aid of the young child dressed like a ragged street urchin. "Frances. After my grandmother," Hannah supplied, and tilted her chin up enough to project the impression that it truly was none of the Timm woman's business.

Hannah kept her face impassive despite the two pairs of disbelieving eyes that suddenly flashed in her direction. Wilma Timm's black eyes shone with annoyed doubt, and the child's were a mixture of wily astonishment and calculation. To Hannah's shock, the girl came around the bench and wedged herself between Hannah and Wilma Timm.

"Don't suppose a body can see the family resemblance none."

Nature's urgent call caused Wilma to take off her hat, get up, and set it on the seat. She shook a crooked finger at them. "Don't neither one of you go gettin' no fancy ideas while I'm gone. I'll be right back."

Hannah and Franc watched the big, overbearing woman pound down the aisle toward the washroom before the girl turned to Hannah.

"How'd you know the name my ma gived me?" Franc demanded.

"You mean Frances?"

"I go by Franc," the girl shot back.

Before Hannah could open her mouth to comment, Franc brought up a hand. "Don't go gettin' no fancy ideas, lady. I only rescued you—"

"Rescued me?" Hannah laughed at the thought of the spindly child rescuing her, when she had already liberated herself.

"From that bloated old lizard. I figgered you and me, we could be of use to each other. Look, I been watchin' you, lady. And the way I see it, you ain't got no worldly smarts, and you're hidin' somethin' in that big basket of yours."

Franc leaned over and lifted the lid before Hannah could stop her. A pair of watchful eyes stared back at her. With a pleased smirk, she lowered the lid. "You can get that aggrieved look off your face. I ain't gonna let on to nobody what you got in there. But you ain't gonna make it without somebody's help. That's for sure."

Hannah had let the girl have her say, but enough was enough. "If I do not have what it takes to care for myself and my pup, Panda Pie, in the basket, and I need your help, as you put it, what is it I can possibly offer you?" Hannah asked, amused and intrigued by the girl's outrageous notions.

Hannah had taken care of herself and her mother as a child in a ramshackle shanty they called home down by the river, although she had to admit that since she had married Emmett, she had not been allowed to make many decisions.

The girl's eyes shifted from side to side before she leaned close to Hannah. "I'll let you know. Always got to have a plan. Remember them words. You see, that dumb ol' conductor's been watchin' me. Those mean train people don't give kids a chance what's travelin' alone, even though I showed him the ticket fair 'n' square." Then for good measure she added, "And I doubt they'd take kindly to no dogs hid away neither."

Although Hannah feared for her precious pet, she troubled over the misguided child. "Are you traveling to join your folks?"

"Naw. Just goin' as far as the ticket takes me. Ain't never had no pa, and my ma's probably layin' underneath the nearest ruttin' man what's got a bottle and her price."

Recalling the distant memory of how her own drunk father had run off, Hannah's heart went out to the girl, and the thought of questioning Franc's curious comment about the ticket slipped from her mind. "I'm sorry."

"Don't be. I been takin' care of myself for well on four years now, since I was seven."

"Then how can I be of help to you?" Hannah asked, suddenly wanting to protect the child.

The girl's eyes lit up. "Next time that railroad man comes 'round, just make like we're kin, that's all."

Hannah thought about such an outrageous suggestion for a moment, then said, "I suppose there would be no harm done," although the nagging voice in the back of her mind warned that she may be making a big mistake.

A sly grin came to Franc's lips. "Good. I'll be your kid."

"My daughter?" Hannah murmured as her hand dropped to her belly and a strange warmth came over her. She had always wanted a daughter of her own. For a moment she considered that she may be carrying a daughter.

"Sure . . . Ma." Franc thrust out her hand, ending Hannah's brief moment of reverie. Franc wiggled her fingers. "Well?"

Hannah offered her hand, but the girl merely raised a sparse eyebrow. Agitated by the child's abrupt manner, Hannah said, "Yes?"

"Fork over enough cash so I can go get me somethin' to eat, Mommy . . . dear."

Hannah was flabbergasted at the girl's unmitigated gall, but she knew what it was like to go hungry, and the lengths one would go because of it. Against her better judgment Hannah dropped two coins into the girl's palm, then stared after her as she flounced off without so much as a thank-you.

Ignoring the child, Wilma Timm waddled back toward Hannah and plunked down, setting her bag beside her. She patted her ample chest. "Now that we're alone, tell me true. That youngun ain't really your kin, is she?"

It was now or never.

Another moment of reckoning was thrust upon Hannah. She either had to claim Franc and stand by her decision, or deny the girl.

Hannah's attention caught on Franc. The girl had her hand on the handle of the car door, staring intently at her. Franc's words rang in Hannah's ears: *Always got to have a plan.* A mother's instinctive protectiveness flowed into her veins.

Hannah titled her chin. "Frances is my daughter."

"I don't believe you," Wilma sneered, and glared at Hannah. "I don't know why you're lyin' for that brat, unless you're in cahoots. But I aim to ferret out the truth about my ticket," she proclaimed, and angrily stomped off.

Franc watched the big woman disappear into the next car, then Franc returned to sit next to Hannah.

"I thought you were going to the dining car."

"Had to look out after my interests," Franc answered without care. Not attempting to hide her actions, Franc rifled through Wilma Timm's bag.

"Put that bag down," Hannah insisted. "It does not belong to you."

"Don't matter." Managing to stay out of Hannah's grasp, Franc pulled out a small bundle wrapped in newspaper and made short work of the wrapping, exposing a plump ham sandwich. Without hesitation she bit into it. Then she tore off a corner and slipped it to the pup.

Franc's mouth full, she mumbled, "Quit bein' such a pure prude. That one don't know enough to leave good, honest folk like me be."

Hannah stared at the stolen sandwich in disbelief. Honest folk? Silently, she did not have to ask if Franc had indeed stolen Wilma Timm's ticket. "Stealing is wrong."

"A hungry gut don't care where the food comes from that drops into it." Franc continued chewing. She stopped when she noticed Hannah's disgusted expression. Franc gave a token guilty shrug. "Sorry." She ripped off a generous portion of the sandwich and held it out. "Here."

"No. And starting right now you will do no more stealing," Hannah stated flatly, and grabbed half the remains of the sandwich out of

Franc's hand before the child jumped out of reach. She ought to take Franc over her knee, but they were already attracting more regard than Hannah wanted.

It had been a mistake claiming Franc. Hannah herself was on the run, having pawned the heirloom brooch for money, and did not need to call attention to herself by inviting the kind of trouble Franc represented.

But Hannah's heart had gone out to the girl. The girl's sorry childhood reminded Hannah of her own youth, growing up in poverty on the river without a father. The townspeople had disapproved of her for no other reason than that the fatherless family had been dirt poor, just like Wilma Timm had disapproved of Franc. At least Hannah had had a mother, although she recollected a time when she had been forced to sneak into the Delaneys' garden and stole vegetables to survive.

While Hannah would not condone Franc's apparent thievery, she understood all to well that sometimes circumstances dictated that one did what one must to exist.

"I've seen that Timm woman's kind on the circuit before," Franc said, licking her fingers while she broke into Hannah's bitter memories.

"The circuit?" Hannah questioned in an effort to get her mind off such morbid thoughts.

Her gut still unsatisfied, Franc sulkily watched Hannah tuck the portion of the sandwich she'd taken away from Franc back inside the Timm woman's bag. "Women of the needle trade. That's what that old puffed-out lizard does, you know."

"Needle trade?"

"Her kind advertises in newspapers and word of mouth, and goes 'n' stays with farmers' and ranchers' families an' such, sewin' duds for months at a time. They get room 'n' board and get paid pretty good for their needlework, I hear."

"How do you know all that about Wilma Timm?" Hannah questioned, amazed by the girl's observations.

Franc rolled her eyes and shrugged. "Saw a note when I got the sandwich outta her bag. I ain't dumb, you know. I know my letters. You got to learn to be more sneakier or you'll never make it out here in the West. What'd you do, run away from your man?"

Hannah gasped. "How did you know?" she said before she thought better of it to lecture the girl on the evils of thievery.

Franc picked a sliver of ham from between her teeth and studied it for a moment before flicking it into the aisle. "Thought so. Anybody can see that white mark the ring left around your finger must of been from a weddin' band you recently shed."

Hannah slapped her right hand over her ring finger, her face growing grim. "I was married once, but I want nothing further to do with men . . . ever. I am perfectly capable of making my own way without a man's protection. Men only—"

"You horrid, thievin' youngun'! With your kind around, a honest body can't leave nothin' unattended for even a minute. Why, neither one of you is any better than the other. You're both nothin' but common thieves," Wilma bellowed, and snatched the crust left from her sandwich from Franc's hand. Balling the remnants in the day-old newspaper, Wilma furiously gathered up her belongings. "I'm going to find out what you're up to and see that you both pay for this!" she huffed, her face blotched purple with rage.

"I apologize for Franc. What she did was wrong, and I—"

Low growling sounds issued from Hannah's basket, cutting off Hannah's intended reparation and redirecting Wilma's attention. Her brow lifted into a suspicious line. "What was that?"

Before the Timm woman could continue with her inquisition, Franc grinned and let out a loud growl. "Woof, woof, woof."

Highly offended, Wilma drew up to her full height. "Why, you disgustin' little desert rat. How dare you!"

"Woof, woof, woof," Franc repeated with a smirk.

Wilma was shaking, she was so enraged. She shook an accusing finger at Hannah. "You mark my words. That little devil's spawn will end up in prison someday if you don't take her in hand and teach her some respect. Prison, you hear me. Prison!" She swung around and stomped over to the other end of the train car and dropped down on a bench, sullenly glaring at Hannah.

Hannah was horrified. She had not wanted to draw attention to herself, and now everyone in the car was openly staring at her. She rummaged through her reticule, intending to reimburse the Timm woman for the sandwich and ticket Franc had taken.

Money in hand, Hannah started to rise, but Franc grabbed her arm. "I wouldn't bother tryin' to buy her off if I was you."

"I'm not going to buy her off, as you put it. I'm going to reimburse her for the sandwich you stole. And I suspect the ticket as well."

"Won't do no good now, you know."

Hannah crossed her arms over her chest. "You did steal her ticket, didn't you?"

Franc shrugged her indifference. "So I took the ticket. She can afford another one. You might as well clear your mind about payin' for it. It wouldn't change nothin'. She hates us both now. And if I hadn't of thrown her off the track, she would of knowed you got a dog hid away, and we would of got kicked off the train for sure. So you see, I did you another favor."

Feeling frustrated by the morning's events, Hannah settled back in her seat. Sadly, she knew that what the little imp said was true. Wilma Timm had an ax to grind now and no apology or amount of money would appease her. And Franc had kept her little dog's presence hidden.

Franc's gaze settled on the money still in Hannah's hand. "You got much money?"

"I already gave you money for food," Hannah said suspiciously.

"Don't worry 'bout that. I got it safe." Franc patted her hip pocket. "By eatin' the old lizard's sandwich I already saved you money. See how much help I been since we teamed up?"

"We have not teamed up. And I do not condone stealing. But I will say that you definitely need someone to take you in hand."

"Give me the rest of what you got," Franc demanded, not knowing or caring what the word *condone* meant. When Hannah merely cocked a brow, the girl grew impatient and decided to take another tack. "Where're you goin'?"

"West. And you will not be getting any more money," Hannah set forth. There hadn't been much money while she was growing up, and once she married Emmett, he had handled all their finances. But she was not going to be tricked into turning over her meager fortune to a mere child—if one could call Franc that.

Franc bristled back. "Well, if you don't trust me, I can always go offer my services to somebody who'll appreciate me."

The girl boldly rose and dropped scraped knuckles on her slender hips.

Hannah stared back at the spindly girl in disbelief. She had taken control of her life when she'd left Emmett, and now some eleven-year-old street-smart urchin was boldly attempting to separate her from her last few dollars. Despite the budding thoughts Hannah had of instilling upon the child a good dose of proper guidance, she held back.

"Everyone in this car thinks you are my daughter, if you have forgotten. So I strongly suggest you start behaving like a young lady."

Franc frowned at the veiled threat in the woman's voice, but settled back down with an aggrieved sigh. "Oh, all right. You win. But what if we split it?"

Two

"Hey, Max . . . Maximilian Garat. That train you been waiting for's just pulled in. You got maybe twenty minutes at most before it pulls out," the station owner hollered from the kitchen. "Hope whatever you are expecting, my friend, is on her."

Max looked up from his bowl of noodle soup at his big friend, then tore a hunk from the huge round of sourdough bread on the plate next to the garbanzo bean dish made with pork sausage. Without comment Max split the red-checked curtains at the window and glanced out before returning his attention to his dinner.

Filled with a knowing curiosity, the owner's wife asked, "Ain't you goin' to go find out if *it's* arrived?"

"There is time yet," Max said, and kept eating, ignoring the woman's strange inquisitiveness. "There is more pickled tongue, Pierre?"

"You Basques are such a stoic lot," the owner's

wife chided with a winking laugh. "Won't give 'way nothin'. If I was you, I'd be standin' out there, rubbin' my hands together with anticipation, especially if *it* is something to help you warm your bed."

Pierre set the tongue on the table, wiped his hands on his apron, and slipped a beefy arm around his round-cheeked wife. "Marie, apologize for such talk. You know better. When Max is ready to tell what it is that he has got coming in on the train, he will."

Max kept his face impassive as Marie blurted out a quick apology and flounced back to the kitchen. Pierre slid on to one of the chairs across from Max. "She means nothing by it, my friend. You know how womenfolk are, not happy until all available menfolk are hitched up to the marriage yoke. Afraid she will never accept that you said you are not going to take another wife after the tragic way your wife passed on. But I will talk to Marie."

"Thank you" was all Max said, but Pierre's unwitting comment about his wife's untimely passing resurrected Max's painful thoughts of his beloved Mary. Despite his efforts, in the end he had been forced to sit by her bedside, bundling the child she had heroically birthed and helplessly watching her precious life ebb from her.

"Most people at these contract dining stations serve nothing but fried meat, potatoes, and eggs for a dollar. But me, my friend, I serve a full

Basque meal. My customers, they are mighty appreciative, and word travels," Pierre rattled on to redirect the conversation when he noticed the bleakness enter his longtime friend's eyes.

Pierre held back the curtains. "Why, just look at the bunch of them heading this way. They can hardly wait to fill their bellies with Pierre's fine food."

His enthusiasm dampened by the painful memories, Max nodded and sopped up the gravy with his bread while he sized up the passengers who were marching toward the station.

Hannah stared out the train window, watching the other passengers march toward the old wooden shanty set among nothing more than miles and miles of scrub-dotted, blowing sand. In front of the building two swayback horses stood quietly at the hitching rail near a battered old buckboard, swishing their scraggly black tails.

"Didn't know there weren't no eatin' place on the train when I took the measly coins you offered," Franc grumbled.

"I just bet you didn't," Hannah said beneath her breath. She was tired and hungry and in no mood for Franc's endless complaints.

Franc leaned over Hannah to peer out the window, ignoring her choice of words. "Wanna join 'em 'n' eat?"

"And how do you propose we pay for it? You

stole my money while I was napping," Hannah snapped, wondering why she hadn't gone to the conductor after she had discovered what Franc had done. The thought of the scene with Wilma Timm reminded her.

"Yeah, but I did it for a good cause," Franc said in her own defense.

"You call gambling the money away before I could stop you a good cause?"

Hannah's father had gambled away the family's meager fortune before he disappeared, leaving her and her broken mother to live in poverty down by the river. Poverty had been hard on her proud mother, just as had motherhood. Poverty had stripped her mother's pride and forced her to turn her back on her only daughter in a desperate attempt to escape poverty's strangling grasp.

And a short time ago, with one flip of a walnut shell, all the money Hannah had in the world had been lost. Earlier in the day Franc had wanted to split the money and Hannah had refused, but the wily child had picked her pocket with the ease of a professional.

"I would've doubled your dumb old precious money if you hadn't of showed up at the last minute and fouled my concentration from takin' that sucker," Franc announced, breaking into Hannah's painful musings.

Hannah threw up her hands. "You stole my money! And you were no doubt cheating too!"

Silently, she wondered why she had opened her mouth and claimed the fledgling scam artist as her daughter. At the moment Hannah was not certain the child could be reformed, let alone guided. Nor was she certain she even wanted to try.

"So? You can't cheat honest folks. If folks weren't such downright greedy-gut rascals, always 'xpectin' to get somethin' fer nothin', I never would've learnt the game in the first place."

"People are not all like that, Franc," Hannah said softly, the wind suddenly spent from her anger. Pity she wasn't speaking from experience rather than her own tarnished idealism. Although Franc exhibited a hard exterior, Hannah could not keep her heart from going out to the little waif who shared such a similar background to Hannah's own.

"Humph! I don't believe that for a minute. So far, you're the only one I've met up with who ain't. And I bet that even you would start talkin' outta the other side of your mouth if you had to."

Franc pointed out the window. Wilma Timm had stepped from the train. Holding on to her hat against the blowing wind, she was heading toward the dining station. "Take that mean old lizard woman. You think she wouldn't cheat the poor farmer she's probably meetin' up with if she had half a chance?"

The woman had few redeeming qualities Hannah could argue. "Well, I suppose she—"

"You can't say for sure, can you?" Franc waited a moment, then crowed, "My point exactly."

"It doesn't matter. I am not going into that dining station and cheat some poor, hardworking person out of the cost of a meal."

"Then you can come watch me." Franc popped up and scrambled down the aisle. Hot on Franc's heels, Hannah rushed after the little urchin running toward the building. She was determined to nip in the bud Franc's criminal career. Hannah abruptly stopped just inside the door. The interior of the station was filled with passengers seated at long communal tables, enjoying lively conversations and filling their plates from heaping mounds of mouth-watering food, the inviting aroma wafting about the room.

"You just stand here and learn," Franc called out, and scurried off before Hannah could grab her. Frozen into inaction for a moment by the rumbling of her empty stomach, Hannah could not believe her eyes as she watched Franc boldly stride to the table, casually snatch a round of bread from a plate, and stuff it under her jacket.

Hannah returned to her senses and started after Franc just as Franc's triumphant smile suddenly turned to surprise and then horror as a huge man clamped an enormous hand on her shoulder, staying her exit. The big man whispered something to Franc and marched her forward.

"This young thief, he belongs to you maybe?" the man asked in a heavy foreign accent Hannah did not recognize.

"Could we discuss this outside?" Horrified, Hannah looked from the patrons' questioning stares to Wilma Timm's smug grin to Franc's angry red face to the man's determined dark countenance.

He was an unusually tall man wearing a soft, visorless round caplike hat. His black hair peeking from underneath it was shot with strokes of gray at his temples. Set in a handsome wedge-shaped face, his eyes were a piercing blue; his nose, straight and proud; his generous lips unsmiling.

Franc tried to squirm from his grasp, but he snorted, took her by the ear, and escorted her outside none too gently.

Hannah heaved a sigh of relief. At least she wasn't going to become additional fodder for the other passengers over Franc's latest infraction.

As Hannah followed him from the station, she had the opportunity to further assess him. His clothes bespoke of a man who earned his living by the sweat of his brow; he was not a soft, pampered city gentleman such as Emmett considered himself. This man's big hands were rough, not smooth and manicured like Emmett's. And the stranger's shirt-sleeves virtually bulged with muscles.

"You may let go of the child now," Hannah directed, and pulled Franc close to her once they were outside. Despite what Franc had done, she was not going to allow anyone to continue to manhandle the child. "This is all a dreadful mistake. I—"

"Yeah, you big bully," Franc seconded before Hannah had the chance to disown her, and glared up at the towering man. "Goin' 'round 'saultin' innocent kids," Franc added for good measure.

"Salt on the tail of a young bird stealing crumbs maybe. Assault? Innocent? I do not think so," Max said, and snatched the round of bread from underneath the kid's jacket.

Franc cocked her head. She hadn't the foggiest notion what he was talking about.

Ignoring Franc's misuse of words, Hannah said, "I was about to pay for the bread, when you interceded," although she knew it was a blatant falsehood.

To her horror he held out a callused hand. He was expecting her to pay for the bread with money she no longer had, thanks to Franc's thievery. She ought to deny the child and be done with it!

"Then now you pay for the bread, yes?"

Hannah stared mutinously up at him. She was snared in her own lie. "Somebody"—she shot

Franc a condemning frown—"stole my money,"
she finally admitted, hating being forced to explain herself to the strange foreigner. "I came
west to work—"

A crate being unloaded from the train crashed
to the dock, effectively cutting off the rest of
Hannah's explanation. Although it was some distance away, near the end of the railroad cars, the
crudely scribbled words *Sewing Machine* were vis-
ibly legible on the side.

"You are the needle lady maybe?" Max asked.

"I beg your pardon?" Hannah returned with
a hint of misgiving at his probing question. She
felt unsettled and uneasy in the man's formidable
presence. She had come west to escape men, and
not five minutes off the train, here she was, fearing this man might seek out the law, probably
lurking inside, and have her and Franc arrested.

Max motioned toward the crate which had been
unloaded from the train. "It is your sewing machine maybe yes?"

"Why would you think that man-made contrap-
tion's hers?" Franc asked, suspicious of everyone
but particularly of folks who spoke oddly.

He cocked a bushy black brow and ignored the
scruffy child and pup, which had suddenly
jumped from the train and leapt into the child's
arms. "It is maybe?"

Hannah opened her mouth to deny owner-
ship, but before she could, Franc stepped forward. " 'Course it's hers. You the one lookin' to

hire someone to run a few stitches?" Franc questioned, unabashed by getting caught thieving.

"I advertise for someone," Max said. For some reason he was unable to take his eyes from the woman. He forced himself to regard her clothing, thinking she did not look like someone who made a practice of thievery. Of course, one could not tell by appearances. She looked more like some fancy dance-hall girl with an equally fancy and useless umbrella hanging from her wrist.

Although the lavish lacy lavender dress she wore could hardly be considered functional attire for a good woman out west, the stitches from her bodice to her hem had been crafted by an experienced hand. And who was he to care what a woman chose to wear?

"A response it comes to my letter saying the woman she is on her way and meets me here."

"I doubt that I am who you are looking for," Hannah gritted out, fighting her skirts under the man's assessing stare now that the direction of the wind had shifted.

Max noticed the unpleasant female stiffen under his perusal, and her snapping green eyes flicker with apprehension. She might be considered pretty if her face were not filled with such trepidation and distrust, and her disposition were not that of a goat. Yet he could not help but notice those slender ankles when the wind had taken up her skirts.

A lump formed in his throat at such unbidden

thoughts. He silently chided himself. Although Max had lost his Mary, he would never think of betraying her memory.

Never.

He was there to hire someone to work for the family—nothing more.

The woman before him fit the general description in the letter he had in his pocket. Except she was considerably thinner and at least ten years younger than the woman had alluded to in her letter, and he hadn't counted on having to concern himself with the woman's honesty.

Pity he had not been able to make out the signature, or he would have called her by name and settled all this nonsense. Other than that bleating shrew who had entered the station just before he'd left, this female was the only one who came anywhere near fitting the general description. There just was no accounting for a woman's taste in dresses.

"Look, missus, either you are the one who answers my advertisement for a seamstress to sew for my family or not."

"But what about the bread incident?" Hannah hedged, frantically trying to weigh her options.

He considered her for a moment. There was nothing conciliatory in her tone. Grudgingly he admitted that he'd had only one answer to his ad. If he didn't hire this woman, regardless of how disagreeable he had found her suggestive letter as well as her presence now, it would be spring before he could attempt to hire someone else.

"If sending the child out to steal the bread is the worst thing you ever do, I overlook it maybe if you make arrangements to pay Pierre for it; I, too, know what it is to go hungry."

Hannah nodded, too proud to proclaim her innocence in Franc's latest foray. She had no intention of explaining the true reason she had come west. Better to let him think what he would than to risk discovery. He could very well have a change of heart and summon the law, and she was not going to endure further censure while sitting in a cell, waiting for some lawman to alert Emmett to her whereabouts so he could have the pleasure of seeing her sent to prison for pawning his family's heirloom brooch.

"As I write to you, I am willing to pay top wages for a few weeks work," he grudgingly said.

"You hear what he said? He's willin' to pay top wages," Franc reiterated, squeezing Hannah's hand. "We need the money, or I wouldn't of had to help myself to that bread, right, Ma?" Franc added through clenched teeth. "And it's good *honest* work."

Hannah's gaze shifted to the man. She did desperately need the money. Thanks to Franc, she was flat broke. She had no prospects, no other options. All she had left to her name was a hungry little pup and a train ticket which took her as far as Sacramento but would not satisfy her empty stomach. Although she had vowed to stay away from men, it was for only a few weeks. And he had said he was a family man, so it would not be as if she would see much of him if she did take the job.

Hannah was tempted to inquire why he had advertised for a seamstress if he was a family man. But, of course, not all women were versed in the fine art of the needle. An understatement, she silently added, thinking about herself.

She didn't have the foggiest idea which end of a needle to thread.

An inner battle ensued as she glanced in the direction of the crate. She had tried to cling to her beliefs of right and wrong, but she had even found herself compromising that in an effort to survive. She could not just claim property which did not belong to her.

Recalling the letter Franc had mentioned finding in Wilma Timm's bag, Hannah realized that the contents could very well belong to the Timm woman. Hannah certainly did not need tempt any farther conflict with that horrid woman. If only she had another option. But she was broke, pregnant, and alone.

While Hannah continued to war with herself, Wilma Timm stormed by with a pained expression on her sour face. She was obviously quite upset over something, although her eyes bored into Hannah's with an unrelenting animosity.

"Humph, nothin' but useless, thievin' white

trash," Wilma sneered, stuck her nose in the air, and barreled on to the train.

Hannah stiffened and bit her lip. She had heard that disparaging remark all too many times while she was growing up on the river. And she was not going to allow her child to be subjected to such vicious slander, regardless of what she had to do.

Hannah raised her chin, took in a steadying breath, and held out her hand; it was trembling despite her efforts to still it. "May I see the letter you mentioned?"

Max fished in his pocket and pulled out the crumpled missive. "You are a careful woman, a little nervous maybe . . . Missus?"

"Turner," she offered, feeling irritated with herself for continuing to claim Emmett's name, when he had vowed immediate proceedings to strip her of it. "Mrs. Hannah Turner. A woman alone cannot be too careful."

He nodded. "A female lady with no money in a strange place who comes to meet a strange man should be careful I think maybe."

"And who are you?"

"The man who hires a seamstress."

While she read the letter, Hannah glanced at the signature. Although barely legible, Hannah was able to make it out. Wilma Timm. They apparently had not made contact inside the dining station. No wonder Wilma Timm had appeared so aggrieved. She had been so agitated that she

must have missed her machine mistakeningly being unloaded, or she surely would have been berating the appropriate railroad employee by this
time.

Hannah reread the letter and again pondered
what she would be letting herself in for if she
acknowledged the sewing machine as her own. If
only all her funds had not been lost. But there
was no use continuing to fret over it. What was
done was done. What had to be done had to be
done to survive until she could replenish the
money that Franc lost.

As if Franc had read Hannah's mind, the girl
stepped forward, her flat chest puffed out. "We'll
take the job."

"We?" Max said.

"We go where Ma goes. You got a problem
with that?"

"There is another one like you lurking around
somewhere nearby maybe?"

"There ain't nobody else like me. I'm eunuch."

Max stifled the unexpected urge to chuckle at
the obnoxious child. "The word it is unique."

"Close enough."

"Franc, apologize for your rudeness," Hannah
chastised the girl as she also fought the hint of
a smile over the girl's misuse of words. The man
said not a word, but his eyes were crinkled at the
corners.

A thought suddenly popped into Hannah's
mind and subconsciously her hand cradled her

belly. Franc could not possibly know about her pregnancy, could she?

Franc turned her back and refused to offer an apology. An instant later Franc swung around. "You wouldn't expect a ma to leave her kids behind, now, would you?"

"Kids," Max repeated, a sinking feeling in the pit of his gut.

Franc shrugged and scratched the little pup behind the ears. "Me and Pandy Pie . . . the doggie. We're her kids."

"I have not accepted the offer, Franc," Hannah chided her, although she had no other prospects. She let out a silent sigh of relief. The girl did not suspect Hannah was pregnant. But events, nonetheless, were suddenly moving very swiftly.

"If it is your sewing machine, you already accept my offer," Max said blandly. "If not, I take enough of your time maybe. Do not forget to pay Pierre for the bread when you earn money. Missus." Fingers pressed to his beret, Max nodded.

He tossed the kid the bread, turned from the pair, and started to walk away. A voice inside his head warned that if he were smart he would not wait for the woman's reply; he would get in his buckboard and forget the whole damned thing.

Hannah was staring after the man when the conductor announced from the train, "All aboard what's comin' aboard." The locomotive belched a cloud of thick black smoke into the air, gave a jerk, and began to inch into motion.

Hannah did not have time to ponder the situation further. She either had to rush back onto the train before it pulled out and take her chances that something would turn up, or she had to embrace the man's offer before he reached the waiting wagon and left the contract station.

If she accepted the position as a seamstress and claimed Wilma Timm's property, she would be telling another lie as well as adding thievery to her growing bevy of sins.

If only she had another option from which to choose.

She frantically glanced from the man's wide shoulders to the train; Wilma Timm was sitting at the window, darkly scowling out at her. Hannah's gaze shot to Franc and her pup, and back to the man again.

The man had not even formally introduced himself; he was a total stranger—a foreigner—with no more than a barely legible letter as reference. And his presence had a strange way of bringing out less than ladylike behavior in her. Worst of all, he was a man. Every masculine, muscular male inch of him!

Her heart pounded furiously.

Either choice enmeshed her deeper in lies she may never be able to unsnarl, leading her further toward an unknown fate, and she had only seconds to make a final decision.

She was frantic as she again weighed her

choices, or lack of them. An inner panic filled her while her mother's voice rang with a hollow pitch in her ears: *You make your bed, you lie in it.*

Three

"Mister! Wait!" Hannah hailed the man just as he was unhitching the horses from the railing. She grabbed her skirts and hurried along after the tall stranger.

When she caught up with him she blurted out the only viable choice she had, "If the position is still available, I—"

"So this is what, or should I say *who,* you didn't wanna tell Pierre and me you were waiting for," said Marie in a self-pleased voice from in front of the station house. She leaned on her broom and winked.

The big-hearted wife of his friend had an equally big mouth! The seamstress's expectant face was flushed as she waited for his answer. Max's annoyance with Marie melted into another round of inner turmoil over his earlier unbidden thoughts.

"You goin' to introduce us, or merely stand there?" Marie urged with a big grin. Pierre joined her, and she looped her arm with his.

"This is the needle woman who comes to sew

for my family," Max said without preamble. He dug into his pocket and tossed Pierre a coin. "To pay for the bread the child does not pay for."

Hannah was startled and confused by the man's unexpected generosity. She was further confused when he said no more to her. Rather, he swung away to direct the loading of the machine in his buckboard. He had not referred to Franc as a thief. Emmett would have seen the girl prosecuted to the fullest extent of the law.

"Pierre, why don't you go on and help Max?" Marie suggested, then turned to assess the woman.

Hannah felt awkward and ungainly under the weight of such an open assessment. And for an instant she experienced a sense of disappointment from the woman, a feeling she feared most, since her mother had made her feel that her best was never quite good enough. She swallowed back that dread, grateful that the woman did not press the topic of the bread. Hannah forced herself to thrust out her hand. "Hannah Turner."

Marie smiled brightly, set her broom aside, and took Hannah's hand. "Marie Laxague. The big oaf helpin' Max is my Pierre."

"Max?"

"Yes, Maximilian Garat," Marie said in a strange voice, and her bright smile faded to be replaced by a wily grin. "Funny, you don't have a foreign accent and your fingers're as soft as a newborn's behind. Not at all what one would expect of a seamstress working with the daily prick of the needle," Marie said with a sly wink.

"Didn't Mr. Garat's letter mention his requirements?" Marie was dying to question the woman further about the letter Max's father had written to the old country requesting a bride for his widowed son, but Pierre had chastised her once this morning.

"Of course . . . the letter." Hannah did not totally understand the conspiratorial wink or the woman's sudden formal use of the man's name, but she decided that it must have something to do with the letter the man had spoken of that he had written to the seamstress.

"Your dress is mighty pretty, though, but it won't hold up long out here."

"I'm Franc, and my ma's the best. 'Course her fingers're soft," Franc hissed, and possessively took hold of Hannah's hand. "And she's wearin' a special dress she sewed herself with that very machine." She pointed toward the men.

Marie swallowed the questions she longed to ask the woman about Max and the letter as her gaze followed the direction in which the child was pointing.

Pierre gave the crate a shove into the bed of the wagon, then glanced back over his shoulder at the two women. "Your *seamstress* is a most fine-looking woman, eh, my friend? A little frilly perhaps, but robust and pink-cheeked.

"She will not last long alone out here. Some

lonely man will learn that she does not seem to have a man and want to take her to wife just as soon as word gets out. That is, if she does not already have a man who's spoken for her." Pierre scratched his head but watched Max out the corner of his eye. "Suppose if she had a man she would be heading home, where a woman belongs."

"In her letter she says she is a widow woman," Max grunted. He was getting awfully tired of well-intentioned friends and relatives' less-than-subtle hints that he marry again. Forcing himself to ignore that big smirk, Max began securing the sewing machine in the bed of the wagon. "The young one is hers."

"It is always good to have more hands around to help out with the chores," Pierre continued, undaunted by the dark frown that his tight-lipped friend shot him. "But I guess you already know that."

"Enough maybe to have the child work off the price of the bread."

Pierre cast a quick questioning glance at the woman and her child. "My Marie, she seems to have taken to your *seamstress*. I hope you know what you got yourself into, my friend."

"I do not get myself *into* anything. And she is not *my seamstress*. I tell you, the woman, she is going to sew for my family, nothing more. She comes to the ranch only long enough to sew up enough clothes for the children so they go away to school. Once she sets the last stitch, any man who has interest can press his suit."

The skepticism in Pierre's raised eyebrow annoyed Max. Refusing to talk further about the woman with his friend, Max finished tying the last knot to secure the crate, climbed onto the wagon box, and grabbed up the reins.

"Missus, do you stand there staring maybe or do you get into the wagon? I pay you to sew, not to stand around in a dress and wait for some aristocrat with a title to escort you to the governor's soiree maybe," he said more harshly than intended.

Hannah's head snapped up and her vision fastened on the big, outstretched hand. He expected her to take his hand, but she had already accepted a man's hand for the last time, as far as she was concerned. "I am perfectly capable to getting myself into the wagon, thank you."

Despite the fierce inner battle she had waged before settling on the job as her only viable option, Hannah felt pretty good to have spoken her mind as she awkwardly climbed into the wagon and positioned herself as far away from the man as was humanly possible. She freed her snagged skirt, and snapped open her parasol while she directed Franc to pick up Panda Pie and hop into the wagon. Ignoring the sudden displeased twist to the man's generous lips, she said a cheery goodbye to the station owners and the wagon lurched into motion.

* * *

You make your bed, you lie in it.

The portent of those words marched through Hannah's mind like armed soldiers on their way to do battle. She was seated on the box of a rickety buckboard, in between two virtual strangers, heading to God-knows-where, and she had only herself to blame.

"Well, I certainly have made my bed this time," she muttered to herself.

"What?"

"I was merely thinking out loud." Hannah lowered her eyes, but she could not help thinking that men the world over were undoubtedly the same—filled with self-importance. They all expected women to prostrate themselves for them, but Hannah had no intention of being a meek doormat for any man again.

Max glanced at the muttering woman sitting so stiffly near him. She no doubt did not possess all her faculties!

He arched a brow at the sight of the nonsensical frilly lavender disk that was supposed to shade the outrageously dressed woman, and turned his attention back to the road. That piece of wilted fluff umbrella was about as practical as the pair of lavender satin slippers she was sporting!

What the hell had he gotten himself into? She

certainly wasn't your average levelheaded ranch woman! No wonder she did not have a man!

As the buckboard rocked and swayed along the rutted road throughout the day and night, and into the second day, the stark quiet of the landscape stretched endlessly before them. Even when they had traveled through a tree-lined pass and dropped back down to the valley floor below, Hannah could not keep her thoughts from the position in which fate had placed her.

When she'd left Emmett she never imagined how difficult it was going to be to find her own way. Without a calling or much money there had been few options; no one had wanted to hire a lone pregnant woman with a small, scraggly pup deemed too awkward to capture a three-legged rat with its eyes blindfolded.

Even when she had swallowed what little pride she'd had left and applied at the last town to sweep up in one of the bawdy saloons sporting a prominent help-wanted sign in the window, the painted female owner had taken one look at her and laughed that Hannah was too old for her customers' tastes.

Hannah almost felt like crying. She was nearly thirty-one years old, pregnant, and flat broke. Necessity and desire to save a child from a miserable childhood had forced her to compromise her beliefs. And she already had broken her vow to have nothing further to do with men. Even worse, she was heading far out into the wilderness with a strange man she knew nothing about.

A sudden wave of nausea overtook her, and she quickly cupped her mouth with both hands. She closed her eyes, praying for the queasiness to pass, and despairing her future once she did reach the man's house.

For she had added still another lie, another secret to her growing list. Except the secret lie that got her the job she was truly incapable of doing could not be kept indefinitely. She plucked at her sleeve. After all, she rationalized, she was intelligent and a quick learner. How difficult could sewing be?

The nausea did not pass.

"Stop! Please!" Hannah cried, gagging back the urge to vomit.

Not knowing what to expect at the panic in the woman's voice, Max quickly scanned the landscape as he pulled up on the reins.

Hannah leapt from the wagon and tossed the umbrella aside. She managed to gather up her voluminous lace skirts and dart behind a scrubby tree moments before her stomach insisted on emptying its contents.

Hannah was wiping her mouth with a hankie, when she glanced up to see a strange, curly-haired creature emerge from the brush and charge directly at her.

"Help! Help me!" Hannah screamed, and made a mad dash toward the safety of the wagon.

Max noticed the animal chasing the woman and felt like throwing up his hands in exasperation as he was forced to come to her aid. To his chagrin, the woman's unruly child also jumped from the wagon and scrambled after him.

The woman stepped on a cactus sticker and stumbled, but Max reached her in time to stay her fall. She may have a prickly disposition, but she was utterly spineless!

Franc barreled past the pair as the man was removing the thorn, grabbed Hannah's umbrella, and bashed the animal on the muzzle. The animal squealed and went down on its front legs, shaking its head as if dazed.

"You dumb, stupid, ragamuffin puff of a pig snout!" a young boy of about twelve screeched, appearing from behind the animal and swinging his staff at Franc.

Franc caught the end of the wooden staff. "I'll teach you to try to sic that strange, mean fuzzy cow on my ma!"

The two children squared off, two pairs of small dirty hands wrapped around the staff.

The fight was on.

Max immediately left the woman and grabbed Franc. The young boy took a swing at Franc, but Hannah, ignoring the pain of the cactus sticker, managed to scramble to her feet and capture the boy. One glance from the man and the child immediately quit struggling and stilled in Hannah's arms. Franc tried to wrench out of the man's grasp, but he held tight to her scrawny arms.

"Let go of me an' I'll settle it good," Franc howled.

"You settle nothing," Max warned. "Mrs. Turner, you release the child. There is no more fighting between the two of you, yes?"

"Yes, sir," the young boy said obediently.

"Only if he keeps that fuzzy cow away from my ma," Franc grumbled.

"It is not a cow, you brains of a pig's behind. It is a ewe."

"It ain't neither me!" Franc balled her fists, ready to take up the battle again.

The miniature of the older man screwed up his young face. "You really are a stupid dummy. A ewe is a female sheep, dummy-rummy."

"No more, André," Max boomed, and both children immediately ceased the exchange. Although both continued to glare silently at each other.

Hannah's hands instinctively went to her hips. "My dear Mr. Garat, who is this young ruffian?"

Max stiffened. The woman was rapidly becoming more trouble than she was worth! "Mrs. Turner, this *young ruffian*, he is my son."

"Oh, dear," Hannah breathed out. She certainly was not off to a very good beginning with the man. She had gotten the seamstress position through deception and had just insulted her employer by stating that his son was ill-mannered.

Well, she was not going to take it back. The young boy was without manners.

Like father, like son, she thought.

Max ignored the woman's tightening expression. "André, you remove your beret and introduce yourself to the missus and her child."

"Why, Papa?" André grumped, now kneeled at the side of his bleating sheep.

"First because I tell you to, and second because she lives with us on our *sheep* ranch"—he said this for the woman's benefit—"while she sews a school wardrobe for you, Lissa, and Samuel."

The boy's blue eyes rounded in dismay. "They are going to be living under the same roof with us?"

"Yes."

André shook his head in alarm before he suddenly blurted out, "You are not going to try to replace our mama with her! We will not let you!" he hollered, and fled, the ewe racing after him.

Hannah was horrified. From the letter she thought she had been hired to sew for a family, not a motherless brood who lived on some sheep ranch surrounded by monster woolly creatures who charged at her! What had the man done to make his wife leave him? An instant of dread that he was like Emmett assailed her. "I hope I haven't given you the wrong impression."

"You do not worry, Mrs. Turner. You give me no impression, and I got no designs on you or your person. Your presence in my home, it is nothing more than a very temporary necessity. Women, they are the least of my interests."

"And men are mine," she shot back, reeling from his easy dismissal of her apparent concern.

"Then there is no danger of a misunderstanding between us maybe."

"Certainly not!"

"Good. We go back to the wagon now. I want to reach the ranch before sundown so you can start sewing first thing at sunup."

Unable to help herself, Hannah retorted, "That's fine with me. I do not plan to remain at your *sheep* ranch any longer than necessary."

"It is a good idea maybe," Max seconded. For some reason, although he was normally indifferent to women, and most respectful, that woman sure was managing to rub him the wrong way!

Thinking that her latest secret would be unveiled shortly and her tenure at the ranch would no doubt end sooner than even he anticipated, Hannah gave a half-hearted nod and raised her chin. Secretly, she was enjoying her newfound freedom. Although Maximilian Garat was strangely exasperating, sparring with the man was also strangely invigorating.

By the time they reached the dilapidated stone ranch house that Maximillian Garat called home, Hannah was having second thoughts. She was exhausted and silently berating herself for accepting the position to work for the cantankerous rancher despite her dire need of money.

The ranch was out in the middle of nowhere, set in the center of nothing more than miles and miles of blowing sand and scrub brush and cactus. Nearby were corralled more sheep. The remains of a weed-infested garden bowed to the dominance of the wind. A broken-down split-rail fence wavered unsteadily around the weathered river-rock house. The sagging porch had seen better days. A weathered wooden sign over the door scrawled in a foreign language and dangling from one hinge warned that inside the worst was yet to come.

"This is it?" Franc whined, voicing Hannah's silent sentiments. "Why, this ain't nothin' more'n a poorhouse."

"Franc, show some respect," Hannah directed.

"I'm showin' as much as I can muster," the girl whined. "No wonder ol' Andy's such a mean varmint; he lives in a shack."

"Franc!" Hannah sought to reprimand the girl, but Franc hopped out of the wagon and raced from the ranch, Panda Pie bouncing after her.

"I am truly sorry, Mr. Garat. I have no idea what got into the child. I'm certain Franc did not mean to offend you."

"Do not concern yourself. You are not here long enough to offend me." What Max did not say was that he was well aware of the sorry state of the ranch. After his Mary had passed away, he had lost all interest in it. And if he hadn't promised Mary that he'd raise the children in America, he would have packed up the whole brood and returned to his homeland in the Pyrenees.

Hannah climbed down from the wagon and was about to follow Max inside, when the front door suddenly burst open and a chubby toddler, followed by a huge black and white cat, streaked by.

"Samuel Bernard Garat," Max hollered at the naked little boy. "You go back inside . . . now!"

"Mama, Mama!" Two-year-old Sammy squealed. He ignored his father and kept going, his short legs pumping as he did a sudden about-face and buried himself in Hannah's skirts.

Four

Hannah bent down to pick up the toddler clinging to her legs with all his might, when a pretty, dark-haired young girl dressed in noticeably worn gingham and two to three years older than Franc suddenly emerged from the house and marched over to the little boy.

"Samuel Garat, you let go of that strange woman this instant. She is not our mama! I told you that Grandpapa was only telling you stories about Papa getting you a mama."

The girl snatched a daunted Samuel from Hannah and lifted him into her arms, settling him on her slender hip. Frowning at her father, she said, "What is she doing here?"

"Lissa, this is Mrs. Turner," Max announced in a strained foreign accent. "She is the seamstress I tell you I hire to sew for us. She lives with us and I expect you to be respectful."

Her lips a tight frown, Lissa Garat gave Hannah no more than a spare nod of recognition and fled back inside the house.

"Mr. Garat, it seems that no member of either

your household or mine has an appreciation for my presence here." Still reeling from the girl's slight, Hannah swung out an arm to indicate the large cat that had followed the toddler from the house.

Not thirty feet from them the black cat with the white undercarriage stood hunched and hissing, its thick fur standing upright down the length of its back as did the fur down the pup's back, facing it.

"It appears that even the animals oppose my accepting this temporary position within your household."

Max did not find this latest scene any more amusing than the one he had just experienced with his strong-willed daughter. "Then I expect maybe you want to waste no time, so you do not stay here longer than absolutely necessary."

Secretly wishing he had missed the woman at the station, Max clapped his hands twice, calling, "Furball," and the cat obediently retreated and bounded onto the porch. The awkward pup scrambled underneath the Turner woman's skirts and peeked out at him with huge, innocent brown eyes, as if it half-expected him to strike it.

Hannah picked up the pup and held it to her, scratching it behind its erect pointy ears to calm it. This was turning out to be a dreadful mistake. Perhaps she should return to the station and throw herself on the station owner's mercy before

Maximilian Garat discovered the latest secret she was harboring.

"Perhaps, Mr. Garat, it would be best for all concerned if I did not take this job after all."

Tired and exasperated, Max shook his head. "Missus, I make a two-day trip to fetch you, and two days to bring you back here. I lose four days work around this ranch. You accept the job, and I expect you to keep our bargain."

Indignant over the annoyance in his voice despite realizing that her suggestion was unrealistic, Hannah rose to her full five-foot-four-inch height. "Very well, Mr. Garat, as you insist, I shall sew for your family. But remember, it was you who hired me. When I'm through I expect to be paid the top wages you offered back at the station."

"I already tell you a bargain it is a bargain."

"I have heard that before."

Max's head snapped up at her telling comment. It told him a little about the woman she no doubt had not meant to reveal. "I do not know who disappoints you, but I am a man of my word, Mrs. Turner."

It was a strange use of words to Hannah. She had always thought of the word *disappoints* in respect to what she did to others, not the other way around. And for a moment she was troubled by it. Steeling herself, she quickly recovered and sent him her most sugary, doubtful smile. "And I shall hold you to it."

Thoroughly exasperated and questioning the

wisdom of his decision to ignore her belligerence, Max stepped up onto the porch and opened the door for the troubling woman. "Do you plan to remain outside during your stay maybe, or do you come inside and settle in?"

From a small fenced pen near the barn a goose honked at her causing Hannah to hug her pup and glance around. Above the door was a neatly hand-painted sign in a foreign language. She beat down the urge to ask him what it meant. Rather, she wondered where else he expected her to reside.

Panda Pie nuzzled her neck. "It's all right, Pie Girl, I won't let that nasty cat harm you," she cooed to the tiny black pup she had found and sheltered as she glided past him.

His voice stopped her cold just inside the door. "Where do you think you go with that dog?"

She swung around and faced him squarely, not sure whether he could be violent like Emmett when provoked. "Panda Pie stays with me."

"*Panda Pie* she stays in the barn."

My God, she wasn't even inside yet and they were already having another dispute!

Hannah lifted her chin and squarely met his determined blue stare. Although she did not feel the bravado and resolve she was displaying, she could not afford to allow him to set her precious pet in the barn.

Her pup was special to her; the only one that loved her without qualification. It was a pure love she shared with her pet; Panda Pie's eyes were filled only with adoration, never disappointment or disapproval, and she was not going to allow such an unnecessary separation.

"Mr. Garat, if I'm to work for you, you must accept and respect my entire family."

Accept and respect her entire family? Holy Mary, Mother of God, he was a rancher and took damn good care of his animals, but they were just that . . . animals, as was the small critter the woman was proclaiming as part of her family!

His fingers itched to wring that incredibly eccentric neck of hers! "Mrs. Turner, I allow you to bring your child and you do not tell me, so I show respect for your family. But that dog—"

"This *dog* is part of my family." She could not afford to let him get the upper hand. She had relinquished her say to Emmett, and she was never going to be put in the same position by anyone again.

"If you cannot see your way clear to allow me to keep my *entire* family at my side, I shall be forced to insist that you return us to the train station, for I simply could not concentrate on my sewing if my beloved Panda Pie is forced to endure the unnecessary hardships that residing in your barn would entail. I will agree to keep Panda Pie in my room—"

"Missus, you do not got your own room," he said, incredulous. "Where do you come from? A rich man's estate? This ranch, it is for working sheep. I got a three-room house, not some sprawling palace."

His comment about the rich man's estate stung. He was closer to the truth than he realized. But she held firm to her beloved pet. She took a deep breath.

"I will have my own bed, or will I be forced to share that, too?" she inquired tartly, keeping the stab of fear she experienced from her voice.

His brow lifted. "Missus, I doubt anyone in his right mind thinks of forcing you to share a bed."

She ignored the purely male inference. "I do hope you fall into that category," she retorted before she could help herself.

At that, a hint of a grin grew at the corners of his lips, and she braced herself.

"If I got my right mind maybe, you would still be on that train."

She raised her chin. "Well, I'm not. And I shall at least require the use of an extra bed."

"There are no extra beds in the house." For some reason, he took satisfaction out of watching her face fall before he added, "I fix you a straw mattress in the corner of the kitchen."

"Then Franc and I share my corner-filled straw with Panda Pie or I leave . . . now."

"You plan to walk in those shoes maybe?" He motioned to the lavender satin slippers.

"If I have to."

Max rolled his eyes. He was wrong in his first

assessment of the woman; she wasn't an obstinate billy goat, she was a stubborn mule!

Hannah held her breath. She had pushed him pretty far. What if he forced her hand and made her walk back? She had no idea where she was.

He grumbled something unintelligible, shaking his head before he announced, "Okay, Missus, if you get fleas, it is your problem. But the first time that dog, it strays from your corner of the kitchen, it goes to the barn."

"Agreed," Hannah said quickly, relieved to have come out the victor. In an effort to redirect the subject before he changed his mind, she said, "It is an interesting sign above your door. What language is it written in?"

Max's face tightened. "Euskera." At the tilt of her head, he translated, "Basque."

She waited for him to translate it for her, but the grim expression on his face warned that he had no intention of doing so. "What does it say?"

"Mary's house."

"Oh." At the look of immense pain and suffering, she was tempted to reach out to him, but the sudden curtain that dropped over his features stayed her. Instead, she swept into the house.

Hannah was pleasantly surprised at the inside of the house. From the edge of the parlor she noted what was probably a bedroom, and kitchen off the main room. Her eyes scanned the parlor.

No doubt it had been decorated with the utmost care by a loving female hand. She stood on

a braided rag rug that displayed the craftsmanship of the maker. The homemade furniture was
draped with crocheted doilies, and plump over-
stuffed pillows lining the backs of the furniture.
On the walls were daguerreotypes of what looked
to be a loving family and a framed needlepoint
proudly proclaimed Home Sweet Home.

Hannah could almost feel the warmth and love
that dwelled inside the house, until her eyes
stopped on the angry young face of Lissa Garat.

Hannah turned back toward her employer, expecting him to further smooth the girl's upset,
but he was nowhere in sight. Hannah realized
she was going to have to fight her own battles
while she was there.

"Lissa, I'm not going to be here long; I hope
that we can become friends—"

"Do not count on it!" the girl shot back. "I
know what you are up to, and it is not going to
work. I read your dumb letter to Papa when you
learned we do not have a mama."

"And what do you think I am?" Hannah questioned softly, sure she was not going to like what
she was about to hear.

"Just what you wrote in your conniving letter—
a desperate widow woman who intends to convince Papa to marry you."

Lissa was half sobbing, half screeching as she
finished with "And if you think that you can
sway him like you said with your great cookin'
and needle skills, you are wrong!"

Hannah was horrified as she watched the girl whip from the doorway and disappear behind the curtain into what she had assumed was the only bedroom.

"Great!" Hannah muttered to herself, throwing up her hand. "Now I'm not only supposed to be a handy seamstress and a great cook, but a desperate, conniving widow woman determined to convince Maximilian to marry me as well." Then she recalled the Timm woman's remark about catching her fourth husband. "Great! No wonder the man has been so wary of me. I am supposed to be on the prowl for husband number four."

She paced back and forth, mulling over how one lie seemed to build on another like sheep falling in line blindly behind a leader. The last thing she ever intended to do again was to get married, but if she was to stay in character, that was exactly what Maximilian Garat expected her to want from him!

Her eyes caught on another sampler lauding the importance of honesty. "Great!" she muttered a third time, and threw up hers hand again. "I made my bed and now I have to figure out how to stay out of it."

She pondered her tenuous situation a moment longer. A panic overtook her. It suddenly became more important than ever for Hannah to get herself away from this sheep rancher as soon as humanly possible, regardless of her lack of options!

She thought about it for a moment longer. She

was hired to sew, and since there did not seem to be any way around it, that was exactly what she was going to do.

She went into the kitchen and set Panda Pie down on the neatly fixed straw bed with instructions to stay put. It was then that the pleasant room caught her eye. In the center was a long, scarred wooden table with benches. The ceiling was held by beams from which hams, sausages, and magnificent rounds of cheese made from sheep milk, hung by strings next to wreaths of garlic, onions, and peppers, filling the kitchen with their aroma. To her amazement, the kitchen did not have a stove. Rather, a massive fireplace, the back of which was covered with white tile and open on three sides burned within the room. Suspended from a heavy chain over the fire was a heavy pot. A mantel over it was decorated with threads of red and blue and set with a pair of pewter candlesticks and two red copper trays.

It was obviously a room in which Max's wife had spent many joyous hours. A sudden, unexplainable jolt of jealousy caused her to turn away and leave the house to search out Maximilian Garat and direct the setup of the sewing machine.

By the time she stepped out onto the porch, the man had already rounded up his son and was unloading the sewing machine. Franc was sullenly standing near the wagon, kicking the wheel. Hannah stood aside as they carted the machine into the house. Then she followed them back into the kitchen and stood off to the side as he set it up. The man dragged over the bench and held out his arm.

"Thank you," Hannah said, and sat down gingerly with a forced smile. "The material and thread?" she asked in a small voice.

"I send you money to purchase what you need," he said in a dark voice.

Panic threatened to overcome Hannah again as she glanced at Franc, who had come to stand quietly in the doorway. The girl merely shrugged. Hannah slowly shifted her gaze to meet the man's expectant one.

"Here is the rest of the stuff from the crate, Papa," André grumbled, and rudely shoved his way past Franc as he returned to the kitchen, his arms ladened with stacks of cloth and thread.

Hannah swallowed a silent sigh of relief and raised her chin. "Thank you, André, for so thoughtfully saving me the trouble of having to go out and unpack the rest of my work materials myself."

"What about supper, Papa?" André asked, ignoring the intruder's attempt at gratitude.

Hannah quickly dropped her eyes and made a hasty study of her supplies, but not before she caught a fleeting glance of the three pairs of eyes that had settled on her.

Emmett had never allowed her near the kitchen, stating that that kind of work was for her subordinates. Her mother had insisted that food was too expensive to waste allowing a child to experiment and present a disappointing performance. So Hannah had never learned to cook—let alone cook over an open fire.

"André, call your sister in here. She gets supper tonight. Mrs. Turner she is going to be very busy stitching her first outfit for Samuel to wear in the morning."

Hannah's breath fled. Thinking about how quickly she could learn was one thing. Actually sitting down and doing it was quite another. He quite simply expected her to whip out an outfit in a couple of hours. She looked to Franc again, but the sly child merely shook her head, rolled her eyes, and swung from the kitchen.

Hannah did not have time to ponder her next move. There was only one option open.

Without chancing another glance at the man, Hannah bit her lip and set to work.

Five

Hannah yawned, fighting back her queasy stomach, and glanced up from running the last stitch on the machine. The sky was just beginning to fade from the jeweled black of night to the cool gray of dawn. She had worked all night on the outfit for the youngest Garat child. The word *disappointment* kept ringing in her ears, but she could never be accused of lacking determination. Massaging her aching back, she grabbed the garment and went in search of little Samuel.

The rancher had announced earlier that he and the rest of the children, including a reluctant and sleepy Franc, would be out in the barn doing the morning chores, and to bring Samuel out after she had dressed him.

As Hannah finished dressing the squirming little boy and headed toward the front door, there was no doubt that her latest secret would soon be out. She took a steadying breath to relieve her pounding heart, opened the door, and stepped out onto the porch.

Furball arched his back, hissed, and vaulted

from the porch. Samuel saw his father and let out a whoop, toddling toward the big man.

"What the hell does this mean?" Max demanded, his eyes blazing blue fires.

Hannah stiffened her spine, prepared for the worst. "Whatever do you mean?"

"Whatever do I mean!" Max practically shouted as his son awkwardly came toward him. Max swung out an arm to indicate his youngest child.

The little tyke's ill-fitting shirt looked like a poorly stitched blue square with holes cut in it for his head and arms. The rolled-cuff pants were way too large and barely held up with a strip of blue cotton knotted around his waist.

"What is it you call this?"

Hannah's latest secret was out. Now everyone knew she could not sew.

Although there was no escaping it, Hannah decided to pretend ignorance of her crime. "What?"

"What? My God, this abomination my son he struggles to keep on." Fighting to keep his baggy pants up, the little boy reached Max and he picked him up.

Struggling to hide her dread, Hannah glanced around at the smug faces of the older Garat children watching her from a nearby corral while they leaned on their pitchforks. There was no mortification in their young faces. Not an ounce.

Devils! They were thoroughly enjoying her humiliation. Franc had turned her back.

"I worked all night, and I did the best I could," Hannah said in a guilty voice. "What did you expect?"

"What do I expect! I think I hire a seamstress maybe," Max shouted, which caused Samuel to screw up his pudgy face and whimper.

Fighting to get his anger under control, Max turned to his daughter. "Lissa, you take Samuel inside. André, you go finish up in the barn." When the pair did not move immediately, Max ordered, "Now!"

Hannah stood still, cringing inside and not knowing what to expect as she watched the children scatter. Even Franc had scurried out of sight.

She searched his eyes. At least she did not notice a sign that she had disappointed him. Instead, his eyes were blazing. She could handle that better than the inner despair and torment caused by the knowledge that she had let another person down.

When she was left standing alone in the yard with the big angry rancher, Hannah ventured to ask, "What would you like me to sew next?"

"Sew?" he said in a dark, thunderous voice as he came forward with his fists on his hips. "Missus, you do not know the first thing about sewing, yes?"

"Well, no, not actually, but I'm certain in time I'll learn."

"You do not learn on my family," he said on a calmer note, although Hannah noted the veins standing out on his neck. "Mrs. Turner, you I fire!"

He had turned toward the wagon, and Hannah followed him. "But you said a bargain's a bargain."

Max stopped in his tracks and slowly pivoted around.

"I make a bargain with a seamstress. You, Mrs. Turner, are no seamstress. Or a bargain, for that matter. As soon as I hitch up the horses I take you and your sewing machine back to the station."

"You're going to pay for the outfit I made, aren't you?" Hannah asked. She did not press him when she noticed his lips tighten, and he turned from her without answering.

As Hannah returned to the house to gather her few possessions, she tried to keep her mind on how she had wanted to get herself as far away from the ranch and that man as soon as possible. But for some reason she did not feel like celebrating. Rather, she felt a strange twinge of regret. She had managed to hold her own with the rancher, and even after he discovered that she had misrepresented herself as a seamstress, his eyes had not been filled with disappointment. When Hannah walked into the kitchen, Franc was sitting on the bed of straw, stroking Panda Pie, who was curled up in her lap.

"He pay you off?" Franc asked.

"For what? Making rags out of perfectly good fabric, or for masquerading as the seamstress the man thought he had hired?"

"He got what he paid for," Franc answered, totally unconcerned.

"He paid nothing."

"So?" Franc shrugged. "He got nothin'. You know, the way I figger it, we can use that sewin' machine to pull off a pretty good scam. But from now on we get the money up front. By the way, when we gettin' outta here?"

"You get out of here right now," Max said as he walked into the room, grabbed up the sewing machine, and lugged it from the house.

Despite feelings to the contrary, Hannah kept her head up. She gathered the few scraps of material, raised her chin, and she and Franc walked past the smirking Garat children.

Although Hannah knew he was livid, Maximilian Garat helped her into the wagon, heightening her feelings of guilt.

Dark, ominous clouds rode across the sky as they traveled from the ranch in tension-filled silence. Hannah glanced at Franc. The girl looked quite pleased to be leaving. Hannah then swung her gaze to the rancher's profile. It was a profile in strength and courage, and suppressed anger. No doubt he was a man who had been forced to carve out a life for himself and his family in this barren wilderness.

Hannah shivered, since the morning had turned very cold as they traveled toward the pass.

Max noticed the woman shudder and grabbed a woolen blanket he kept underneath the seat. "Here. It is all I got."

"What 'bout me?" Franc whined. "I'm cold too."

"Since neither of you brings much more than the clothes on your backs, you two can share," Max said tightly.

Hannah had not expected his display of concern as she wrapped herself and Franc in the warm woolen blanket. Another prick of guiltiness settled heavily on her shoulders about the same time as the first snowflake.

There were only a few white flurries at first, but soon the snow began to fall in force, transforming the barren landscape into a winter wonderland.

"Dammit!" Max swore as he pulled up on the reins. "We never make it through the pass."

"What're we going to do?" Hannah asked, her voice echoing the inner concern and conflict she felt. Franc opened her mouth to put in her two cents, but Hannah pulled her closer into her arms and cradled her face against her chest, effectively cutting off the girl's latest round of complaints.

"There is little we can do," Max responded sharply. "We must head back to the ranch." The snow was coming faster and harder now as Max turned the horses around.

Visibility was nearly zero, and the drifts had quickly piled up on the road, making it difficult for the wagon to pass through the white mounds. The snow filled the worst of the holes in the road, and the wagon wheel hit a deep rut, causing it to break.

Max caught the woman up in his arms to stay her fall when the wagon tilted. She was trembling, and despite his anger he gathered her in closer to reassure her. But when he stroked her silken chestnut waves which hung loosely down her back, he had to remind himself why they were out in the middle of a blinding snowstorm.

"What you doin'?" Franc demanded.

"Franc, Mr. Garat was merely being a gentleman," Hannah said, and pulled away from the man. She rubbed her arms where he had held her. She could still feel the heat that lingered there, and it caused a surge of goose bumps to rush down her spine.

Max ignored the child, straightened his beret, and jumped from the wagon to survey the damage as he heard the kid say, "There ain't no such thin' as a gentleman. He just wanted a feel."

"And you just want a taste of a good bar of

lye soap," Max suggested. He was thoroughly exasperated. That child was itching for much-needed discipline.

"What?"

"You ask me to teach you respect," Max grumbled, wishing at the moment that he had his fingers around a big homemade bar. That child had the mouth of a crude sheepherder!

The woman pulled the child to her in a protective gesture. Max cursed his luck. He was stuck out in the middle of a sudden snowstorm with the disagreeable pair. But worst of all, he was going to have to return to the ranch with them.

Alarmed when he left the wagon wheel and began unhitching the horses, Hannah asked, "What are you doing?"

He looked up in disgust. "These animals, they are important. I do not leave them here with the wagon."

Hannah's hand flew to her throat. "You don't intend to leave us here with it, do you?"

"Missus, do not give me ideas." Max walked around to the wagon box and grasped the woman around the waist.

Hannah had not expected the personal contact, and she struggled in his arms, causing her to slide along the length of his body to the ground. He was solid and muscular beneath the heavy duster, and on impulse she reached up to brush the snow from the twists of hair peeking from his beret.

Max caught her wrist. His fingers easily encircled the soft white flesh, heightening his awareness of her as a woman, soft and alive. "What do you think you do?"

"Nothing," she answered for want of a better response to explain herself. It had been a sudden, uncontrollable urge that had driven her.

She retrieved her hand. She rubbed her wrist. She could still feel the checked power, the gentle strength with which he had stopped her from touching him. There had been times when she had been afraid that Emmett would break her wrist when he was angry. And she could not understand what had driven her to make such an intimate gesture. Although she was forced to acknowledge that the desire lingered.

When the rancher turned from her without another word and trudged through the snow to the horses, the strange, unexplainable feelings she was experiencing from their personal contact turned to fear. He wasn't planning to leave them there, was he?

"You aren't going to leave us here, are you?"

Max led the horses to where the pair now stood. "You think of good suggestions today. You must be more careful in the future. I just may decide to act on one of them maybe."

At her look of terror, Max chided himself. He did not make a habit of scaring women. He added, "You quit worrying. Now you make a cradle with your hands and help me settle the child on the horse's back. You two ride.''

"That horse ain't got no saddle," Franc bitterly complained. "How do you expect me to stay on its back?''

It was freezing cold, the wind was blowing the snow, and Max was in no mood for further unwarranted complaints. He swung the kid up onto the horse's back despite his intention of having the woman help in order to keep her mind occupied. Then he wrapped the kid in the wool blanket and offered up a handful of mane. "You hold onto this. I do the rest."

Not about to waste any more time, Max lifted the woman onto the other horse's back and easily swung up behind her. Although Max wasn't sure why he had suddenly decided on the seating arrangements, she did not protest, did not say so much as a word as he nudged the horse forward. Rather, she settled back against his chest and seemed almost thankful when he encircled her within his duster.

"Need to share our body heat," he said because he felt a sudden twinge at the feel of the woman's soft body warm up against his.

They traveled for hours in silence. While Max had to fight to keep the horses tramping through the deepening snow, and the freezing wind from blinding them, he did not have to fight to keep warm.

The gentle motion of their bodies caused by

the swaying of the horse's back caused her buttocks to rock against him, keeping his face flushed with heat and a red-hot arousal in that uncontrollable male portion of him.

In an effort to stop the sudden fantasies he was experiencing over the woman and stem that inflamed part of his body from exploding, Max wrapped the woman in his duster and slid from the horse's back. Left with a sheepskin jacket, he grabbed the reins. Shielding his eyes from the blowing snow, he plodded through the drifts.

The man's sudden withdrawal caused Hannah to fret that they had lost their way, or perhaps he had an abhorrence to her plumpness. Emmett had constantly reminded her of his aversion to her appearance often enough. Although she was secretly relieved that the rancher was no longer seated so close to her. She had felt his hardness pressing against her backside, and secretly knew she had stirred him.

And although the rancher had caused strange sensations to awaken inside her, Hannah fought back such sudden unbidden feelings by reminding herself of Emmett's rough groping and probing at will. Emmett never missed the opportunity to remind her that he had selected her because he did not want a beautiful wife he would have to concern himself with. He had made her feel unlovable, as if he had been doing her a big favor by stooping to marry her.

Fighting back such ugly memories, Hannah

glanced back toward Franc. The child was mounded up in the blanket, her young frown nearly hidden as she sat sullenly quiet.

The rancher suddenly stopped, causing Hannah to shift her attention. He was apparently surveying the area. Hannah could not understand what he was gazing at; she could not see more than five feet in any direction, the snow was coming down so hard now.

Another fear overtook her, and she asked, "Mr. Garat, we're not in danger of losing our way, are we?"

The cold having returned Max to his senses, he was disgusted with himself for so easily being aroused by the woman. Max pulled his beret down on his head and walked over to her.

"Missus, you got no idea just how close I come to losing myself."

"But everything is all right now?" Hannah inquired, not understanding the pained expression on his face.

"Maybe you say I got things pretty well under control again."

Returning to the forefront of their little party, Max did not wait for a response. There was none she could make. He could hardly blame her for nearly inciting him, although if it weren't for her lies, they would not be out in this storm now.

At least he had sighted familiar terrain and they would be back at the ranch soon. If he had not had to hold onto the horse's reins, he would have thrown up his hands.

Now he had to figure out what the hell he was going to do with the pair.

Six

Snow was blowing in every direction, piling up against the already-leaning fence when they finally made it back to the ranch. Hannah did not know how the rancher managed it, since she could barely make out the house from the barn. But once he had seen to the horses, Hannah found herself back inside a ranch house she had never expected to see again.

"Papa," Lissa cried, and rushed into her father's arms. "We were so worried."

Lissa suddenly realized there was someone else standing just inside the kitchen door. She pulled out of her father's arms. "What are they doing back here?" she asked in an accusing voice.

"Lissa, you watch your manners," Max warned as he shrugged out of his jacket and went to help the Turner woman out of his duster.

"But what are we going to do with them?" Lissa persisted.

"You ain't goin' to do nothin' with us," Franc inserted, sticking her sour face in the older girl's. The girl stepped back. Satisfied that she had daunted the older girl, Franc plunked down on the bed still set up in the kitchen and removed Panda Pie from inside her jacket.

Adjusting her cap lower on her head, Franc swung her attention to the rancher. "How soon can we get outta here?"

Max leveled a steady gaze on the woman, ignoring the child. "I am afraid outside there is a blizzard brewing, which means we will be enjoying one another's company until spring, when the pass, it clears, unless I miss my guess maybe."

Hannah's sudden intake of breath caused all eyes to swing in her direction. Her hand went to her belly. Her baby was due in spring. Somehow she had to leave long before that. She did not want the rancher to know that she was going to have her baby alone.

"Guess you get that chance to learn how to sew after all, yes?" Max added, surprised and momentarily curious over the woman's silent panic. It was not just the panic he noted, but the type. She seemed more like a frightened trapped animal.

He suppressed his curiosity and ordered, "Lissa, you take Mrs. Turner and get her some dry clothes. And André, you find the boy some work clothes."

Max waited until his sulky daughter begrudgingly led the woman away to carry out his directives before he slipped into his duster to return outside and string a line among the house, out-house, and barn before the storm got any worse.

The woman's sweet lilac scent lingered on his duster and tantalized his nostrils with its flowery fragrance, filling his mind with visions of her even as he fought to keep his attention directed on stringing the lifeline.

This sudden, early storm was not so good an omen of what was to come, he thought.

Max cursed his luck.

Out of all the eligible women well-meaning friends and family had attempted to shove at him, the only one he had not been totally immune to, the only one who had affected him in the slight-est, was going to be right under the same roof for the entire winter.

Hannah followed the young girl to the single bedroom. The youngest Garat child slept soundly in a tiny provisional bed in the corner of the small room cluttered with mementos and remind-ers of Maximilian Garat's departed wife.

A woven wreath of dark hair hung alongside a cracked mirror adorned with a rosary and posi-tioned over a small makeshift dressing table crammed with jars of cream and other female items. An iron bed covered with a patchwork quilt stood in the corner as a testament to the mar-riage bed and all it symbolized.

Hannah quickly averted her gaze from the

man's bed as reminders of Emmett's cruelty flooded over her. And she silently swore to make herself stop comparing her present circumstance and surroundings to her past life with Emmett if she were going to survive the close confinement with the rancher.

"If you are wondering how you will fit in Papa's bedroom, do not bother," Lissa snipped from the second rung of a ladder.

Astounded by the girl's venom, Hannah's head snapped up in time to see the girl disappear through a hole in the ceiling. Immediately afterward, Lissa's head popped back through the opening.

"If you want dry clothes you will have to come up and help me find something to fit you."

The girl was a shrew-in-training. She needed to be taken in hand as much as Franc did, Hannah thought as she ascended the ladder made of cottonwood-tree branches held together with leather straps.

By the time Hannah stepped from the top rung of the ladder, the girl was bending over a dusty old trunk in the corner of the small space that housed the two narrow beds Hannah discerned served as a bedroom for the two older children.

"I doubt that any of your things would fit me," Hannah said.

Lissa frowned, but pulled a scoop-necked, blue gingham dress out of the trunk and held it up. "This should do."

"Whose dress is this?" Hannah asked as she hesitantly accepted the girl's offering. The dress was much too large for the girl, and a sudden sense of foreboding over the girl's sudden display of generosity encapsulated her.

Lissa shrugged. "It is just some old thing that has been lying around."

Hannah shivered from the cold, wet dress she was wearing and ignored her better judgment as she quickly stripped out of the wilted lacy creation and shrugged into the generous gingham dress. She had to have something dry to wear or she would catch her death.

The girl rummaged through the trunk and pulled out stockings and a pair of sturdy shoes. "I think these will be more practical," Lissa announced, and motioned toward the woman's sodden slippers.

Hannah nodded her gratitude. Perhaps she was wrong about the girl. Hannah plunked down on the hard bed. She kicked off her slippers, rolled the stockings down her legs, and put on the girl's offering. The shoes were too generous, and the girl offered a couple of hankies for Hannah to stuff into the toes.

"I will braid your hair. It does not make sense to let it hang down your back. It will just get in the way while you are working and leave strands in the food and around the house."

The girl's argument made sense, since Hannah was certain Max would not want any reminders to linger on the furniture after her departure, so Hannah let the girl plait her hair and pin it on top of her head.

"There. I think that should do it," Lissa announced. The sound of the kitchen door slamming signaled her papa's return to the house. Suppressing a gleeful grin, she said, "We better get down to the kitchen and get supper started. Papa likes to eat on time."

"It is practical," Hannah murmured, holding out her skirt and feeling foreign but newly domestic with her transformed appearance.

The girl looked Hannah up and down, and her young smile became a tight yet sad grin. "I know that you will make quite an impression on Papa, if that is what is on your mind."

As Hannah followed the girl down the ladder, she was relieved. Although it was obvious that Lissa Garat did not totally accept her presence yet, it seemed to be proving easier to change the young girl's mind about her than she had anticipated.

Determined to make the best of her situation, Hannah raised her head and walked into the kitchen, held out the skirt, and pivoted around, exhibiting the sturdy shoes with a click of her heels. "What do you think?"

The glowering expression on the man's face took her by surprise. Hannah stilled and dropped her arms to her sides, unable to understand his reaction this time. "I had hoped that you might be pleased."

"Take off the dress," Max directed in a voice filled with cold, commanding authority.

Her brows shot together. "What?"

"You do not hear? I say . . . take off the dress . . . and those shoes."

"But why—"

"Just take it off before maybe I am forced to rip it off," he said with such icy deliberation that flashes of Emmett caused Hannah to turn and flee.

Franc leaned up on her elbow and watched the scene with quiet fascination.

Lissa started from the room, but Max caught her arm. "You do not leave so fast, yes, young lady?"

"What is wrong, Papa?"

"I think you know maybe. Where does the woman get that dress?"

"Guess she pulled it from the trunk," Lissa lied, the whites of her eyes as big as snowballs, giving her away.

"I guess maybe she does not. I guess that maybe you give it to her. And I guess that maybe she gets those shoes from you, as well as those braids being your handiwork, too, yes?"

"I am sorry I gave her Mama's clothes, Papa," Lissa suddenly burst out, crying. "I just do not want you to forget Mama."

Max's anger and pain over seeing his departed

wife's clothes on another woman melted, and he pulled his daughter into his arms and held her while she sobbed, stroking her dark hair. He expelled a deep breath, fighting to keep his own renewed grief suppressed.

He and his wife had been so happy about the baby, and then everything had gone so wrong and his wife was dead. Now a strange woman comes into his house and next thing he knows she is wearing his wife's clothes and renewing the pain all over again.

"I miss Mama so bad, Papa," she sobbed, soaking the front of his shirt.

"I know, Lissa. I know." He held her at arm's length and looked into her pleading blue eyes. She was silently begging for understanding. "I wish I make the hurt go away. But I cannot. What we do maybe is to keep her memory alive in our hearts. And in time the pain will fade and leave behind all the happy memories, yes?"

"Are you sure, Papa?"

He pulled her back to him and kissed her on the forehead before resting his chin on the top of her head. Squeezing his eyes shut and willing that what he'd told his daughter was true, he murmured, "Yes, Lissa, I am sure."

The void inside him cried that two years had not healed his heart. He still hurt, and deep in that place which he did not share with anyone he had been angry that she had left him. That anger had finally started to fade, and he was be-

ginning to accept his wife's death, until the
Turner woman had come into his home. Now,
though, that anger was returning. This time it
was directed inward. For this time it was due to
the undeniable stirrings he was experiencing inside for another woman.

Hannah had wrapped a blanket around her
shoulders and returned to the doorway in time
to observe the touching scene between father and
daughter. Regardless of the girl's spitefulness,
Hannah's heart went out to her. The Garat children must have loved their mother very deeply,
and Hannah could understand and sympathize
with the depth of their plight.

Max glanced over his daughter's head and noticed the Turner woman standing quietly in the
doorway. Despite himself, he smiled at her, grateful that she made no move to intervene and chas-
tise Lissa for what she had done.

For a moment Max lost himself in her gentle
smile of understanding before she nodded and
motioned for her child to join her so he could
comfort his troubled daughter in private.

Hannah saw that Franc was seated on a chair
in the parlor, then settled on the sofa next to
André, who was glumly curled up with his arms
crossed over his chest, hanging his head. The
rancher's older son was hurting, too.

"It must've been very difficult to lose your
mother, André," Hannah said softly, and ringed
her arm around the young boy's bony shoulders.

André just bobbed his head, unable to speak for fear that he would give way to the hurt that he kept locked up inside him and show in front them that he had a weakness.

Franc noticed the boy's bottom lip tremble and decided to take charge of the situation before the boy started to blubber. "Come on, Andy, I got to get me some dry clothes on my back unless you want me to freeze my butt off."

"Not a bad idea," André mumbled, but a glimpse of a grin hovered about his lips. He rose from his seat and shuffled toward the bedroom, grateful to have his thoughts redirected. When the dumb kid did not immediately follow him, André said, "Well, has your butt already stuck to that chair, or you waiting for a special invitation?"

"Not from you. I'd freeze my butt first," Franc retorted, ignoring Hannah's raised eyebrows over such talk. "But I'll tell you what, Andy, I'll play you a game of cards for that heavy coat you got."

"Franc, no. You're not to play cards or any of your other games with any member of this family," Hannah said sharply. Remember that we're going to be living here for the winter," Hannah reminded the girl. "And we're guests under the Garats' roof."

"I ain't likely to forget; you won't let me. But maybe perhaps I'll have me a whole lota new clothes afore winter's over 'n' done with." Franc winked at Hannah before she sauntered after Andy.

Hannah sighed and rolled her eyes at the obstinate girl's lack of values. But Hannah could not help but think that Franc did indeed have the spark of a kind heart underneath that sarcastic, unguided, larcenous shell she hid behind. The girl had managed to save André from losing control, and Hannah could tell that André had been grateful to Franc for it.

Hannah was sitting alone in the living room, pondering over what she was going to do to extricate herself from her present situation, when Maximilian Garat joined her.

"Lissa, she is getting supper," he said, unable to discuss the incident further. Basques were legendary for the curtain of privacy they maintained, and Max was no exception. He moved toward the window and lit another oil lamp on the rough-made table near Hannah. Then he tossed another log into the already-crackling fire which warmed the isolated house.

"Mr. Garat—"

Max glanced up and leaned a forearm on the mantel he had fashioned from a pinion pine log. "You call me Max maybe since we are living in close quarters for some time to come." Privately, he did not want his children to think that he condoned their rude behavior, and by demonstrating to them that he accepted the woman and her child, his children would be forced to do the same.

"Thank you. I'm Hannah." He stiffly nodded, causing Hannah to offer, "Max, I hadn't meant to misrepresent myself back at the station. Truly I hadn't. I desperately needed a job." *And I needed a place to hide, although I had not counted on this.*

"Well, it appears that the storm it provides that maybe, so we might just as well try to make the best of it, yes?"

It was apparent that words did not come easily for the proud man, but he was making an effort and Hannah found herself most grateful for that.

"Now that is settled, I find something more suitable for you to wear maybe, then you help Lissa with supper."

Hannah attempted to appear calm as she gave a hesitant nod, but inside she was roiling with turmoil. They had reached a tenuous truce at best. Although he had a rough exterior, Hannah wondered about the man he was inside and how he would react should he uncover the other secrets she was hiding. Now Hannah worried how long or if she could stave off his finding out about them.

And the worst part about it was that her next test already lay waiting for her in the next room.

Seven

Night was rapidly encasing the isolated ranch house within a howling blizzard when Max returned to the parlor with clothes draped over one arm and Samuel straddling his hip. The little toddler was sleepily rubbing his eyes. Max set Samuel on a braided rag rug before the fire with two carved wooden toys.

At her look of interest in the toys, he said, "I whittle in my spare time sometimes."

She was impressed with his craftsmanship and the obvious love that had gone into making the wooden animals. She pressed her fingers to her stomach. For an instant she wished that her baby's father had been filled with as much love.

"Here." Max held out his arm, redirecting the conversation. "These clothes, they should serve."

Hannah took the offering and surveyed the clothing. "But these are men's pants," she said, startled that he expected her to wear such masculine attire.

"They are dry and warm and should suit

maybe until you learn to sew a skirt, if that is what you wish to wear."

"Thank you," she responded stiffly. From his expression, Hannah knew there was no use attempting to make further argument, although she did not relish the thought of wearing his clothing. Her unorthodox appearance would make it difficult for her to win the acceptance of the Garat children. She cast one last glance at Max's unmovable face, then accepted defeat and went into the bedroom to change.

As Hannah was pulling the pants up her legs, she could hear the children arguing in the tiny bedroom above her. Although she was tempted to intervene, Hannah decided that for the present time it was the wisest course to let the pair try to find their own peace.

Hannah tucked the huge woolen shirt into the baggy denims and secured the pants with a length of cord Max had provided. The clothing was well-worn but clean, and not at all what she was accustomed to wearing.

She smoothed her hands down her body. A sudden unexpected warmth surged through her at the thought that the clothes were intimately touching her skin in the same places that they had touched Max Garat's. It was a strange feeling she had not anticipated, and it gave her pause.

In an effort to put such unbidden but shockingly pleasant feelings from her mind, Hannah quickly folded the blue gingham dress and left it lying on the bed and padded barefoot into the kitchen. She was thankful that Lissa was nowhere in sight.

Hannah bit her lip when she walked through the door to find Max waiting for her, holding out an apron. She thought she denoted a hint of amusement in his eyes, which were crinkled at the corners.

"Max, about supper—" Hannah began, when a sudden commotion broke out above their heads in the tiny attic room.

"You north end of a southbound hog, you are not going get away with it!" came André's high-pitched voice spiking through the ceiling.

"I won that dumb hat fair 'n' square, you wormy weasel welsher. Hand it over, or I'm goin' to rip it off you."

Expecting to see anger in Max's face over Franc's mouth, Hannah glanced in his direction. To her astonishment, he almost appeared to be fighting back a smile.

Max attempted to keep his face impassive, although he was secretly relieved that life was coming back into his son after the silent sadness that had surrounded the boy since his mother's death.

A loud crashing thud suddenly echoed through the small house.

"Oh, my dear God, they must've fallen down the ladder," Hannah gasped, and ran after Max into the bedroom.

The two children were no more than a tangle

of flailing arms and legs, rolling on the floor, kicking, hitting, and yelling at each other.

After discerning the children were unharmed, Max grabbed André and Hannah managed to hold Franc back. But in the ensuing scuffle the cap that Franc always wore had fallen off, and her pinned-up braids had come uncoiled.

"Look, Papa, he is a she!" André snorted, pointing an accusing finger. "He is a she!"

Lissa, who had followed close behind on Hannah's heels, gasped, "A girl," and covered her mouth with her hands.

Hannah's heart sank. Now the fragile truce they had reached was destroyed, and a strange sense of loss grasped her.

Max's eyes first surveyed Franc and then swung to Hannah. She had been caught in another lie. A lie of omission. When Max had thought that Franc was a boy, she should have corrected him. Instead, she had remained silent.

"Max, I—"

"André," Max cut in, swinging his attention from Hannah to his son. "Maybe you explain what starts this, yes?"

Hannah remained silent and listened in amazement while Max adeptly settled yet another confrontation between Franc and André. The young pair was like a cat and dog set together, yet Max was handling the situation with such patient fatherly skill that Hannah could hardly believe her eyes when the two children actually thrust out their arms, shook hands, and André gave Franc his hat.

Max was strict but fair, a loving father that any child would be lucky to have as a parent. The sentiment caused Hannah to wonder what kind of husband he had been before she quickly caught herself and banished such a disturbing thought from her mind.

"You two clean up the mess in here," Max directed. "Then maybe you go back up the ladder and clean up the wreckage you no doubt leave up there."

"Lissa, you play with Samuel while Hannah and I we finish getting supper."

"Hannah?" Lissa questioned. She could hardly believe her ears. One moment her father was consoling her, saying he understood how she felt, and the next moment the woman had her papa calling her by her first name.

"Mrs. Turner," Max clarified, and cast his daughter a look that brooked no argument.

Hannah could see the surprise and disapproval on the girl's face when her father had referred to Hannah by her given name. There was a dark light in the girl's eyes that warned Hannah that in the future she would have to watch her back.

As Hannah followed Max into the kitchen to face yet another trial of her own doing, she determined that she somehow had to win over the older girl.

Once in the warm, cheery kitchen, Hannah

thought that Max had intended to help, but to her chagrin he pulled out a bench and sat down. In an effort to forestall the inevitable, Hannah slipped an apron over her head, tied it around her waist, and attacked the half-chopped onion.

"Why do you not tell me Franc she is a girl?" Max asked casually, watching her intently.

Hannah's hand stopped in midair, and her head snapped up. This was a man who lived by honesty, and she was constantly demonstrating how dishonest she was turning out to be. If only she'd had another option, she would not be trapped by her own deceptions.

"Does it matter?" she asked when she found her voice.

"The fact that she is a girl it does not matter so much as why you find it necessary to lie about that, too."

"I did not lie," she insisted, although she knew she had indirectly.

Secretly, she wished she had a defense. But sometimes life's circumstances dictated one's actions. If she told him the truth now, she would be forced to lay bare another lie. Franc was not her child, but she had to protect the girl. Despite the squabbles Franc was getting into with the Garat children, it was apparent that underneath Franc may come to enjoy her budding relationships with the other children. It was daunting how one lie seemed to build on another, and each just further complicated things, when all she had wanted to do was to get away from Emmett and rear her child.

"You thought she was a boy. I merely did not correct you."

She expected him to respond, to call her a liar or worse, but he merely sat before her, staring at her, making her feel that she owed him a further explanation. Unable to offer him any, she quietly wished that she had never been forced to lie in the first place. Hannah lowered her eyes and tried to focus on slicing potatoes and tossing them with the onions into a cast iron pot she set on the fire.

Hannah did not hear Max rise, but in the next instant he was at her side, the crook of his rough index finger lifting her chin and raising her head to face him.

There was a probing intensity in his blue eyes, and Hannah felt he was gazing into her soul, penetrating the wall she had erected around herself long ago, to breach the façade she presented to the world. It unnerved her.

His gaze dropped to her mouth. In response, her tongue slipped out to trace and moisten the contours of her lips. He slowly dipped his head, and she was sure he was going to kiss her. Hannah's heart raced and her hands trembled.

He *was* going to kiss her.

"Hannah," he said softly, and raised his head. "There is something troubling you maybe?"

"Why would something be troubling me?" she said in a whisper, staring at his full lips.

"You are so nervous around me."

He did not kiss her. Unsure whether she was relieved, disappointed, or had somehow foolishly mistaken his intentions, Hannah stepped back. She bumped against the hot pot, which caused her to jump forward, propelling herself into his arms.

Max reflexively wrapped his arms around her.

When Max consciously realized what had almost happened and became aware that he was holding her softly rounded body against his and could feel her heart pounding against his chest, he immediately released her and pushed her away from him.

"Call when supper it is ready," he said stiffly, and left the kitchen.

Hannah pressed a hand to her bosom, trying to calm her breathing. His arms had been so strong. She had been held in his checked, powerful embrace. My God, what was happening to her? She was becoming too aware of him as a woman would a man. She could not afford to let down her guard. She had promised herself never to let another man close enough to hurt her again, and here she was thinking about Max Garat and wondering—possibly even hoping, if she were honest with herself—if he was going to kiss her.

Hannah was still troubling over her body's response to Max when black smoke started to billow from the pot. In a panic she grabbed the handle. It burned her palm and she dropped it, sending it clattering to the floor. Panda Pie whimpered and dove under the covers of the straw bed.

Although Hannah rarely cried, the events of the day suddenly seemed overwhelming, and as she kneeled down to clean up the mess, she started to sob.

"Hannah," Max said, suddenly reappearing, and kneeled down next to her. "You are all right?"

"I'm fine," she sobbed, and wiped at the salty streaks running down her cheeks. She did not expect sympathy, which caused her to fight back another, stronger urge to cry.

He set the pot back over the fire and helped her to her feet. Examining her reddened palm, he stroked the soft skin as he observed, "You do not look fine to me maybe. Here"—he repositioned the bench—"sit down, yes?"

With efficiency he moved about the kitchen, scooped out some butter from a crock he pulled from under the counter, and smoothed it on her burn. Her hands were so tiny and delicate, and her skin was velvety soft against his rough, sunburned fingers. He fought the urge to rub the back of her hand against his cheek, and quickly wrapped a dish towel around the salved burn.

"Don't I get a slice of bread with my butter?"

she asked in an effort to put an end to the tension filling the room. She felt foolish and as awkward as a young girl. She had dealt with Emmett's demands with youthful humor for so long that she did not know how to respond to Max's kindness any other way.

The serious expression on his face softened into a gentle smile. He helped her to her feet and swung her around toward the bed. "I think maybe what you need is bed."

Hannah stiffened and whipped around, drawing back. Emmett had always enjoyed taking her to bed after hurting her. It had seemed to give him a perverse pleasure to have such power over her, and Max's mere mention of bed now frightened her. "Not the bed with you, I don't."

Her accusation, coming out of the blue when his intentions were only the most honorable—well, no more dishonorable than the thought of a stolen kiss—was like a frosty bucket of fresh snowmelt dumped down his back.

"Look, Missus—"

The fight came back into Hannah. She was fighting for her life. "No! You look. This may be your home. But just because we're stuck here together for the time being does not mean I have any intention of willingly going to bed with you."

The look of surprise on his face caused her to be immediately contrite. Hannah stripped off the apron and, tossing it at him, plopped down on the bed that had been prepared for her in the kitchen. Panda Pie climbed into her lap. Cuddling the little pup to her breast, she lifted her chin toward him.

"This is the only manner I intend to sleep in this bed while I'm here," she said more softly.

If her indictment wasn't so absurd, Max would have been livid. But rather than continue such a ludicrous debate, he tossed the apron back to her.

"You suit yourself, Hannah. Call me when you get supper ready, yes? I do expect you to earn your keep around here."

"Not if it includes having to bed with you," she blurted out to his back as he pivoted around to leave the kitchen.

She immediately regretted her choice of words when he made a sudden stop and slowly turned to face her, his face darkening into an angry mask.

"Missus, I do not know what others they expect of you where you work before here, but I assure you, you jump to the wrong conclusion.

"There are four young children in this house. So, if I have interest, which incidentally I do not, you do not have to worry anyway. Furthermore, I do not bed or even desire to bed any woman since my wife she passes on.

"The only reason you are still here under my roof at all is because of that"— he thrust out an arm and pointed to the snow blowing against the window—"storm. So, until I am able to get you the hell out of here, you rest assure that your person it is perfectly safe from me."

Left alone with her apparently ungrounded fears, Hannah felt bewildered, dismayed, and saddened at learning of his wife's passing. But she had felt the tension between them; she was sure of it. The rancher hadn't actually propositioned her though. And she had insulted him. Although her experience had been limited to Emmett, it led her to believe that men were interested in only one thing from a woman.

A warm, submitting body.

Still unsure what to think about Maximilian Garat, Hannah climbed back to her feet, and ignoring the burn she had sustained to her palm, she set to work getting supper.

By the time they all were seated around the table and the indistinguishable food artfully arranged into an eye-pleasing creation on everyone's plates, Hannah's nerves had calmed. She had worked hard and was proud of her table. Expectantly, she watched Max bury his fork in a brown mound and lift it to his lips.

He suddenly burst out choking.

Forks stood suspended in midair as all eyes snapped to Max. He grabbed into his pocket for his handkerchief, immediately spit out the bitter-tasting concoction, and reached for a glass of water.

"Holy Mother Mary, cooking you do not know either."

Eight

Hannah's glance shot around the table at the children. Not one moved a muscle or met her gaze. But only Franc had attempted to taste what she had prepared. And Franc had wrinkled her nose at it and spit it out. Hannah set her own fork aside, folded her hands in her lap, and waited. She was going to suffer another humiliation in front of the children. She had tried so hard with her first cooking effort, but it had been a disappointment.

"You children, I excuse you," Max announced.

"We ain't goin' t' bed without supper, are we?" Franc protested, breaking her young silence.

"Yes," André seconded and narrowed his eyes toward Hannah.

"I say I excuse you." Max's voice was full of authority and left no further room for debate. Apparently even Franc had limits, Hannah noted when the girl did not offer further argument. Despite Hannah's unsuccessful efforts with the obstinate Franc, the girl was responding to male influence.

While Max waited for the children to vacate the kitchen, he thought about the situation in which he now found himself.

Although Max had a hard time with the lies Hannah told, he had the distinct feeling that she was caught up in something much larger, he was sure of it. Why else had she jumped against the pot when he had tried to ask her about it? He was curious but he was also patient. Though misguided, she had shown a lot of fortitude so far. It was obvious from her soft hands that she was not used to the hard labor required on an isolated sheep ranch, or anywhere else for that matter. But despite all odds, she had determination that he could not help but admire.

She had stitched—tried to stitch, that is—an outfit for Samuel, and had attempted to cook. That took strength and a hell of a lot of pluck. And her perseverance was admirable. Those were qualities needed out here in the West.

Max was rarely driven on emotion alone. He considered all angles. Perhaps the woman's efforts had been no more than foolishness. But he had become intrigued.

Max got up from the table and started slicing thick chunks of bread. He scooped out a glob of bacon grease from the tin near the fireplace and set it to heating in the cooking pot. "You get that crock of butter and start to spread butter on the bread while I cook some eggs. We got a houseful of hungry mouths to feed."

"But what about my cooking?" Hannah asked, a strange sensation bemusing her that Max had chosen to use the word *we* as if they were a couple.

"I am not sure I call it cooking maybe. No wonder you bury three husbands. The hogs they enjoy it, yes?" Max chuckled and cracked an egg into the sizzling grease.

Hogs indeed, Hannah thought miserably. And Wilma Timm's three dead husbands. She had forgotten. She was supposed to be on the lookout for husband number four.

He glanced back over his shoulder. "Since we are here together for the time being," he said, tossing her words back at her, "you got the opportunity to learn to cook maybe, yes?"

Hannah did not dare look up at him. But she recognized his words as her own. The matter-of-fact tone in his voice—strangely void of the anticipated disgust and disappointment—unsettled her and she dug the knife blindly into the crock of butter and piled it on the thick crust of bread.

"You do not need two fingers worth of butter on the bread when the crock it is almost empty," he said, coming up behind her and closing his hand around hers.

Hannah immediately froze. He took the bread from her hand and scraped three-fourths of the butter off it.

"I like a lot of butter on my bread," she protested in an feeble effort to cover up how flustered his touch made her feel. She was not going to let him know just how confused he had left her. She had lived with disappointment and knew how to handle that, but not this.

"To put food on the table it takes a lot of hard work around here. I think it is good maybe that you should learn this as well."

Hannah only nodded for want of a better response. His remark did manage to clear her muddled thinking though. He seemed to believe she was totally helpless. Well, she would show him! After all, how hard could it be to make butter?

Hannah took the eggs and buttered bread up to the three older children while Max fed Samuel and got him ready for bed. While she sat next to Franc on one of the beds in the small, cramped space and waited for them to eat so she could return with the plates, she wondered at Max's fierce protectiveness over the youngest Garat child.

She had offered to prepare the toddler for bed, but he had given her a look that had silently stated that he would brook no more of her games with his youngest son.

"Samuel, he is only two years old," he'd said. "He is too young to understand the falsehoods you tell, so I want you to leave him to me."

His remark stung, since she would never cause the little boy harm. "How old was he when he lost his mother?" she cautiously asked, since she knew it was a delicate subject.

Max's face tightened noticeably, but he had a stoicism about him that Hannah had already come to respect. "Two hours, thirty minutes."

Hannah bit her lip to keep from gasping. His wife had died in childbirth. At a time when there should have been cause for great celebration and rejoicing, Max Garat and his family had been grieving. A new and stronger feeling for the youngest member of the Garat family took hold of Hannah. The little boy had never known a mother's love. And a new and stronger feeling of respect for Max Garat accompanied it.

"I see by your face what you are thinking, and I am warning you that I do not tolerate your efforts to make me your next husband by trying to take the place of Samuel's mother."

"I wouldn't do that to the child," Hannah said strongly. "I know you don't think much of me. And in a way I even understand your feelings. Heaven knows, I have been anything but honest with you since the moment we met. But I would never intentionally cause the child harm."

"You are right, of course," he said, but he nevertheless intended to keep an eye on her. He planned to discover those reasons, but now was not the time.

"Here," Lissa said, thrusting the empty plates into Hannah's hands and returning her from her troubled reverie.

After instructing a glum Franc to go down to their bed in the kitchen, Hannah followed the girl down the ladder. The vision of Max rocking the cradle and crooning to his son in a foreign tongue stopped Hannah. She watched for a moment, in awe of such a big man so lovingly caring for the small child before she tiptoed from the room and washed the dishes.

By the time she entered the parlor, Max was seated before the fire, puffing on a homemade pipe, his stocking feet propped up on the wood box. He was staring into the flames so intensely that she took a seat on the sofa quietly so as not to disturb him.

Max had heard Hannah enter the room and settle onto the cushions quietly. He glanced up and his eyes came to rest on her hand. "Your palm, it no longer troubles you?"

Hannah tentatively touched her fingers to the flesh. "It was only a minor burn. It's okay now."

He nodded. "And Franc? She is in bed?"

His eyes held genuine interest and caring as he questioned her. Emotions she was not used to. "Yes. Her name is Frances, but she insists on being called Franc." He nodded, causing Hannah to continue. "She doesn't have a father, and I think she's trying to be brave like she thinks a boy should be."

"Brave like a boy?" Max echoed.

"She tries to act a lot tougher than she really is underneath. It's hard for Franc to let down her guard since she has had to fight for everything."

"That I can understand." Max nodded, thinking about his own childhood. "I grow up in the mountains of southern France and life it is hard there."

"Is that why you came to America?"

"To make my fortune, so I take my family back home a wealthy man, like so many other of my countrymen they do. Only life it does not quite work out the way I plan maybe."

It was Hannah's turn to bob her head in a sympathetic nod. "Life seldom does. I hadn't planned to end up poor and alone either."

A fiery pride flashed in his eyes for a moment. "I am not alone or a poor man, Hannah. I own over five thousand sheep and my ranch it has much land, so comes my younger brother who is out with my papa shepherding the flock so I care for the children. I am able to support my family well. But I learn that wealth you do not measure it in money."

"True," she agreed. She had been very wealthy by anyone's standards as Emmett's wife. But her spirit had been bankrupt.

"Yes, well,"— he rose—"I think that morning it comes soon enough maybe. So, Hannah Turner, I suggest you join your daughter and get some sleep. You need your rest."

As Hannah rose, she watched him take the poker and stir the fire. The muscles in his arms bulged and corded veins stood out on his bronze forearms. He was a man who had learned the lessons of hard work firsthand, and Hannah intended to prove to him that she was not just some helpless female as he had charged earlier.

"Tomorrow I'm going to start showing you that I can earn my keep."

He stopped what he was doing and gazed at her. "Everyone on a ranch they earn their keep."

"Well, tomorrow I am going to churn some fresh butter." She announced the idea she had been thinking of earlier.

His brow arched. "Do you ever churn butter before, Hannah?"

"Well, no, but I'm a quick learner and a hard worker. Furthermore, how hard can churning butter possibly be?"

To her surprise, he set the poker aside and in two strides had reached out and squeezed her upper right arm. In a reflex action Hannah pulled her arm out of his grasp, stepped back, and stared at him.

"I startle you maybe. I am just wondering whether you got the muscles for it."

"Women don't have muscles," she insisted, and tried to relax. But he was right, she had been startled. She had been grabbed like that before when Emmett was getting ready to take his pleasure with her.

"Ranch women they do," he said, thinking how his Mary's arms had become grooved like a man's from the hard work. For a moment, regret of the hard life Mary had known assailed him, and he thought it would be a shame if Hannah's woman's softness were to be pared down by the backbreaking work a ranch like his required.

"I'm not a ranch woman," she cut in into his thoughts.

His face hardened. "No, you are not, and I do not think maybe there is much hazard for you to become one. Good night, Hannah."

Before she turned and joined Franc in the warm kitchen, Hannah stood for a moment, watching Max snuff out the lamps. She was not sure whether she was more irritated with herself for making the comment or more irritated with him for agreeing with her.

Hannah slipped off the baggy clothing he had given her to wear and folded it on the floor near the edge of the makeshift bed. Franc was curled around Panda Pie when Hannah lifted the covers after attending to her body's needs and joined Franc.

Franc rose on her elbow and twisted her head toward Hannah. "You don't really plan to earn your keep around this broken-down place, do you?"

"*I* don't"—Hannah heard Franc heave a sigh of relief before she finished—"but we do."

"You ain't my ma, so I don't have to—"

"Yes, you do," Hannah cut off the girl's strangled rasp. "And since we have no other options, while we're here, I am your mother and you will do what I say. You will no longer be disrespectful, do you understand?"

Franc said through tight lips, "Yeah, I understand."

"Good. Whether you like it or not, we're going to be living here for some time, so you might just as well get used to the idea of making an honest living."

"But you ain't my ma and he'll find out that you lied about that, too."

Hannah tilted her chin. "I intend to be completely truthful and tell him."

"Then we'll be leavin' this god-awful forsaken shack soon?"

"You know that's impossible."

Franc huffed, "He'll kick us out for sure when he finds out."

"I will tell him when the time's right. In the meantime, you are going to start behaving yourself."

Hannah reached out to stroke the girl's cheek, but she leaned out of Hannah's reach. Understanding the difficulty Franc had accepting any display of affection, Hannah stroked her pup, then settled against the fresh pillow.

Hannah frowned into the darkness. She had her work cut out for her with both girls. "Good night, Franc."

" 'Night," Franc harrumphed.

Franc had been choked into silence by the woman's newfound forcefulness and laid back down to gently rub the sleeping puppy in the darkness of the night. She had to figure out a way to handle this sudden turn of events.

She couldn't just run away as she had in the past when she didn't like stuff. There was nowhere to go in all that stupid snow. But she didn't like the way things were ciphering out. Hannah seemed to be taking that dumb old rancher's side, those two kids weren't as feeble-witted as she first thought, and if she wasn't careful, she was going to be put to work. The very idea of work stuck in her throat like the taste of Hannah's cooking.

Well, somehow she was not going to let anyone get the best of her. It may take more time than she thought, but somehow she was going to come up with a way to turn things around the way she wanted them to go.

No, this was war, and it wasn't over yet! Not by a long shot. With that thought held firmly in her mind, Franc closed her eyes and suddenly the answer crystallized in the round gold dots of light that often appeared when she squeezed her eyes shut.

The best way to get Hannah back on her side so things would go to her way of thinking again was by stopping the fledgling partnership between Hannah and that foreign woolly rancher cold before it went any further.

And what better way than riling things up a bit with those kids?

Nine

Hannah awoke to the aroma of bacon sizzling over the fire. She sat up and adjusted her eyes to the light to see Max bent over the flames, turning the crispy strips. His children were quietly seated around the table, Lissa holding Samuel. Max brought to her mind the picture of domesticity that Hannah had always secretly longed for.

"So, Hannah Turner, you are finally awake. I think, after you plan to churn butter today, you change your mind maybe."

She smoothed back several errant strands of hair and fought back the queasiness in her stomach. "I haven't changed my mind." Her gaze trailed to the cold gray light at the window. "But that doesn't mean I have to get up at dawn to do it."

"Gol-ly," Franc whined, and stuck her nose out from underneath the covers. "Ain't nobody in this house got smarts enough to know I was sleepin'?"

Hannah ignored Franc's complaints. She had a

complaint of her own. "How am I expected to get up and get dressed without any privacy?"

A spare smile threatened Max's lips. "André, you go fetch Hannah the extra pair of boots Petya leaves here."

Hannah watched the boy shoot her a disgruntled frown, but silently leave the table to follow his father's directives. Lissa turned her back on Hannah, as did Max. "Aren't you going to leave, too?"

"You got three minutes maybe before André he returns, so you better be quick about dressing," Max said without glancing at her. "I must keep watch on the food. I got my back to you and you got nothing to worry about. I do not look."

Hannah heaved a sigh but did not waste a moment. She snatched the clothes underneath the covers with her and fought the modesty-providing blanket as she scrambled into the overly generous attire. Panda Pie whined, and Hannah quickly carried the pup to the door and gently gave her a nudge before she messed on the floor and drew the rancher's promised retribution.

"Here," André said, returning, and shoved the boots and a pair of woolen socks into Hannah's hands.

"Thank you," she said more by rote, since the boy's demeanor did not warrant her gratitude. She quickly jabbed her feet into the thick woolen socks and boots, grateful that at least something was going right. The boots fit in comparison with the rest of her costume.

"You take my extra coat from the hook by the door to see to your needs," Max instructed.

"But there's a blizzard out there." Hannah's head shot up, and she had to hold her long hair back from her face. Max was staring at her and for a moment she feared that he could tell her stomach was upset.

"There is a break in the storm maybe," he said, and handed her the pot she had used the night before. Without a word she slipped into the coat. Using his footprints in the deep drifts, she followed the long strides through the snow toward the outhouse. Her pup fell in step behind her until the goose, which seemed to come out of nowhere, hissed, stretched its neck, and chased Hannah and her pup into the small outbuilding.

It was almost as if a silent communication had passed between them. As if Max had known what she'd been thinking when he'd handed her the pot, she thought after making sure the goose had gone before she returned to the house. No one had ever anticipated her needs before, let alone made any attempt to meet them and stave off the necessity to broach such a delicate subject.

Not about to mention the goose and give them cause to laugh at her, Hannah had kept her silence and took over kitchen duties after the morning meal while Max had put the toddler back down in his bed and then headed outside.

The older children did not need direction, they had donned their coats and knitted scarves and gone out without direction. Hannah was thankful that Franc had followed their lead without further protest.

The chores of the morning complete as far as Hannah was concerned, she slid back into Max's coat and went outside to hunt up the butter churn. The minute she stepped from the house she was hit square on the side of the face by a snowball.

"Daughterly love," a grinning Franc crowed, wiping her gloved hands down the front of her.

"Daughterly love, huh?" Hannah returned, and hurtled a big wet ball of her own back at Franc. It was childish, she knew. But Hannah had fond memories of the immature pastime she had so enjoyed as a young girl.

Soon the other children had been coaxed into the game on Franc's side and Hannah was receiving the worst of it.

"Get back to your chores," Max's voice boomed out as he was blasted with an icy sphere. The Garat children scrambled back to work. Franc stood still, looking mighty guilty and proud of it.

"We were merely having a few moments of frolic," Hannah insisted, standing up for them.

"Frolic it is for when work is done," he said, not inclined to tell her that her daughter had intentionally hit him with a snowball. They had made progress and reached a truce, and he did not want to break it, especially if they were going to be living under the same roof for the winter. There would be time for the girl to learn proper discipline. He would see to that. "Here. You follow me and I show you how the butter, you churn it, yes?"

He handed Hannah what looked to her like a long stick with blades and walked past her into the house, carrying a wooden barrel.

He remembered. She had not had to remind him. He set it up, gave a brief demonstration, and turned to leave. "Where are you going?"

"I go back to work. While André and I we go to fetch the wagon, you churn the butter maybe."

"What else can I do? This shouldn't take me long."

To Hannah's chagrin, he said, "Rest."

Hannah went to the window and watched Max talk to the girls before he and André mounted the two swayback horses and headed out from the ranch. Then she turned and walked toward the churn with determined steps.

Her confidence in herself was already returning since she had taken control of her life away from Emmett. Feeling quite capable for the first time in years, she decided that she would have a whole crock of freshly churned butter ready long before he got back, and have the house cleaned, and perhaps start cutting out the fabric for a skirt as well.

After discovering that it was going to take more than a few quick pumps, Hannah agitated the blades of the wooden dasher until her back and arms ached. She peeked into the churn. A frothy liquid met her eyes. She returned to pumping until she thought she could not continue, but she was determined, and by the time she was finished she had butter.

"You're not going to find fault with me today, Max Garat," she said to the torturous churn, and shoved back a damp curl that had fallen into her eyes.

Exhausted, she poured herself a glass of buttermilk. She went into the parlor and sat down near the fire to drink it. She needed a few minutes rest, then she would resume the duties of a ranch woman.

"So, Hannah, you take my advice," Max announced.

"You are back so soon," she said, coming awake at the sound of his rich, deep voice. "I must have fallen asleep for a few minutes." She rose up on her elbow, only to realize that it was dark outside and someone had covered her with a heavy woolen blanket.

"It is not soon nor a few minutes. The children they already eat supper and are fast asleep."

Hannah started to get up, but felt warm, silken fur wiggle at her toes.

Panda Pie had somehow made her way to Hannah and was hidden beneath the covers at her feet. If Max discovered the pup he would banish her to the barn.

She had to think of something fast! Before she could come up with an idea, Max grabbed the corner of the blanket.

"No!" she exclaimed, and grabbed back the blanket. "I'll do it. I am perfectly capable," she added so as not to show her alarm.

"Suit yourself."

In a panic Hannah leapt up and started bunching the hand-spun wool around her precious pet. The little pup squeaked, causing her to jump.

"You are all right?" he asked.

Hannah shot up with the blanket in her arms bunched around the pup. "I'm fine. Fine." At his curious look, she amended, "I mean, I'm a little sore from churning the butter. I just did not want to tell you."

"I see."

Without a word he turned and went into the bedroom, leaving her alone. Hannah saw an opportunity and rushed into the kitchen. She had just plunked Panda Pie on her straw bed when he entered the kitchen.

"Come back into the parlor with me, Hannah, yes?"

Hannah was relieved to have concealed Panda Pie long enough to return her to the kitchen and followed Max back to the parlor without question.

"Sit down, yes?" He motioned to the chair before the flickering fire.

She settled into the chair hesitantly and craned her neck, trying to keep an eye on him when he walked around behind her. She jumped when he put his hands on her neck.

"Do not worry, Hannah Turner, I am not going to hurt you. Your muscles they are sore from churning the butter. Massage, it will help. I got some cream from the bedroom that will help your arms."

Hannah tried to relax for the second time that night as his fingers began to work their magic. She was sore. She was tired. And she was scared. This man was different. Maybe it was because he had a foreign accent, or was from a foreign country, or was a family man, or was patient despite his annoyance, or, despite herself, that she found herself attracted to him.

His fingers worked over her shoulders and down her arms. Then he kneeled in front of her and pushed her sleeves up. He dipped into the cream and warmed it between his palms, applying it to her forearms while his fingers worked their magic.

"Your muscles, they are very tight. Already they are starting to strengthen. You show today a new beginning," he said softly. "You accomplish something with good honest hard work.

"Hannah Turner, while I am out fetching the wagon, I take time to think. I believe that you and me, we get off to a bad start. You answer my advertisement for a seamstress when you are looking for a husband. And then the letters. I need someone so bad that perhaps I do not make myself clearly understood.

"I think maybe part of our problems at the station they are my fault. I am not expecting the needle lady to come with a child. And my bones they are weary after the long trip back to the ranch, and I do not sleep well when I see what you try to sew."

"I did try," she interjected. "I'm new at the trade and needed the work." Although not entirely honest, what she said was essentially true, she thought as the blood in her veins surged forward underneath his fingers.

"Yes. And cook you do try, although maybe not too good. So, I think it is that I am too hard on you maybe. Since we are to be here together for now, I think we should start anew maybe. Of course, only if that is what you want, too, yes?"

He did not tell her that he had checked the pass while he was out and that he may have been able to breach it before the spring thaw if he had really put his back into it. His decision to have her and the child remain was too new, too difficult to define to shatter such a tenuous truce.

Hannah could hardly believe her ears. She was being given a second chance. A fresh start with this man and his family. For an instant she almost believed that she was the needle lady. She threw her arms around his neck in gratitude, only to bring her nose to nose with the big rancher.

A warm, golden glow flickered across her face and mingled with the soft scent of freshly churned butter. Max's gaze lingered on her bewitching green eyes and caught on her lips. She looked like a young girl with that line of buttermilk tracing a path over her full mouth. Max was reminded of the first love of his youth.

The reminiscence and Hannah's nearness mesmerized him. He lifted his fingers to her lips and gently wiped the milk with the pad of his thumb. "You got milk, like a young girl, above your lip, Hannah."

"Do I?"

She brought her hand toward her mouth, but he closed his over hers and brought it down. His hand was rough and warm, as she had imagined.

Her hand was smooth and silken, as he had imagined last night when he lay awake for hours unable to get the woman off his mind.

"Yes, you do," he murmured.

A rush of desire overwhelmed him, hot and urgent. Unable to stop himself, Max cradled her face between his palms, tilted his head, and kissed her.

Instinctively, without conscious thought, Hannah gave silent permission to be kissed.

It was a gentle kiss, undemanding, chaste, but filled with desire and yearning. For Hannah it signified her longing to put her past behind her, to forget the pain and wash away the memories that had brought about a vow to wall herself away from all of male humanity. For Max it had grown from their enforced nearness, from watching her, from the growing belief that perhaps it was finally time to lay Mary to rest.

Max lowered a hand to hers and rubbed his calloused thumb over the back of her hand, waiting for some sign of rejection or condemnation or self-loathing for allowing his desire to rule his actions.

It was not forthcoming. Rather, a long-dormant yearning awoke inside him.

He pulled back and stood, helping Hannah to her feet. He felt her tense and immediately drew back. "I think for us it is time to say good night, Hannah."

She swallowed, still experiencing the tingling sensations left by his gentle-hearted kiss. Her hand absently massaging her collarbone, she murmured softly, "Yes, I think it would be a very good idea. Good night, Max."

As Max lay in the darkness of his bedroom, he discovered that the glimmer of feeling that had reawakened took hold and found root in his chest. He had thought he was no longer a man. That all feeling deep inside him had perished the night his Mary died. He had been convinced that he was empty, a shell left hollow and barren like the memories of the burned-out stone houses from his boyhood village. He continued to rise each morning to care for the children because he had promised her. And although he loved his children, he had been unable to stop thinking of himself as little more than one of the walking dead—until now.

A sudden revelation settled gently over him in the wee hours of the early morning darkness.

He was still a man.

Ten

Life for Hannah seemed to settle into a comfortable pattern after such a rocky beginning. Her first kiss with Max had signaled some sort of subtle transformation in their relationship. Their open adversarial positions had faded, to be replaced by the beginnings of what Hannah described as a familiar companionship.

He had begun waiting to enter the kitchen until she was up, dressed, and the morning sickness had passed. Then he would help her start the morning firewood he had hauled. Sometimes he would stand a trifle close, his arm lightly touching hers, then move away with a lopsided grin.

Hannah would sometimes reach past him from behind and brush his arm when she set a dish of food or an eating utensil on the table. This was always before the children were washed up and sitting at the table. And she never glanced at him when she did it. Rather, she would always say, "Excuse me," and step away.

Sometimes Hannah wondered if their actions were akin to the beginnings of some type of courtship ritual. But then she would catch herself, and stop such outrageous notions. She was probably reading more into his actions than were there.

The children were another matter. None of them, except Sammy, was overjoyed with the arrangement. Although André seemed more responsive than Lissa when Hannah had spoken with him and tried to understand his feelings. Lissa remained obstinate and steadfast in her anger.

"I do not need help to clean the house or put out the wash, Papa," Lissa insisted, glaring at Hannah from across the breakfast table.

"You work much too hard. With Hannah here, your workload, it will lessen maybe." Max raised a hand and waved her off. "Do not argue." He swung his attention from his daughter to his son. "André, you take Franc and show her how to gather eggs, and let her help you clean the stalls in the barn."

"Gol-ly"—Franc looked around at the other children already scrambling to do *his* bidding—"I ain't hangin' around here just so I can be the lucky one to shovel sh—"

"Franc!" Hannah snapped. "You best get started helping. There won't be any lunch for you until you do."

Once Hannah had begun asserting herself, she had discovered a new, accomplished side she had

not known existed. She was perfectly capable of
handling a recalcitrant Franc.

By the time Hannah walked into the bedroom,
Lissa was leaning down through the opening in
the ceiling as if waiting for her. "I do not need
your help up here," Lissa snorted.

Hannah nodded as the girl disappeared from
the opening. Lissa needed more time to accept
her. But the undertow of tension she created was
difficult to endure.

While Hannah straightened the toddler's bed,
a warm glow slid through her. Next spring she
would be straightening the blankets for her own
baby.

She moved next to Max's bed. Her hand
worked out the wrinkles, which seemed to have
been left by a restless sleeper, and she wondered
if he was having as much difficulty sleeping as
she was. The quilt, sewn in loving symbolism of
the Garat brood by the dead woman's hand,
caught Hannah off guard. She touched the fine
blue threads. Before today she had not noticed
the childish faces and dates stitched in the
squares, signifying the birth of the children, or
the bride and groom and wedding date, or the
house and sheep. It was a wonderful tapestry, a
testament in family history and the love Max had
shared with his wife.

Feeling unsettled and like an outsider, who
somehow had intruded on something very sacred,

Hannah quickly finished making up the bed and moved to the dressing table.

She picked up the dust cloth she had brought in from the kitchen and set to work. Careful so as not to disturb the positioning of the bottles and jars on the dressing table, Hannah took each one individually and, with the utmost care, wiped the specks of dust that had gathered on the precious keepsakes.

"How dare you touch my mama's things!" snapped Lissa, her breath coming out in an ugly hiss as she descended the ladder.

A purple-tinted perfume bottle in her hand, Hannah swung around at the spiking sound of the girl's voice. "Lissa, I was only cleaning the—"

Lissa grabbed the bottle. But when she ripped it out of Hannah's hand, the lovely flowered top disengaged from the bottle and perfume spilled down the front of Hannah's shirt.

The scent of gardenias wafted about the room and mingled with Lissa's cries.

"Now look what you have done," Lissa wailed, and held the bottle to her budding breasts.

Hannah was horrified at the results of what had begun as nothing more than an honest effort to prove that she could be just as good a ranch woman as any of them.

"Papa is going to be furious with you when I tell him you were messing with Mama's things."

The girl's nasty intent to bend the truth was all Hannah could tolerate. "You are going to do no such thing, young lady, you hear me?" The authority in Hannah's voice immediately stilled Lissa. "Your father has enough on his mind without being forced to take on the problems between us."

The girl's lower lip began to quiver, causing Hannah to say more softly, "Lissa, I know you loved you mother very much, but I am not trying to replace her."

"You never could." She sniffled back tears.

"No one could, and I do understand that. So can't we at least try to get along? You may even come to find out that I am not so bad, and eventually we may even become friends."

"I do not want to hurt Papa, so I won't tell him." Lissa lifted tear-filled, defiant eyes to Hannah. "But we will never become friends. I will go set the tub to boiling for the wash."

Hannah felt deflated once the girl left. Their little talk had not ended as she had hoped it would. She wasn't trying to usurp the children's loyalty to their mother, but life would be so much simpler while she was there if they all could at least make some effort to get along. She was not going to give up on the girl.

The strong scent made her realize that she certainly couldn't continue to wear the perfume-soaked clothing. She did not want to cause Max any pain from the memories the scent might evoke. While she hunted through Max's meager wardrobe for something clean to wear, careful to keep the fragrance from getting on anything else in the room, an idea came to her.

She had been meaning to attack that obstinate sewing machine again. Now she had good reason not to forestall it any longer.

Hannah finished cleaning the bedroom, then made certain that mean goose was nowhere in sight before she left the house and dropped the fragrant clothes into the washtub that Lissa had bubbling. It was a cold, crisp day, and steam bellowed from the tub in clouds of puffy white; it matched the mounds of snow piled against the fence and mounded around the yard.

Lissa finished hanging a pair of André's drawers on the line and whipped around. "I have put up all the family wash except the sheets." She sent Hannah her most brittle smile. "I thought I would save that for you, since you seem to have such a personal interest in them."

Hannah sighed as the young girl stalked off. But there was nothing she could do about the girl's attitude for the time being. Lissa was Max's child, and it was not her place to discipline the girl.

The goose hissed, causing Hannah to jump and cast an uneasy glance over her shoulder. She let out a relieved sigh to find it in the corner of the enclosed pen. Feeling safe from the beast, she picked up what looked like a long pole and began to stir the tub.

For a moment she was afraid that the perfumed shirt and trousers would scent the sheets, but the harsh lye soap did its job admirably. When she finally picked the clothes out and draped them over the line, no scent remained.

She was struggling with the bed linens, when Max suddenly appeared. He had a stool in his hand.

"Lissa, she tells me you may need this stool," he said.

"She sent you?" Hannah asked, confused by what seemed to be the girl's sudden generosity.

A shadow came over his face. "No, not exactly. It is in her hands and I offer to bring it to you," he said, thinking not to tell Hannah that Lissa had it with her in one of the stalls as if preparing to hide it. "I think you and she still have trouble maybe, yes?"

Hannah forced a smile and dropped a gentle hand on his arm. "She is just young."

"I speak with her again."

"No!" Hannah's grip tightened "I think it would be best if we worked it out ourselves."

"Suit yourself." Silently he admired her determination with his daughter. It had been difficult with Lissa the last two years, and sometimes Max didn't know what to say to the girl. "Here"—he set the stool on the ground and positioned it under the line—"you let me help you."

"I can manage." Holding the sheet against her body with one hand, she started to step up on the stool, but he steadied her around the waist.

Hannah sucked in a breath at the strength of his fingers around her middle and quietly draped the sheet over the line. The white cotton flapped in the breeze, and Hannah hurried and fished the next sheet from the tub to make short work of that one as well.

When he helped her off the stool a second time, they were standing together, his arms circled around her, between the two sheets as if they were between rippling walls that shut out the rest of the world.

"Standing here, it makes it seem like we are alone, I think," he said, and gazed down at her. She looked back up at him with big, disturbing eyes. He almost wished that she had been old and ugly; life would have been so much simpler if she were.

"Yes, it does." His body had tautened beneath her fingertips. She tensed and kept her gaze away from that incredible full mouth. Instead, she made a study of the wrinkles around his eyes. But all that did was make her want to touch the creases there.

Franc, who had seen two pairs of feet peeking out from under the sheets, positioned in a suspicious angle facing each other, crouched down and edged her way stealthily through the yard so she could get a better look.

What she saw disgusted her.

"You learn very fast, Hannah Turner," he said, intently gazing at her mouth.

"I have a good teacher." Her eyes watched him while her body reacted of its own volition.

"And I got a good pupil."

"I am sorry you must spend so much time teaching me things. I should have told you I am new at the trade."

"I guess every woman she must begin somewhere to learn her profession."

Hannah could hardly believe her ears. He was openly making excuses for her, understanding the portion of her dilemma that she had shared with him.

"Me, I learn from the time I can walk to become a sheepherder. It is what the men in my village do, besides, of course, smuggling. The Basques, they are very good smugglers. It is a time-honored tradition and we accept it unless it accompanies acts of violence or falsehoods."

The word *falsehoods* momentarily disturbed Hannah, since the beginning of their relationship was built on a bed of falsehoods, and Max obviously had a great aversion to them. In an effort not to dwell on the other secrets she harbored, she said, "I'm sure you would be good at whatever you tried."

"You think so, do you?"

"Yes." She searched his eyes, feeling the heat in her own cheeks rise. He was a man who was comfortable with himself and his abilities.

"I hope you think I am good at this too," he

rasped and angled his head, lowering his mouth toward hers.

He was going to kiss her again, and Hannah closed her eyes in rapt anticipation.

A ruckus not more than fifteen feet from them suddenly erupted.

"Of all the pissant, jumpin' toady grasshoppers in a day of Sundays," Franc squalled.

The moment vanished, and Hannah turned and rushed toward Franc, who kneeled beside an overturned basket of eggs, furiously beating a scrap of kindling against the crushed shells.

"Franc, are you all right? You didn't get hurt, did you?" Hannah kneeled down and was checking for bruises, when Max stopped her.

"I tripped," the girl sobbed, and kept her face as innocent as the fresh, untouched snow.

"I think Franc she is not hurt maybe?" Max said, joining Hannah.

It was a question, but his expression told Franc that he did not believe her. She clung to Hannah and stared up at the huge rancher. "I coulda kilt myself workin' 'round here."

"No, instead, you make sure there will be no eggs for breakfast, yes, Franc?"

"It weren't my fault," she blurted out and let the tears she reserved for special effect flow freely down her cheeks.

Franc had not cried since she'd met her, which made Hannah want to believe her, although she silently wondered about the suspicious mishap.

Especially since she had run over to Franc and had found her own footing perfectly secure.

"Well, you clean up the mess and then go back to helping André. There is still much you got to learn around a ranch."

"Yeah, and a lot you got to learn, too," Franc muttered under her breath before scrambling back toward the barn. She made a big production out of slipping once or twice just to make it look good. But inside, her determination was steady and sure.

"I'm sure it really was just an accident," Hannah said. She truly wanted to believe Franc would not do such a thing when she didn't know she had an audience nearby.

"I am sure too," was all Max said as he watched the child scamper out of sight. He turned his attention back to Hannah. He could see from her face that the moment between them had passed.

"I wash up, then I show you how to make noodles if you want maybe."

Hannah nodded. "Yes, if it isn't as difficult as churning butter."

"It is easy. A cup of flour, a pinch of salt, one egg"—Hannah noticed him glance down at Franc's mess with barely hidden disgust before returning his attention to her—"and half an eggshell of water. Mix it up, roll it out and let it sit, then boil the strips you cut.

"I check on Samuel. Then we cook, yes?"

"Yes."

Hannah stood out in the cold and watched him go inside the house. The scent of the strong soap reminded her of her earlier mishap with Lissa, and Hannah pinched her lips together. She hoped that she had cleaned well enough to erase the gardenia scent from his bedroom.

Max walked into the bedroom, went straight over to Samuel's bed, and lifted the little boy into his arms. As he was crooning, to the sleepy toddler, a faint hint of a familiar scent assaulted his nostrils and he whipped around.

Mary's favorite perfume.

Eleven

Max felt as though he had been kicked in the stomach. With Samuel clinging to his hip, Max purposely strode to the dressing table and checked the bottles until he found the one he was looking for. Just holding the cool, fragile glass in his hand brought the bittersweet memories flooding back.

"I bring you your bride, Maximilian Garat," a long-boned-faced Etchahoun said, and drew the sturdy, dark, russet-haired girl forward. "This she is our Mary."

Although the marriage had been arranged, Max never questioned the family's choice. They were married a short time later, and although they were little more than intimate strangers, set out for America to make their fortune.

They arrived in Nevada with little more than hope, a few bottles of sweet-smelling water Mary had refused to relinquish, and a dream.

Samuel started to fuss, which brought Max back to the present. He wiped the bottle, set it back in its place, and turned his attention to Samuel. But not before he thought how different Hannah was from Mary. The only time Mary had gone against him was when she had refused to abandon her perfumes, despite the extra burden of transporting the delicate bag. Hannah had already shown how stubborn she could be.

Of course, Mary had been given to him; Hannah had not.

Max set Samuel back in his bed with a toy while he used the bowl of water on the bureau to wash up, change his shirt, and slick back his black hair.

Lissa pulled back from where she silently watched from the opening in the ceiling. She sat on the floor, waiting for her papa to leave the bedroom and praying that the drops of perfume she had drizzled down the outside of the bottle had been enough to remind him of her mama.

Lissa had waited and listened all evening for her papa to mention the perfume incident, but it wasn't until the next morning, as she was putting on her coat to go out and do chores, that he finally broached the topic.

Looking out the window he had inserted over the kitchen work counter, Max casually said, "Although we have snow on the ground outside, in the bedroom it smells like the spring flowers."

Hannah's hand stopped in midair from drying the last dish. "I meant to tell you about that."

"About what, Hannah?"

"It was an accident." Hannah shot a quick glance at Lissa. The girl was biting her lower lip. "I was dusting and the perfume bottle accidentally opened in my hand."

"Ah, I see," was all he said. Max had not missed the exchange between Hannah and his daughter. He might have pursued the matter further since he did not believe he had the whole story, but Hannah had wanted to try to work things out with his daughter.

"It won't happen again," Hannah said, and let her words settle on Lissa.

Lissa's lips were stretched into a thin, tight line and she slammed the door. Neither Franc nor André said a word during the exchange. They buttoned their coats and followed Lissa out into the yard.

"I am out butchering hogs today and make blood sausage, so I think you may wish to remain in the house maybe," Max said as he shrugged into his coat. "It is not a pleasant sight for you, and I need someone in the house to help with Samuel."

Hannah brightened, relieved after the tension-filled moments before Lissa had left the house. She had no desire to be forced to witness such a gruesome event.

"I will enjoy watching over Samuel." He nodded and turned to leave, then Hannah said,

"Thank you, Max, for not pursuing the incident with the perfume."

"It is an accident," he said, but not before she noticed a flash of pain cross his face.

"Yes." She lowered her eyes. She did not want him to see her expression for fear that it would give away another half-truth she had spun. Luckily, he did not question her further. Rather, he left her alone in the kitchen with Samuel, who was still playing with his breakfast.

"All right, Sammy, you finish that slice of bread while I set up the sewing machine. Then you can play on the floor with Panda Pie while I show your daddy that I do not have to be taught everything."

"Mama, Mama." He stuffed the last bite of buttered bread into his mouth and lifted his chubby arms.

"Oh, Sammy,"—she hugged him—"you precious little tyke."

After a big kiss she set Sammy on the floor and called Panda Pie off the blanket in the corner. She slipped the little dog a bite of bacon, then watched the child and dog romp for a few minutes.

The little dog nudged and tried to lick Sammy. He squealed with delight and made a grab for Panda Pie, who darted under benches and raced around the kitchen in circles before skidding to a stop in front of Sammy. Then the game started over.

Satisfied that Sammy would be well entertained, Hannah set out to do battle with the infamous sewing machine.

She got tangled in the threads and briefly whispered, " 'Oh, what a tangled web we weave,' " to herself, wondering who had coined the phrase as she attempted to unsnarl the nest of threads. They were reminiscent of the complicated tangle she had woven into her own life, and a reminder of how her mother was inclined toward her own favorite clichés. Hannah wondered if she was ever going to unfetter herself from such a snarled muddle.

After the first skirmish, Hannah had the machine threaded and was ready to tackle her next campaign. She pulled a length of green calico from the supplies and spread it out on the cleared table.

She had been studying Lissa's worn skirt for days, and with no more than her imagination and determination, she set to work.

Hannah waited until after supper and everyone had adjourned from the kitchen for the parlor before she changed into the green calico skirt.

Pleased with her efforts at gathering the fabric and stitching a band around it, she strolled into the parlor, held out the surprisingly passable skirt, and twirled around.

"What do you think?" she asked.

Max removed the pipe from his mouth. "I think that you are on your way to becoming a very good seamstress maybe. The skirt it goes well with my white shirt."

Hannah was pleased at the twinkle in his eye as he perused her efforts with a nod of approval. Her pleasure ended when she caught sight of Lissa. The girl wore an expression of angry longing, and Hannah noted how Lissa's small hands unconsciously smoothed at her own worn skirt. It gave Hannah another idea.

"Do you like it, Lissa?"

"What difference does it make whether I do or not?" Lissa said tightly, lifted a yawning Sam into her arms, and stalked from the parlor.

"Franc?"

"Why ask me? I don't know nothin' 'bout skirts and I don't want to know nothin'." At Hannah's sigh of disappointment, Franc amended, "Guess it's okay for a skirt." Then to André, "Come on, Andy, you promised to teach me how to play marbles after I help Lissa put Sammy down to bed."

Hannah cast Max a wan smile and shrugged. "I guess I managed pretty much to clear the parlor," she said, and gingerly settled onto the sofa.

"I am still here."

"Yes." Hannah felt awkward at the sudden increase in the pace of her heart. She began to babble in an effort to cover her feelings. "When I was growing up, we didn't have much. I guess you could say we were very poor."

"You wear a fine dress at the station," Max remarked.

"I lost everything else I had." It was the truth as far as it went. She could not explain further about the dress she had tucked away next to her bed in the kitchen and how she had lost all her wordly possessions. Because then she would have to tell him about Emmett and Franc, and she could not take the chance of unsettling their fledgling relationship to do that. "I must have looked rather out of place when you first saw me."

"You are not what I expect." He stared at her. Something about her story told him it was another half-truth, and he was sad for the trouble that must be inside her.

Again she felt awkward and ill at ease, as if he were expecting a confession she was not prepared to make. So she said the first thing that came to mind. "When I was a small girl I wore threadbare hand-me-downs."

"It is hard for a little girl maybe?"

She stopped to truly consider his response. "Not as difficult as the flour sacks my mother made for underwear."

"Flour sacks, they are sturdy."

"Yes, they are. Mine were printed with BIG JOE'S FLOUR in big block letters across my backside," she said, a little uneasy to be discussing such an intimate piece of apparel with Max.

Nonetheless, she proceeded because, despite

the awkwardness, it was strangely soothing to lay out the childhood pain that had been locked inside her for so long. "I brought quite a few rounds of laughter when I played with the other little girls and the wind would take up my skirts."

As Max listened to Hannah describe her sorry childhood, he considered her. It was a glimpse of what made up Hannah the woman, and gave him an idea as to at least part of what seemed to be driving her.

"I grow up in the mountains and got only good memories of that time. We honor the old traditions and always help each other."

He found himself telling her far more of himself than was normal for a man of his culture. Basques usually maintained a measure of distance with anyone considered an intruder, which the outside world was deemed in general. It was a strange realization for Max that he had broken the long-held custom.

Max fell still, and the silence seemed to stretch between them. They both stared into the flames of the fire. Max was troubled by the memories of his youth and how different they were from those of the woman who now shared his parlor with him. Hannah was at odds with herself.

Breaking into the heavy quietude, Max suddenly stood. "Tomorrow, it comes before we know it. Good night, Hannah."

"Max. Wait!" she blurted out before she had

the time to think better of it. "There's something I must tell you."

He sat back down and waited. "Yes?"

She watched him nurse his pipe, not quite knowing how to begin unloading part of the burden that plagued her. "I want you to know that I wasn't actually . . . I mean . . . that . . . I—I haven't been married three times."

"I know," he said softly in a matter-of-fact manner.

"You know?" she puzzled. "How?"

"You do not got the look of a woman who buries three men."

"Look?"

"A season look would be a good word maybe. And you know so little about what it takes to run a man's home. With three husbands, I think you got few lessons to learn while you are here."

She considered his response, then waited for him to continue. When he said no more but rather kept watching her, she felt compelled to add, "I don't know why I wrote those things in my letters."

I didn't write those letters. I just can't take the chance and tell you screamed inside her head, and she lifted her fingers to her temple at the first stab of pain.

"I think you do. In time you are able to sort it out and put it into words maybe."

She waited for him to proceed. He merely continued to watch her with the eyes of a keen hawk.

"Is that all you're going to say about it?" she quizzed him, astounded and more than a little relieved and confused that he was not making her confession any more difficult. If only that were all she had to confess.

"Unless maybe you think I should say more."

Thrown off balance, she said, "No. Well, I mean . . . I thought you might become angry and yell or scream or threaten me or something."

"If I show my anger to you in any of those ways, I am sorry," he said, wondering who used to do such things to her. It was not the time to ask such questions, although it gave him further insight into the woman's reasoning. "It is not the Basque way to treat women as such." He got up and moved toward the lamp.

"If you don't mind, I'd like to sit here for a while. I'll extinguish the lamps."

Hannah sat and stared into the flames of the fire for the longest time, attempting to sort out all the emotions barraging her. But answers were as elusive as wishes coming true. Finally she conceded that there would be no simple resolution forthcoming. She was about to bed down for the night, when André suddenly tiptoed into the room.

"Wonder if I could talk to you?" the boy asked as he stood before her, shuffling his feet.

"You can always talk to me, André." She patted the place next to her on the sofa. "Sit down."

He quickly dropped to the sofa and tucked his

feet beneath him. "I just want you to know that I do not hold any bad feelings toward you personally."

"That is good to hear," she answered, and it was.

"Lissa has been pretty mean, but she really is a good sister for a girl. It is just that it is hard for her because she was really close to . . . Mama."

Hannah could hear the crack in his voice and laid a hand on his arm. "You don't need to apologize for your sister. I understand why she is acting the way she does toward me."

Her gentle touch made his chin start to quiver. He had come out to get a few things straight, but he was going to give himself away. He was going to cry.

He couldn't let a woman see a man cry!

"You must miss your mother a great deal," she was saying when he suddenly sprang to his feet.

"Of course I miss my mama."

Her hand tightened on his arm. "André, any time you want to talk, I'm here." At the change of light in his sad eyes, Hannah added, "If there's anything I can ever do to help—"

"There is," he broke in, sniffling back the tears threatening to fill his eyes. "Please don't try to replace my mama."

He raced from the parlor, leaving Hannah surrounded by an even more complicated mixture of emotions. Feeling pushed and pulled in different directions by outside forces only added to her inner turmoil.

And the fact that she was physically stuck in such proximity to Maximilian Garat until spring only made the choices now open to her all the more agonizing.

Twelve

For over three weeks Franc had worked on Lissa's worries about her papa taking up with Hannah now that the pair seemed to have made peace with each other and were getting a mite too friendly. Franc had courted the girl, helping her with dumb old chores and watching little Sammy. Franc liked that part of pretending to be nice to Lissa, but she wouldn't openly admit it to anyone—even if she were strung upside down over a red-ant hill with honey poured between her toes.

She had also spent time being nice to Andy and that stupid woolly of his. Of all the dumb pets—a sheep. Of course, Andy didn't really have brains enough to know that dogs were best. Although for a boy, she secretly admitted, he sorta wasn't too bad.

She had even forced herself to sit with that dumb-witted cat, Furball, in her lap out on the cold porch until she started to sneeze her head off. And she had shot marbles with Andy, and even made herself miss a couple of shots so he would like her—not that she gave one wit, mind you, because she didn't. It was just part of her plan to get Hannah and herself away from the stupid, broken-down ranch.

It was the morning Franc accidentally saw Max helping Hannah hang out the wash again that spurred her into action. Once was bad enough, but twice was too much. Hannah had been struggling as usual, probably because she was putting on weight around the middle from eating too much of Max's cooking—he could cook, Franc would give him that.

Max had stopped his own chores to help Hannah. And when neither thought anyone was looking, Max had leaned over like he was going to kiss Hannah again. Ugh! If Franc hadn't been there to save Hannah, that man would probably have actually done it this time—fastened his mouth on Hannah's!

Such a disgusting thing, mingling spit.

Franc was not dumb. She knew what went on between a man and a woman, since her ma had made a living at letting men poke her. Franc intended to save Hannah from getting caught like her ma, whether Hannah thought she needed it or not.

Franc's ma had said over and over that it was Franc's fault that it happened. Although she did not understand why she was to blame, since she did not like it when men grunted on top of her ma, Franc was determined not to have it be her fault with Hannah. Because even though she had never said anything to Hannah, Franc secretly liked the woman and wouldn't want the same awful thing to happen to her as had to her ma.

Franc waited until all the chores were done after supper and Lissa and Andy had climbed the rickety ladder to their room. Franc tiptoed to the doorway leading to the parlor where Hannah and Max had settled with Sammy before the fire, then tucked Panda Pie within her jacket and scrambled up the ladder.

"Hi, what're you two doin'?"

Each curled comfortably on their narrow beds near a brightly burning lamp, Lissa and Andy looked up from their readers. "What does it look like?" Andy rolled his eyes at the stupid girl. He was sure girls possessed only half a brain. "We are reading, like Papa said. Would you like a book?"

"Why'd I want one of them things?" Franc sniffed. She was not about to admit that she secretly liked reading about all the places she intended to go to when she was grown-up.

"Then what do you want? You know that Papa has been insisting that we finish our lessons every night," Lissa said.

"Yeah. And I know that he plans to send you both away to school next year to finish your lessons, too. But did either one of you know that your pa is gettin' awful sweet on my ma?"

Both children stiffened upright in their beds.

Lissa's face registered suppressed panic at Franc's news, laying bare her biggest fear. Her book tumbled onto the floor.

The loud thud caused Max to holler up from downstairs, "What do you two do up there?"

Furious, Lissa glared at Franc, tempted to tell her father that the girl had disturbed their lessons. But the earnest gleam in Franc's eye stopped Lissa.

"I accidentally dropped my book, Papa." Then Lissa turned on Franc. "All right, Franc, you better tell us exactly what you mean by saying such things, or I will tell Papa you have been sneaking around, spying on everyone."

Hurt after all the effort at making friends with the mean girl, Franc crossed her arms over her flat chest. "You can tattle if you want. But don't be surprised if he lies to you."

"My papa does not lie!" Lissa exclaimed, Andy bobbing his head in agreement.

Yet Franc could see from the troubled glimmer in Lissa's eyes that the girl believed her. Probably even caught her pa staring at Hannah when he didn't think anybody saw.

"Okay, okay, everybody but your pa tells fibs. Ain't you interested in stoppin' it, or do you want to sit by and just watch until you got a new ma?"

Franc could tell by the sudden intake of breath that she had hit her mark, and she pushed forward. She got to her feet and started toward the ladder. Then she stopped and tossed over her shoulder, "Well, if you change your minds and wanna hear out what I got in mind to stop it, you know where I'll be."

"Wait!" Lissa hailed Franc.

"Lissa, what are you doing?" André questioned. He didn't want a new mama, and he sure didn't want another dumb sister! But secretly he liked Hannah. She had been nice to him and listened to him without getting mad or walking away like his papa did when he tried to talk about his mama.

"Hush up, André. You do not want that awful woman to be our mama, do you?" Lissa snapped.

"Wait just a dang minute," Franc interceded on Hannah's behalf, her little hands balled into fists, ready to fight. She may not openly tell Hannah what she meant to her, but no one was going to talk against her like that in Franc's presence either.

"Sorry, Franc. I did not mean to say anything bad about your mama. But André and I do not want her for ours."

Franc relaxed her fists. "Yeah, well, I don't want your pa for mine neither. I'll tell you what. I won't say nothin' more bad 'bout your pa if you don't say nothin' more bad 'bout my ma. I just thought we might work together to break up any silly notions they might come up with since they're gettin' a mite too social." She thrust her hand forward. "Deal?"

Lissa and André looked at each for a moment,

then plunged their hands forward, Lissa's more swiftly than André's. The three children locked right hands and on the spot made a pact.

"Max, what would you think if we made a pact?" Hannah suddenly set out in a tumble of words after weeks of silent consideration. Max had just returned from putting Sammy down to bed for the night. It was the first time in a week the two of them were alone for more than fifteen minutes without at least one of the children popping up.

He folded his large frame in the middle of the sofa and spread his arm along the back of the pillows. Curled up in the corner of the sofa, he could almost touch her with his fingertips.

"What kind it is this pact?"

His face was unreadable and it gave her pause, but the words weighing on her mind had already left her lips, so she was committed.

"A pact that no matter what happens between us, we will consider the children and put their welfare first."

"We do not do it any other way." He leaned over and stretched his hand out.

Hannah did not hesitate. She slipped her hand into his.

"I think that this has become a most pleasant time for me," he said, and squeezed her hand. But silently he had started to long for more than

companionship, although it went against his beliefs. Feelings he had thought had died had only
been numb, lying dormant until this particular
woman had come along.

Hannah had lost her fear of him as a man,
and now looked forward to holding hands when-
ever they had the opportunity. She found that
she secretly began to hope that perhaps the en-
joyment they took in each other's company might
be a prelude to something more, something
stronger. Yet a nagging fear in the back of her
mind continued to plague her with the knowledge
that she was the only woman within seventy miles.

When he inched closer and tentatively dropped
his arm around her shoulders, Hannah's concern
vanished.

"You are getting stronger," he said. "I can feel
the muscles."

Hannah knew it was a compliment from a man
who had a difficult time expressing his feelings
openly. "Yes, the work seems to agree with me."

"I am glad," he said, and in an unexpected
move pulled her closer to him. She smelled of
soap, and the urge to run his fingers through
her hair overcame him. Silently he pulled the
pins from the silken chestnut strands twisted at
her neck and let them cascade into the palm of
his hand.

"Your hair, it is soft," he murmured. Without
taking his eyes from hers, he arranged the heavy

mass over her shoulders. "I think that I like it down."

His black hair curled over the collar of his wool workshirt, casting the coal blackness of it a golden glow from the fire. Hannah could not help herself, she reached out and wound a curl around her index finger. "We are alone together," she breathed.

"Yes, we are that."

She gathered her courage. "Would you consider kissing me again too brazen?"

"No, Hannah Turner. I would consider it an honor."

What began as a gentle, lingering kiss grew like long-smoldering embers into the flames of a fire. Hannah moaned her desire and pressed herself against him, crushing her breasts against his chest. She locked her arms around his neck, offering her submission.

A low groan escaped him, dissolving against her mouth. He chewed on her bottom lip, taking little nips and sucking at the soft flesh. His tongue then swept the outline of her mouth before dipping inside. She tasted like the fine dark honey he remembered from the hives his papa kept in the old country.

His hand moved down the column of her neck. He traced the path of his shirt collar that she wore down the opening until his hand rested lightly on the soft swell of her breast.

"Dear Lord, Hannah," he sighed at the fullness that filled his hand. He half expected her to stop him from taking such liberties. He waited for her to pull away. She did not. When he felt the nipple pucker against the fabric beneath his palm, the urge to possess this woman threatened to conquer every other conscious consideration.

Hannah had never experienced a fondness for kissing, much less being touched so intimately, but Max was being so gentle and considerate. It was a totally foreign experience. A new understanding began to emerge that perhaps things could be different between a man and woman.

Her hand cautiously moved to his face and she caressed his jaw. A light stubble had formed since early morning. As if he sensed her explorations were tentative, Max withdrew his hand and drew back. He gazed at her face as if he were studying it, which caused her lip to tremble.

"I am sorry, Hannah." He ran the back of his hand along her cheek. "I do not shave after supper. It is very inconsiderate of me, yes?"

"Oh, no, I wasn't thinking that. It is just—" She suddenly ceased what she was trying to say and lowered her eyes. How could she ever put into words what she felt. She could never share the ugly secret of the shame and humiliation she had known at Emmett's hands.

She dropped her hands to her lap. During their descent she felt the beginnings of a new roundness which would swell with her unborn child. She tensed. She was carrying another man's child. She had no right to hope or ask anything from Max Garat.

"Is it that I touch you when a man he should not do this?" Max feared that he had frightened her by the liberties he had taken. He wanted to lift her chin so he could try to read the green in her eyes. But he, too, had fears. He feared that she might recoil if he attempted to touch her again.

"No. That's not it. Max, I—I liked your touch," she offered in a rush. "I truly did."

"But you wish that I not do this again maybe?" he probed, unable to let it go. While he feared the truth, he was a man who had faced much in his life and he could not back away now that his emotions had been reawakened.

"It is not that."

"It is true, Hannah?"

To his chagrin, she did not look at him. Rather, she nodded to her clasped hands in her lap.

"Then you look at me without thinking maybe that Max Garat he has done an outrageous thing to you, yes?"

Her gaze lifted to his at that. She was met by the seeking inner forcefulness of his stare. Her breath threatened to flee, for she almost could believe that he was looking past the façade she presented to the world and could gaze into her soul. She blinked several times to curb the impulse to bare her soul's secrets. That would be foolish and leave her wounded, raw, and too vulnerable.

She opened her mouth to say something clever or witty, anything that would relieve the tension between them. But nothing came to mind that would allay the tremble of her lips.

"Max—"

"Pardon me all the way to hell and back barefoot over a rocky road," Franc interrupted from the kitchen doorway. "Ma, I got to go pee and it's too dark out there to go alone with that mean goose lurkin' around waitin' to take a chunk outta my backside again."

While Franc had been crawling from the bedroom on her hands and knees in an effort not to be found out, she had overheard way more than she wanted to. She had decided that if she didn't put a stop to it, and right quick, she was going to puke right there on the kitchen floor.

She needed Hannah's help, and fast!

"I'll be right there," Hannah called back. She glanced at Max as she rose, not certain whether to be grateful for another of Franc's untimely interruptions or disappointed that she did not have enough faith in herself or Max to be completely honest with him.

Thirteen

Emmett Turner picked up one of Hannah's expensive fancy French perfumes and angrily dashed it against the wall. The shattered pieces of glass showered onto the rumpled bed, and filled the room with Hannah's favorite flowery fragrance. Rather than make him feel better, all smashing her things did was to remind him of his runaway wife. Although he had tried to keep her disappearance quiet until he could locate her, gossip was beginning to circulate.

He paced the room, swigging from a bottle of imported Irish whiskey, letting it drizzle down the fine blond peach fuzz that had formed on his chin, and onto his wrinkled shirt. He cursed her for thinking he would let her run out on him without retribution. He stopped before a life-size portrait he'd had painted of his ungrateful wife.

"Nobody leaves Emmett Turner without paying for it," he growled to the painting. "Not even you, Hannah." He smashed the liquor bottle against the portrait and rang for a servant.

Moments later a hapless young man skidded into the room. "Yes, sir?"

"Get me another bottle!" Emmett demanded.

"Yes, sir." He bobbed his head, looking around the room with wide eyes, but hesitated.

"Well?"

"The gentlemen you have been expecting are waiting for you downstairs in the library."

"Get them drinks and have my bottle ready and waiting for me when I get there."

By the time Emmett walked into the spacious book-lined library and sat behind his desk like a European king holding court, he was feeling particularly mean. He hated having to share that woman's sins with strangers.

"What did you find out?" Emmett stared down his nose at the three. He normally took gratification from making lowly hirelings squirm, but he was too enraged this time to take pleasure in his position.

The tallest of the three stood up. Keeping a sheath of papers behind his back, he walked to the edge of Turner's desk. "We finally managed to persuade the doc to give us his files like you suggested, Mr. Turner."

"And?" Emmett prodded, growing impatient for the report, although he expected proof—real or invented, he did not care which—to corroborate his suspicions of a dalliance.

"That puny doc ain't gonna be treatin' nobody else's bruises but his own for a long while," the fat one on the velvet settee chuckled until he noticed the black expression on Turner's face. The man immediately sobered.

The one standing gulped. "It isn't what you expected, so we brung you the whole file 'cuz we thought you should have a look see at it for yourself . . . Mr. Turner, sir."

Wavering under the suffocating weight of Turner's growing rage, he brought the file from behind him and handed it to Turner, who practically ripped it out of his hand.

Emmett tore open the folder. His anger coming out in drunken huffs, he scanned the pages. Emmett's head suddenly snapped up. Pure, unadulterated rage filled his every pore.

"She's pregnant," he exploded, "with *my* baby!"

Awaiting return to his lawyer, the final divorce decree lay on the edge of his desk. With an animal roar he barely suppressed the urge to tear it to shreds, and instead flung it across the room.

"It's ripped to shreds." Hannah sighed as she held up the lacy lavender gown before her to assess the damage. Feeling as if there were a pair of eyes watching her, Hannah glanced up.

Lissa stood in the doorway with what Hannah could describe only as a smug smirk on her face. There wasn't an inkling of remorse on Lissa's young face. The girl's smirk broadened, then she whirled around and disappeared.

Hannah stood there in disbelief. The girl had all but openly admitted shredding her gown. Hannah was tempted to go after the girl. Rather, she took a calming breath and silently counted to ten.

No doubt Lissa had run to Max. If Hannah did hunt the girl down and confront her, she would be doing what Lissa wanted—creating a scene in front of her father.

Hannah was not going to allow Lissa to provoke her so easily into breaking the pact she and Max had made. They would be living under the same roof together all winter and Lissa was not going to cause dissension between Max and her so easily. What Hannah was beginning to feel for Max was too new, too fragile to even be named, let alone take the chance of destroying it. So because of and despite of the children, she made a decision to keep peace.

"Max, what're you doing here?" Hannah choked out, and dropped the gown on her bed when Max suddenly appeared in the kitchen.

"Lissa, she says you want to see me." His face held mild curiosity.

He was not aware of what his daughter had done.

Hannah glanced around Max to catch sight of Lissa standing behind her father, silently egging Hannah to tattle on her. Behind Lissa, André stood with his head bowed. Franc brought up the rear, holding Sammy's hand and watching Hannah intently.

Hannah bit her bottom lip. The three of them were in it together. The two oldest Garat children did not want her there, and Franc had been clamoring to leave since their arrival.

"Hannah?" Max prodded.

"Oh, yes, *I* wanted to see you. Yes. Um, I need your help." She glanced around the kitchen. This was Lissa's doing, and Hannah was not going to allow the child to get the better of her. "The lid. Yes. The lid to the beans is stuck. I wanted to fix them for supper tonight as a surprise, but I couldn't get the lid off."

She watched Max take the jar and twist off the lid with little effort. To her horror, he set the jar down and picked up the shredded gown.

"What is this?" he asked.

Hannah swallowed hard and stared back at the quizzical expression lining his face.

"Hannah? There is something you want to tell me maybe yes?"

"That is my gown."

"Yes, that I know."

She retrieved it from him. "I was making strips so I could use it to make hair ribbons and later decorate some undergarments I plan to sew for the girls."

He gave her a skeptical glance, but said, "You

got plenty of time to practice maybe while I am not here."

A sudden panic enveloped her. She was going to be left at the isolated ranch. "Not here? How long?"

"Several nights. I am the camp tender. I must take the provisions to the shepherds at the winter camp in the desert, and it nears the time to ship last year's lambs to market. I should go a week ago. I can wait no longer. I am sorry I am not be here to eat the beans you cook tonight."

She put up a brave front. "I am, too."

The uneasiness he heard in her voice caused him again to wonder at her story. He had a hunch from the expression on Lissa's face that the children had something to do with it this time.

He had promised not to intercede, but he could give her a reprieve. He swung his attention to his daughter, who had come to stand at his side. "Lissa, you do not see your grandpapa since he leaves to be with the herd. You go with me and help separate from the herd the sheep we send to market in November."

Lissa looked dumbfounded. "What about Sam? You just cannot leave him with *her.*" She pointed an accusing finger at Hannah.

"Hannah, she is good with the boy. André and Franc, they are here to help out if she needs anything."

Lissa's shoulders slumped in defeat, but she

quickly recovered and raised her chin. "I am glad André and Franc will be here to *help* her."

Hannah did not miss the angry intonation in the girl's voice before she and the other children swung from the kitchen and scampered out into the yard.

"You do fine here with André. I must load the supply horse now." He crossed to the door, stopped, and tossed back over his shoulder to Hannah. *"Divide et impera."* Hannah cocked her head in confusion. "Machiavelli, he says divide and rule."

Despite the dread she experienced at the thought of being alone on the isolated ranch, a hint of a smile formed on her lips. "I'll remember that."

Left alone in the kitchen, Hannah dropped onto the bench and rested her chin on her palms. She could not, would not, let the children defeat her. If she could conquer that obstinate sewing machine, surely she could conquer three obstinate young children.

But while Hannah sat there contemplating her ruined gown, she was not so sure.

Lissa sat back-rigid on the horse, a sour you-will-never-win expression on her face as she glared down at Hannah.

"We go only for as long as we must," Max said. He was standing directly in front of Hannah. Unconsciously, he started to reach for her before he caught himself and dropped his hand to his side.

Hannah had noted Max's actions and circled her arm around Franc, drawing the child to her side so she would not be tempted to raise her hand in response.

"You help Hannah take care of the ranch, yes?" Max said to André, chucking the boy on the chin.

"We are counting on you, André," Lissa said in a singsong voice, and immediately lowered her eyes at the warning look Max shot her.

Max swung Samuel up into his arms and gave the toddler a big hug.

"Mama, Mama," Samuel began to fuss, and reached for Hannah. Reluctantly, Max handed him over to her.

Hannah took the tot and set him on her hip. "It's Hannah, Sammy. Remember?"

"Franc, you mind your mama," Max advised as he mounted his horse and picked up the reins.

"You ain't got to worry none. I ain't goin' to take my *mine* off her."

Max arched a brow. He doubted that what she said was a misuse of words this time, and he wished he did not have to leave the ranch or Hannah. That girl needed someone to take her in hand. But his brother and father were expecting him. Shepherds depended on fresh supplies during the winter for survival and he could not let them down. And he had to help get the lambs ready to go to market.

Hannah squared her shoulders and stood and watched the two riders and supply horse until they became no more than three dark dots against the bright glare of snow on the horizon. Max had entrusted the children into her care. It was the first time since she had wed Emmett that anyone had depended or relied on her, and she was not going to let him down.

Not more than two hours had passed since Max had left, when the kitchen door suddenly flew open. Hannah swung around, expecting to see the children. She was startled to see a deep-chested stranger standing framed in the door, three rabbits dangling from his hand.

A big grin split his dark face. "Already you are here, eh? We do not expect you so soon."

Hannah relaxed when she recognized the endearing foreign accent. It was the same as Max's, as was the beret covering his dark hair. The man also had to be of Basque origin and probably a friend of the family's. Confused, she asked, "You expected me?"

"Yes, but of course. I am Petya, Max's brother. The letters?"

"Oh, the letters. You read them?" she questioned, suddenly embarrassed by the suggestive content of Wilma Timm's letters when Hannah recalled how Wilma Timm had bragged about writing them.

"I help write them."

"Then it wasn't Max's idea?" she quizzed. Max had said that he had written to the seamstress.

The man tossed back his head, gave a hearty laugh, and ignored her question. "Where is Max?"

"Delivering supplies to you and your father."

"Ah, but I am here." He chuckled. "How long is it you have been here?"

"A little over a month."

"Then you know well enough my brother's ill temper by now."

"Max is not ill-tempered!" Hannah defended Max.

"I like the way your green eyes snap of mountain fires in summer. It is good the way you defend my brother. That I like. You will be good to have around the ranch, eh?"

Hannah watched him toss the rabbits on the work counter, pull out a bench, and finger the sewing machine. "What is this?"

"It's a sewing machine, of course," Hannah answered.

"Ah, sewing, yes. With the children it will be good, this machine. What a smart woman you are, Hannah. You know what a man with a family needs."

"What else would he need?"

"What else, eh?" He winked.

He may be Max's brother, but he was beginning to irritate her. He was flamboyant and more than a little cocky. A handsome young man who obviously knew it. "It's a requirement for the job."

"Job. An interesting notion that is." He smiled broadly, and Hannah's level of irritation rose with the dazzling grin.

Her hands dropped to her hips. "If not a job, what would you call it?"

Fourteen

Although Hannah frowned at the big-shoul-
dered man, there was something most likable
about him. Then she realized that he was very
much a younger version of Max. He had dark
hair, an engaging smile, and was muscular. She
could not help but find him endearing despite
herself.

"What would you call the reason I'm here, if
not to do a job?" she prodded when he did not
immediately answer.

"The world over, it is the same. What word is
used, does it matter, eh? Welcome, Hannah."

Although he spoke well and seemed to com-
prehend what she said, he must have some sort
of a language barrier, and it was not worth arguing about. She glanced at his big outstretched
hand. It was not as callused or leathery as Max's,
and she silently chided herself for continuing to
compare this handsome young man to his elder
brother. She offered her hand in return.

She had expected him to join her in a hearty
handshake. Instead, he yanked her into his arms

and gave her a big, breathless bear hug. "I think I like you already, Hannah."

"Uncle Petya!" André squealed from the door.

The man unwrapped his arms from Hannah, allowing her to catch her breath, and embraced André. "So big you have grown in only two months, eh?"

Her arms full of firewood, Franc stood back and took in the scene. Her keen gaze had not missed Hannah hugging that big stranger, or how Hannah was breathing hard over the man. Her narrowed eyes met the man's smiling ones.

"And who is this we have here, eh?" Petya asked, breaking the hug with André to swing out an arm and indicate Franc.

"She is a girl," André said with a hint of youthful male disdain for the opposite gender.

"Her kid." Franc thumbed toward Hannah after shooting André a frown.

Petya perused the young girl who looked more like a ruffian than a budding young lady. "You do not look like a goat, I think," he offered with a disarming smile, and winked at Hannah.

"A goat!" Franc wailed, screwing up her young face. "I ain't no goat, you big dumb black sheep of the family."

To Franc's consternation, Petya threw back his head and roared with laughter. "That I have been called before. I think I will like your young *kid*, Hannah." Ignoring the child's dark scowl and the twinkle of amusement in André's eyes,

Petya's brow crinkled in Hannah's direction. "You are a widow woman?"

Hannah's breath caught, and her glance shot to Franc. Franc could give her away; the girl was glaring so furiously at Petya, and Franc did not always stop and think when she was angry. If Franc truly wanted to get them kicked out, all she had to do would be to tell Petya and Max that she had lied about that, too.

Hannah schooled her expression. "Is there something wrong with that?"

"Of course, we cannot control all the events in our lives and must learn to live with them, eh? I am only surprised, although my papa's letter to Uncle Laborde did not say that our uncle he could not send a suitable widow woman to be Max's bride."

"Bride!" Franc and André choked in astounded unison.

A shock wave reverberated through Hannah. They had been talking about two entirely different letters. She had thought the letters were the ones that Max and Wilma Timm had exchanged. But Max's father and brother evidently had been writing to relatives in their home village to secure a wife. The confusing conversation she'd had with the station owner's wife when they had left the train came to mind, and Hannah wondered if the woman knew of the letters as well.

Hannah also silently questioned whether Max knew of his brother and father's attempts to secure a bride for him—especially since Max had been so adamant about his intentions to the contrary.

"But of course, this *job* of yours, Hannah. The reason you are here." Petya settled a questioning look on Hannah, which forced her to redirect her attention.

Hannah glanced at André. His young eyes were intently watching her for her response; his face was tight. Franc was also staring at her, her hands balled on her hips.

"I'm afraid there has been a dreadful mistake. I am here in response to an advertisement Max placed for a seamstress—"

"Only she cannot sew," André put in to Hannah's chagrin.

"That is most interesting I think." Petya cast Hannah a sly grin as he contemplated this bit of information for a moment, then said, "A seamstress who cannot sew. Does my brother know of this?"

"Yes, Papa knows," André said dejectedly, and his shoulders slumped.

"Max knows of this, and still he does not send you away, Hannah. Very interesting this is, I think."

"Not that interestin'," Franc muttered. "He tried. But the pass got snowed in, so he can't send neither one of us away."

"Ah, I see." He studied Hannah, making her uncomfortable under the intensity of his scrutiny before his eyes shifted to his nephew. "Most interesting, these events."

Hannah squirmed inwardly under his observation. That a mail order bride apparently was on her way to become Max's wife troubled Hannah. Although it should not matter, she felt a strange sense of loss and a prick of jealousy and anger as well. After the vow she had made to herself, was she foolishly becoming a willing substitute until the woman he was going to marry arrived?

Although Hannah was trying to hide it, Petya noticed the tightening in her expression. "André, take Franc out and show her how to skin the rabbits I brought, eh?"

"Why'd I want to learn to skin a rabbit?" Franc protested.

"You like to eat, Franc, yes?"

Franc rolled her eyes and huffed, " 'Course I do. That's a dumb question. How do you think Ma and me ended up here?"

Hannah noticed his eyes flash in her direction before returning his attention to Franc. "If you like to eat, then you and André better set to work," he stated. "There will be no food on your plates until those rabbits are skinned and cleaned so Hannah can cook them."

"If we're goin' to have my *ma*"—Franc motioned toward Hannah—"cook them, there won't be no food on our plates anyways."

"She does not cook so well either, Uncle Petya,"

André explained, and stuck out his tongue to attest to his distaste of Hannah's cooking.

Petya cocked his brow. "A seamstress who does not sew and a mama who does not cook. And still Max allows you to stay. This I find most curious. Most curious indeed."

Franc screwed up her face. "I told you, he ain't got no choice."

Petya rubbed his jaw. "But of course you did. In that case, you should waste no more time. It is already late afternoon and nearing suppertime. So you will enjoy the fruits of your labor on your supper plate, my young Franc, I will show Hannah how to prepare the rabbits, and perhaps a few other things as well before I start back."

It had been late afternoon by the time Max spotted the fires burning around the sheep band to ward off coyotes, and he and Lissa rode into the winter camp. Max was cold, hungry, and tired of Lissa's pouting. Unable to get Hannah off his mind, Max had driven the horses to reach camp so he would not appear to be in a big rush when he announced that he and Lissa would not be remaining as long as he had originally planned.

Set in the high snow-covered desert, the camp was no more than two canvas tents on either side of a briskly burning campfire. The scent of blazing sage billowed up in tendrils of smoke from the fire and mingled in the icy air with the tinkling of bells worn by the lead sheep. The bells were music to Max's ears as he noted the sheep pawing through the snow to reach the dry sagebrush that was their winter forage in the desert.

"Max, you have finally come," the stooped old man said, and left the side of his great white dog to greet his son.

The two men embraced, then spoke of the sheep while grandfather and granddaughter embraced.

"You grow like the wild sage, Lissa," Bernard said as he held his grandchild's small hands in his.

"Oh, Grandpapa, I am so glad to see you. I have missed you so much." Lissa glanced around for her favorite uncle. "Where is Uncle Petya?"

"Somehow you must have missed each other, yes? He left for the ranch last night and should have already arrived there early this morning."

Max's brow lifted into a troubled line as he questioned his father. "What do you mean, Petya he arrives at the ranch early this morning?"

"When you do not come with the supplies, we wait. But you have been a week overdue, so Petya he goes to check that everything it is all right with the family."

An inviting aroma of bean stew swirled from the campfire, but Max had suddenly lost his appetite. His brother was a beguiling ladies' man who could charm the fleece off a sheep in winter. And although Max did not have a claim on

Hannah, the thought that his brother could take an interest in her greatly disturbed Max.

"My son"—Bernard laid a gloved hand on Max's arm—"what is it that brings much troubled light into your eyes?"

"It is probably that woman that Papa has staying at the ranch. She—"

"Enough, Lissa," Max warned.

The girl immediately ceased what she was going to say and plunked down on a rock near the fire.

Bernard's interest peaked. "A woman?"

Evasively, Max said, "It is not for us to discuss this."

"This woman, she is Basque?" Bernard asked, wondering if his brother in the old country had been able to work a miracle in response to the letter Bernard had written requesting a bride for his grieving son.

"No. I hire this woman to sew for the family. She leaves before the spring shearing. It is nothing," Max answered in response to what he knew would be his father's relentless questioning.

"A woman she is nothing?" Bernard quizzed. Although Bernard felt a momentary disappointment that the woman evidently had not been sent by his brother, it was the first time he had seen the spark of life glint into his son's eyes since his Mary died. To see the spring of life once again flow into Max's veins secretly delighted Bernard. The old man had worried that Max would never get over his wife's death, and would forget that man was not meant to go through life alone.

"There is no reason for you to smile, old man," Max grated out, annoyed that his father seemed to be reading much more into the situation than was warranted.

"I smile only because you are here with provisions so I will not have to join the flock to forage for sagebrush while waiting for your wild younger brother to return." He patted his flat belly. "One must eat to keep up his strength to ward off the coyotes and wolves here in the isolated desert. It is also a small pleasure. You know how lonely it is out here for a man."

Max knew all too well.

The winters he had spent with the flock had left him with a deep gnawing hunger in his heart and loins for his woman by the time spring took him back to the ranch in those early years.

A strange realization that had been nagging at the back of his mind overtook him. It was very similar to the hunger for Hannah he had refused to acknowledge the last few weeks.

Bernard watched his son's face. Max appeared to be deep in thought. Maybe he had given his son something to consider. But in case Max needed a little more help, Bernard said, "Since you do not see Petya this morning before you leave, I do hope he has not lost his way. Or maybe he finds shelter against the cold night in a warm bed, yes?"

"I do not worry about Petya, Papa. He always finds shelter."

"Ah, yes, but of course he does. Even if for one night in a woman's warm bed, eh?"

Max frowned at his father. The old man's words held the hint of suggestion. And well they might. After receiving Max's letter, Petya had come to America under the pretext of helping Max with the ranch after Mary's death. Only later had Max discovered that Petya had fled their childhood village to avoid what was called in America the shotgun wedding after reportedly deflowering one of the local beauties who had been betrothed to another.

"Lissa," Max suddenly hailed. "Help me unload the horse. We return to the ranch tonight." To his father he added, "I do not stay to help ready the lambs for shipment this year."

"In the dark?" the girl whined, and looked to her grandfather for help.

"I think it is the wise man who protects that which would be his," Bernard said. He picked up a tin cup and poured himself a warming cup of coffee from the pot set across the fire.

"Do not speak such foolishness, old man," Max snapped. He was irritated with himself for being so transparent. "Tonight we return to the ranch because"—he motioned to the west—"there is a storm brewing."

With a nod and sly lift of his bushy white brow, Bernard chuckled. "Yes, my son, I think finally you have come to recognize the signs perhaps."

Fifteen

"What goes on under my own roof while I go from the ranch?" Max snorted.

Hannah was barefoot and dressed in one of his nightshirts with his jacket thrown over her shoulders. Her long hair flowed over one shoulder in a disheveled braid. His brother wore trousers, and a shirt open in front. Max scowled at the pair, although he did not say all that was on his mind. He had no right to demand further explanation. Silently he took in the situation.

He had entered through the front door, carrying his sleeping daughter to find his brother and Hannah seated on the sofa. Petya's hand was on the back of Hannah's neck, and he was leaning toward her as if he were going to kiss her. Hannah had her face tilted up to Petya.

"Ah, Maximilian, you return so soon. I had not expected to see you, big brother," Petya said. Although Petya was unperturbed by the barely disguised annoyance in his brother's voice, Petya withdrew his hand from Hannah's neck.

"I see for myself maybe that you two do not

expect me so early in the morning before the sun comes up," Max said coldly.

Rubbing her eye, Hannah scooted off the sofa and was about to deny any wrongdoing, but Petya reached out and squeezed her arm.

"Do you deliver the provisions?" Petya asked, casually rising to stand at Hannah's side.

"I know my duty."

"Always you have, brother," Petya said airily, undisturbed by the undercurrent of hostility exuding from Max.

Petya stepped forward. "I will put my Lissa girl to bed," he offered, and took Lissa from Max. "My little sleeping princess," he cooed to the girl. "Your papa, he must have worn you out to rush back, eh?"

Max forced himself to ignore Petya's subtle jab at how he cared for his family and directed, "Tuck my daughter in my bed."

Lissa clung sleepily to her uncle, but she was not so drowsy that she missed the exchange between her papa and favorite uncle. Inside she bristled with animosity. That woman not only had tricked her papa, but now she was after her uncle Petya too.

Max stiffened when his brother winked at Hannah before he disappeared into the bedroom with Lissa. Max was troubled by the sudden wave of possessiveness he felt toward Hannah as he recalled what had brought them together in the first place.

He had originally hired Hannah to sew for his family so he could send the children away to be educated and he could go back out with his band of sheep. But lately his thoughts had shifted along different lines.

Now all too often he found himself thinking about Hannah as a man does an attractive, ripe woman. The swell of her breasts, the fresh scent of her silken hair, her smiling eyes, awakened his body, and he imagined himself holding her as he had seen his brother about to do when he had walked in on the pair.

"Max, it truly wasn't what it seemed," Hannah said in no more than a soft whisper. She noticed the faraway glint in his eyes fade. She feared it would be replaced by disappointment and hastened to say, "I had something in my eye and Petya was helping me remove it."

"Petya, he is always very clever at helping," Max muttered. *Particularly at helping attractive females out of their clothing.*

"He was a big help while you were gone."

"No doubt."

"He brought rabbits for supper and helped cook them. And the children seem to love him."

"Everyone, they love Petya." *Every woman within a two-hundred-mile radius.*

Although his words were innocuous enough, and the delivery dispassionate, Hannah was not certain whether Max was deliberately misinterpreting what she was attempting to say or was sincerely agreeing with her assessment of his brother.

There seemed to be some sort of competition between the two brothers, yet Hannah wondered just how brotherly it was. She did not want to be the source of friction between them.

"Well, I know you must be terribly exhausted from traveling all night and will want to get some sleep," she finally said for want of better conversation. "And I had best get back to bed as well."

She started for the kitchen, but Max's strong hand stayed her, causing his jacket to tumble from her shoulders to the floor. She could feel the rapid pulse of his grip on her arm; her pulse surged through her veins in beat with his. She glanced up to look into the probing blue flames blazing in his eyes.

"Hannah," he probed, "what do you do up at this early hour?"

Hannah could see by his tight expression that it was difficult for him to ask such a question. A month ago she would have resented him thinking that he had the right to interrogate her. Now, however, she was secretly pleased that he was no longer indifferent toward her.

Her vision dropped to the powerful, steady grip of his hand, and he immediately withdrew it. Her eyes trailed back to his face, and she had to fight the urge to track her fingers along his stubbled chin.

"I heard Sammy stirring and went to check on

him." Her lips curved into a hint of a smile. "I rocked him until he stopped fussing and fell back to sleep. I must have disturbed Petya while I was putting him back down. As I was leaving the room, Petya noticed that my eye was irritating me and asked if he could help."

Max was grateful that Hannah had taken such pains to care for his young son. Her motherly instincts should have relieved Max's mind, but at the moment Max was feeling anything but fatherly.

Without comment, his vision shifted and he stood and stared.

She had shifted her stance so she stood before the fire, which gave him an unobstructed view of the ripened outline of her lush body through the thin cotton fabric. The warm brown centers of her full breasts were peaked. His vision trailed over the gentle flare of her hips and settled on the faintest hint of a delta of brown-black curls at the apex of her thighs, which caused his arousal to grow hard.

His own body, which he had honed through the years with discipline and hard work, was beginning to betray him. It was responding to the sight, scent, and touch of her when he willed it not to, disobeying his silent commands.

"Well, I should get to bed," she said after a lengthy, awkward silence.

"Yes, I think bed it is a good idea for all of us to put the events of this night to rest maybe."

Max watched Hannah nod, then pick up the jacket and pad across the parlor to disappear into the kitchen before he dropped onto the sofa and sat staring down into the dying flames.

"So, you bow your head in shame, big brother, to ask forgiveness for the way you treat Hannah when you return, eh?"

Max's head shot up. Petya was standing behind Max with his arms crossed over his chest. "I think maybe you should start back to help ready the lambs for market now that you know I deliver the supplies and all it is well with the family, yes?"

Petya draped himself in a chair near the sofa. "I know the provisions they are delivered, but from what I see and hear, I would not go so far as to say that all is well with the family, eh?"

André had eagerly told Petya about the problems the children were having accepting Hannah. And the girl, Franc, had put in her complaints as well. Petya had patiently listened, then under penalty of reaping dire consequences Petya had sworn the children to silence about the Basque bride.

Max glowered. "Be careful how far you go, little brother."

Ignoring Max's warning, Petya said, "Now it is that I know there is trouble here. You do not call me *little brother* in that harsh tone of voice unless you are about to exert your birth order, eh?"

"You make too much of nothing maybe," Max said, slipping back on his mask of indifference.

"I do not think so. Do you want to know what it is I think?"

"No," Max grumbled, although he suspected that he was going to hear what Petya had to say whether he wanted to or not. Petya had not inherited the Basque stoicism. He was flamboyant and outspoken.

"I think that the lovely Widow Turner, she is the first woman who catches your eye, eh?"

"She is here to sew."

"I hear how she sews and I hear how she cooks, and still you do not make arrangements for her to leave your home."

"Snow blocks the pass."

"Yes, but there are other families in the valley who will take such a woman off your hands. Why do you not admit that she is a handsome woman and you are a lonely man, big brother? The hot brick you wrap in your beret at night to heat your bed does not warm your heart."

"I am not a lonely man," Max declared despite the isolation he had experienced since Mary's death. "My children surround me."

"You bring a seamstress here so your children they will be sent away to school."

"It is custom," Max argued. In his village, formal education was minimal. In America, his people sent their children to private church schools in California, and he had promised himself to offer his children a better education than had been available to him.

"And you are a man of responsibility and tradition, eh?"

"Zahar hitzak, zuhur hitzak."

"Old words are wise words. One of your favorite sayings," Petya scoffed.

"They are concepts you do not yet learn."

"I learn from watching you, big brother, that not all traditions they are to be followed blindly." Petya dragged his fingers through his hair when Max stiffened and his hands balled into fists. "You surround yourself with the ghosts of your marriage. Mary would not have wanted you to live the hermit's life."

"You overstep yourself," Max warned darkly. He was in no mood to discuss his ghosts.

"That I do for years." Petya gave a nervous chuckle. He knew that he was pushing his brother dangerously close to the edge, but it was time that Max got a little shove. And Petya had designated himself the perfect one to do it.

"Do not make light."

"That is another of your problems." At Max's dark, questioning expression, Petya elaborated. "You do not know how to make light."

"Life is not for making light."

"Life, my big brother, is for living. When you are young you know about such things. But after forty years you have forgotten how to live. Two years now you go through the motions, but I have not seen the spark of life in your eyes . . . until this woman she comes."

"You do not know of which you speak." His life was not something Max laid bare for anyone else to dissect, not even his brother.

A devilish twinkle sparked into Petya's eyes. "If I truly do not, then you do not mind if I remain here a day or two and keep Hannah company before I return to the sheep, eh?"

Petya grinned at Max and gave him a conspiratorial wink. For an instant Max considered punching that disgusting, self-satisfied grin right off his brother's boyishly handsome face.

"Leave Hannah alone. She is not one of the town *domestiques* you visit."

"She is a widow and knows the way of a man. Maybe she will welcome me, eh?"

Max's temper exploded.

He sprang to his feet, grabbed his brother by the collar, and slammed his fist into Petya's jaw.

Petya tumbled to the floor, where he sagely decided to remain and lick his wounds without tempting fate and adding to his brother's wrath.

Standing over Petya, Max growled, "If you cause Hannah harm, that is how I welcome you in this house, little brother."

Petya twisted around and watched Max stomp from the room. He waited until he heard the creak of the rungs of the ladder under Max's weight; Max was going to sleep in the attic room with André. Then Petya picked himself off the floor and curled his frame on the sofa.

Petya smiled to himself as he lay back and

rubbed his aching jaw. Max always could throw a punch. Despite the pain, it pleased Petya. He considered the growing bruise well worth it. He had elicited the response he had been expecting from his brother.

Now, if only Max would acknowledge what Petya, for all his mere twenty-four years, knew.

Despite his vehement protestations and adamant proclamations to the contrary, Maximilian Garat was in grave danger of falling in love.

Sixteen

Hannah and Petya were standing at the table, laughing together at something one of the children had said, when Max walked into the kitchen with Samuel on his hip.

Hannah immediately sobered at the dark expression on Max's face and went to get Samuel.

"Good morning, Sammy. I hope you're in a better frame of mind than your daddy," she said when Max handed over the boy without comment.

As Hannah set the toddler in a chair and got his breakfast, she considered how she had tried to clarify the innocence of last night. She had tried to make Max understand, to explain. In the cold light of morning she did not feel so inclined, since there really was nothing to explain.

She glanced at the two brothers. So much alike, yet so different. Petya had a way about him that made her relax and feel at ease. They laughed easily together, and he made the work seem less like drudgery. Max, on the other hand, had been difficult to get to know. He did not laugh so much, and he put work first. It was Max, though, who electrified her senses and made her heart yearn to break the vow she'd made to herself after she'd left Emmett.

"Good morning, big brother," Petya said, and stepped away from Hannah. Max was good to his word, and Petya did not want to chance another right hook to the jaw for not leaving Hannah alone as Max had directed. "You do not look like you slept so well. Could it be that such a narrow bed sours your humor, eh?"

"More a brother who forsakes his duty."

Franc smiled. If everything else failed, she'd spill the beans about the bride coming to wed up with Max. But he was acting awful disagreeable. Hannah would not like him that way.

André kept his eyes away from his sister's. He didn't like keeping secrets from Lissa. He yawned. His papa's snoring had robbed him of a night's rest.

Lissa frowned. She did not like it that her papa and uncle were not being nice to each other, and it was all Hannah's fault.

"Duty, it is such a tiresome bother," Petya said. "I think what we need in this house is to visit with people who know how to smile and laugh." He turned his attention to the children. "How would you like to spend the day with the Herrias?"

"Yes," the three children chorused, then immediately quieted at the dark frown Max shot them.

Petya ignored Max's censuring glower. "Afraid you are outnumbered, big brother. We go. While the children finish the morning chores, Hannah, you dress my little Samuel, then pack several of those ropes of sausages hanging there." He motioned toward the ceiling, where the newly made blood sausages hung. "I will hitch up the team. It is good to spend time with people who know how to make light."

The children rushed from the table, leaving their food unfinished in their haste to grab their coats and finish the chores.

Once the children, followed by Panda Pie, had scrambled outside, Petya noticed Hannah's hesitancy. "Do not worry, Hannah. It will be good for Max to remain here with his own company for a day. It might improve his disposition, eh?"

Frustrated that Petya was managing to make him appear some type of ogre for adhering to his belief in the work ethic, Max plopped the beret on his head, pulled it down over his forehead, and swung toward the door.

"Ah, what it is they say of the man who wears his beret as you do?" Petya remarked to Max's glower of ill humor. "It means the wearer is in a bad mood, eh?"

Max harrumphed and left the house.

Outside in the cold air Max usually felt refreshed and invigorated. Now, as he stood near the corral, where the crippled lambs were housed, he burned like the heat of August. His curtain of privacy, hiding his emotions, was being penetrated and he was troubled over it. Basques were supposed to ignore that which was not worth fighting about. And yet Max had attacked his own brother over Hannah.

Grudgingly, Max admitted to himself for the first time since his thoughts had begun regularly swaying to Hannah Turner that she was a woman well worth fighting about.

By the time Hannah left the house and handed a bundled-up Samuel to Lissa in the wagon, Max had made a difficult decision. He met her on the steps of the house when she returned to fetch the basket she had packed.

"If you want to go visiting, I take you, Hannah," Max offered.

"Why don't you come with us?"

"It is nearly fifteen miles, this neighbor. The sheep, they do not wait to be tended. That my brother does well to remember. I take you on Sunday. It is a day for resting after morning chores are done."

Choices warred inside Hannah. She glanced in the wagon's direction. Petya and the children were waiting with expectant faces. Franc had Panda Pie tucked in her coat. Hannah looked back to Max, hoping he would give her a reason to remain other than it being his responsibility and the practicality of waiting until the sabbath. She desperately longed to hear that he did not want her to go with his brother, that he wanted her to stay with him. But he said no more.

Max could see that she was wavering, and his eyes silently urged her to remain. But he could not speak the words. He had no right to ask her not to go. He had no claim on her.

To his disappointment, she squeezed his arm, then turned and fled toward the wagon.

It took every ounce of reserve that Max possessed not to call her back. Solemnly, he remained stalwart and watched her hand up the gift basket and mount the wagon. He even forced himself to smile and wave at his children as Petya snapped the reins over the horses' backs. The wagon lurched from the yard before he turned his back to care for his animals.

Max worked harder than he had in weeks around the corraled sheep that were crippled or too weak to be put out with the rest of the band during the winter.

Physical labor helped relieve tension, and that was just what Max needed. Despite the physical exertion though, he felt like a powder keg of simmering emotions close to erupting by the time he finally trudged into the house.

Shrugging out of his sheepskin jacket, Max suddenly drew up short and stared.

Hannah had returned.

"I was beginning to wonder if you were ever

coming back into the house," Hannah said, sitting at the sewing machine. Her foot stopped working the treadle, and her hands stilled at the wheel.

"What do you do here?"

"I decided to take you up on your offer to drive me over to visit your neighbors on a Sunday," she said shyly. She had never done anything so bold before in her life, and she fidgeted with her fingers under his scrutiny. "Besides, I wanted to finish the shirt I've been working on."

Max's eyes dropped to the blue fabric for an instant before he asked, "And Petya and the children?" He still had a hard time believing his eyes that she had returned to the ranch.

"They continued on to your neighbor's. Petya said they would be gone all day and probably would not return until morning if he is winning at *mus.*"

At the question on her face, he clarified, "Mus it is a card game we play with bluffing, much like the American poker."

"Oh."

"Petya, he is a very good player and seldom loses."

"I see."

She sat at the table, staring up at him, unsure what to say. Despite knowing about the letters to Max's village requesting a bride, Hannah had remained in the wagon only until the first bend in the road before she asked Petya to stop and let her out. Lissa and Franc had put up a fuss to return to the ranch with her, but thankfully Petya had winked at her and not allowed it. Hannah had lifted her skirt and ran all the way back, knowing only that for some reason she had to return to the ranch.

After a long, awkward moment of silence, Max said, "Hannah, why do you return?"

"I told you, I wanted to finish this shirt." She could not bring herself to explain the growing attraction he had for her. She did not totally understand it herself. She cut the thread with her teeth, tied it off, and held up her creation.

It was a man's shirt.

The startled expression on his face that she would attempt to fashion such a garment for him emboldened Hannah. "Take off your shirt."

Max cocked a brow but did not move a muscle. Underneath his calm exterior his senses were heating up despite his efforts to remain indifferent.

"I need you to try it on, just to be sure it fits before I finish sewing the last of the buttons on," she explained, although she had used one of his old wool shirts as a pattern.

Still he stood without moving.

"You don't like the shirt?" After noticing how his shirts were worn and frayed at the cuffs, she had worked long and hard to fashion a new one. She desperately wanted him to appreciate her efforts.

Not like it? he thought. He was deeply touched

that she would take such trouble to labor over the sewing machine for him, especially considering her lack of skill with a needle.

"Are you going to try it on or not?" she barely whispered, her nerve rapidly dissipating.

Soundlessly, he unbuttoned his shirt, never taking his eyes from hers and tossed the old work garment over the end of the table.

Hannah could not help the sudden intake of breath when he stood before her naked from the waist up. His broad shoulders were enormous, dark, curly hair forested his muscular chest and traced a path downward past his washboard middle and slender waist to disappear into baggy blue cotton trousers tucked into black work boots. There was not an inch of softness on him. The urge to run her fingers down the rippling muscles was nearly overpowering.

"The shirt?" he said when she continued to stand and stare.

"Oh. Oh, the shirt. Of course." She held it out and he slipped his arms into it.

The sleeves were too long, the shoulders a bit tight, but for a novice her effort was surprisingly well executed. Not nearly as well engineered as the job that nature had done with Max. His physique appeared as if it had been sculpted by a master. Trying to keep her focus on the shirt, she reached up and began adjusting the shoulders.

"I think maybe you make a fine shirt," he remarked, looking down at the top of her head. She was standing much too close for comfort, and he inhaled the fresh soap scent from her hair, which hung in free-flowing waves down her back.

"Thank you." Hannah looked up into his face and felt threatened that she would become lost in the intense blue of his gaze.

Nervously she began to work the buttons. Her fingertips brushed his bare chest, which was rising and falling at a rapid pace. Quickly, she brought his wrist up to adjust the length of the sleeve. But when she did, his arm gently snaked around her.

"Hannah, do you know maybe what you do to me?"

She did not speak for a moment until she finally found her voice. "I think I know."

Although she was acquainted with a man's lust, had been subjected to its dark side, the feelings she was experiencing now were unfamiliar to Hannah.

This man had never tried to fall upon her, as had Emmett in an attempt to sate his baser appetites. Max was strong where Emmett was weak, gentle where Emmett was rough; kind where Emmett was cruel.

Fear fled and anticipation filled the void in her breast.

"Then you know what it is I am thinking, yes?" *What I have been thinking from the first time I kissed you.*

"I believe so."

They were alone at the ranch. Petya had seen to that. For an instant Max questioned whether his younger brother had purposely planned it this way. A second later Petya and everything else except for Hannah slipped from Max's mind as his body grew hard against hers.

Max's overwhelming hunger prevailed over his usual rational consideration of what he was about to do. He scooped her up into his arms and laid her down on the pallet he had prepared for her in the kitchen. Kneeling over her, he brushed an errant wave from her face.

She closed her eyes as he leaned over and kissed her. His tongue outlined her mouth, but she kept her lips pressed together.

He pulled back and gazed down at her. "Hannah, do I frighten you maybe?"

"No." Wide-eyed she stared up at him, her chest heaving, her arms straight at her sides, her ankles crossed.

She willed her body to relax, reminding herself that he was not Emmett, but bitter memories of brutal couplings at Emmett's hands caused her to remain stiff, her knees locked.

Max shifted and cradled her head in his lap. Slowly, he untied the ribbon from her hair and stroked the silken strands until they fanned out over his thighs.

"I do not hurt you," he said, massaging her temples.

She tentatively reached up and caressed the line of his jaw. "I know."

He took her hand in his. Bringing it to his mouth, he kissed the sensitive skin on the inside of her wrist. His other hand brushed her shoulder and moved toward her breast, gently rotating the flat of his palm in a circular motion.

His touch through the cotton fabric of her shirt nurtured her ardor. With deft fingers he unbuttoned her shirtfront, pushed aside her chemise, and exposed her full, rounded breasts. Under his heated gaze, her nipples darkened into pointed peaks. She had no experience to compare with what was happening to her. Max was adeptly awakening her desires, instilling burning tremors of hunger within her, guiding her toward an overwhelming ecstasy.

"Max, I must tell you, my husband did not—"

"No, Hannah, there is no need to explain. For now we leave the ghosts in the past, yes?" From her reactions, Max knew that her deceased husband had not been a considerate lover. Max silently vowed to respect her feelings.

He curled his hand around the nape of her neck and lifted her face to his.

Slowly he pressed his lips to hers, his tongue seeking entry into her mouth, dissolving all thoughts she had of confessing her past. She opened her mouth and his tongue plunged in, slowly at first, then accelerating the strokes until he was simulating the urgency of the mating rhythm.

Gently, his hand pushed up her skirt, riding up the outside of her thigh and dipping beneath the band of her underwear to twine in the fan of dark curls at the apex of her legs. When his lips left hers, he dropped feathery kisses down her neck until his mouth fastened on a breast and tugged at the sensitive center. She arched and pressed herself against him.

"Hannah, remove your underwear for me," he murmured, and sat back.

His voice was a silken caress, a whispered request. Hesitantly, Hannah started to slip the garment down her legs.

He curled his big hands around hers. "I help you." With sensuous slowness he drew the underwear down until he had freed her of it. Then he proceeded to remove her skirt and slip her shirt and chemise off her shoulders before he lay her back against the woolen blanket.

"Open to me, Hannah," he hoarsely whispered, and nudged her thighs apart.

Although she lay totally exposed to him, Hannah felt no impulse to push him away from her and cover her nakedness. Tears did not threaten to dampen her cheeks, and the urge to flee did not overcome her, portending remembered intrusions. Rather, she recalled his gentle strength and consideration, and a sense of wonder filled her as she opened her thighs farther to his hungry gaze.

"You are a most beautiful woman with a body made to cradle a man's."

His trousers seemed to melt from him until he sprang free before her. There was nothing repulsive about him. And she did not recoil when he took her hand and wrapped it around his extended heated velvet shaft.

"Do you feel the life you bring to me?"

His shaft pulsed in her hand and she nodded. "Yes."

"You make me long to bury myself inside you," he groaned thickly, and lightly fingered the outer lips of her womanhood. He slid first one finger, then two into her. She was slippery wet, hot, and ready for him.

To Hannah's further wonderment, after he dipped his fingers into her, he brought them to his lips and drew them along the tip of his tongue.

"Oh, God, Hannah, you taste so good as you feel."

He waited as if testing her willingness to give him such an intimate gift.

Emmett had merely taken his grunting pleasure without regard to her feelings or the pain he caused. That this man was taking the time to give her exquisite pleasure and consider her feelings was nearly overwhelming. She reached up and opened her arms to him.

"I make it good for you." Max positioned himself between her thighs and slowly guided himself to the entrance of her woman's core.

Instinctively Hannah stiffened, preparing herself for the burning, tearing pain she expected would come with entry.

"Do not worry," he whispered into the valley of her breasts. Her husband must not have known how to take a woman, Max thought.

He withdrew. At her look of confusion, he said, "I make sure you feel only pleasure."

Hannah watched in amazement while he brought his palm to his mouth and laved it with his saliva, then moistened his shaft until it glistened in the afternoon light. The sensitivity of her breasts soared when he lowered himself and pressed his bare chest to hers.

She opened her mouth to moan her joy, but he covered it with his lips. And as his tongue slowly slid into her mouth, he immersed his shaft deep inside her.

Her legs spread wide and her hands closed around the woolen blanket, making tight wads, which Max was sure must be a death grip. "Wrap your legs and arms around me, Hannah," he directed softly.

He filled her completely, fully, yet she experienced no pain. Only an incredible pleasure at their joining. Hannah clasped her thighs around him and clung to his shoulders as she felt the tension of fear fade.

Together they began to move. He began slowly, hesitating before plunging deep within her, then withdrawing, resting for a moment before starting again, building the rhythm until an animal instinct took over and their movements became wild and uncontrolled.

Hannah had never experienced such intense pleasure, which seemed to engulf her senses until spasm after spasm erupted and she climaxed in a straining, burning blaze. Only then did she realize that he had withheld his own release until he had satisfied her.

Afterward he cradled her drenched body to his and wiped her damp waves from her face.

The wonderment of something akin to the stirrings of a phenomenon before unknown began to fill every chamber of her heart, and she said, "I never knew it could be like this."

He gathered her in tighter against him and held her. *Neither did I.*

Hannah lay quietly in his arms, unnerved that he had not responded to her declaration, and her conscience assailed her. Against her vows to stay away from all men, an overwhelming attraction had drawn her to lay with one man while she was carrying the child of another.

She snuggled against his chest, listening to the steady beating of his heart. For an instant she considered laying bare her past and the secrets that had driven her to him. But Max was a proud man who valued honesty, and she feared he would spurn her as an unconscionable liar.

Now she was faced with a seemingly insurmountable dilemma. She had waited too long just to blurt out the truth, although in the coming weeks, as she swelled with child, there would be no denying it.

Seventeen

They had slept, gloriously sated, for over two hours nestled together, her hand held gently in his. When Hannah opened her eyes, Max was lying on his arm, watching her.

"Finally you awaken. I begin to think maybe my arm it is permanently numb for not wanting to awaken you."

Hannah smiled at him. He had lain in an uncomfortable position because he had not wanted to disturb her slumber. His thoughtfulness touched her heart. She sat up and a bubble of joyous laughter threatened to erupt at the twinkle in his eye. "I wouldn't want to be responsible for permanently laying you up."

"I do not complain."

"Not now, but if you couldn't work the ranch, you would."

He flexed his fingers and winked. "There is a good way I know to liven up the nerve endings." He reached for her.

He playfully pulled her closer to him, running

his fingers along her sides, causing a burst of giggles to erupt from her and make her squirm.

"I like to hear your laughter, Hannah. You do not laugh much."

"Neither do you," she challenged, and poked at his sides without the desired response. "You aren't ticklish."

"No, but it is not a reason for you to stop," he said on a more serious note, and enveloped her in his strong arms. "You are round in all the right places," he added.

Hannah stiffened in his arms when his palm skimmed over her gently rounded stomach. Mistaking her reaction, Max said, "You are put together very well. I think that I hold you until it is time to go out and break up the ice so the sheep, they can drink."

Trying not to think of her own unborn child, Hannah forced herself to relax in his arms while her mind replayed their playfulness. Max had been right, she did not laugh much; she had not had much reason to laugh. And thinking about Max's loss, she sympathized with why he did not have much cause to laugh either. They had come together out of loneliness. Hannah closed her eyes and decided not to examine further the wondrous joining that had happened between them. Rather, she would accept the temporary gift as long as it lasted.

"Hannah?"

"Umm?"

"Thank you for being so patient with my stubborn Lissa."

"There's no need to thank me."

"I think there is. It is Lissa who rips your dress maybe?"

Hannah lowered her head, but he raised her chin and gazed into her eyes. "I think I am right, yes?"

"Losing her mother must have been very difficult for her."

"It does not excuse such behavior."

"You've treated Franc with kindness when she did not deserve it."

"My Lissa, she misses a mama's guidance and your Franc, she misses a papa's."

For an instant a brief fantasy that each would be able to fill the empty place in the other's life sparked into her mind's eye. Then Hannah realized that his voice had trailed off awkwardly as he finished his sentence as if he were worried that she might misconstrue his meaning to be an invitation.

She shifted uneasily. "I'm sure the children will be fine in time. They are just young and will grow out of it."

"You are right maybe. But if there are more problems, we stand together to solve them, yes?"

Hannah nodded, wondering if his words had unspoken implications.

After a long silence Max got up, left Hannah, and went into the bedroom. Hannah wrapped a blanket around her shoulders and padded after him, needing to reassure herself that she had not misinterpreted his comments regarding the children.

Max's back was to her as he rummaged through the drawers at the opposite end of the room when she sat down on the bed. The blanket slipped off her shoulders, displaying more cleavage than she had intended.

"Max, about the children needing another parent—" When Max swung around, although he attempted to hide it, the expression on his face could have frozen fire and stopped Hannah in mid-sentence.

Suddenly, she realized that she was sitting on the elegant quilt his wife had made for their marriage bed. Then it dawned on her that he had not taken her to his bed, but had remained in the kitchen.

She got up and pulled the blanket up around her neck. "I'm sorry," she said stiffly. "I shouldn't have been so presumptuous as to come in to your bedroom with you."

"Hannah," Max said, but she had already swept from the room.

Max plunked down on the bed where Hannah had been sitting. For over two years that side of the bed had been left untouched and cold. He pressed his hand to the quilt and fingered the date on which he had been wed. The place was still warm, and reminded him that Hannah was a vibrant, living, loving woman. His mind warred with bittersweet memories and long-held beliefs. But there was more to consider than just the two of them. There were the children, his father, and the old country traditions.

By the time he dressed and returned to the kitchen, Hannah was once again seated at the sewing machine.

"Hannah, there is something I want for you to understand."

She glanced up, her face devoid of emotion. "You don't have to feel that you must explain. I understand perfectly. As a matter of fact, you needn't concern yourself. What happened between us was merely a diversion. We have children who need our first consideration," she said in a brittle voice.

"Yes, you are right." He nodded, shrugged into his coat, and went outside without further comment.

He had known that from her previous reactions to him that she had been badly hurt, and from her reaction to him now he realized that he too had hurt her and must take precautions to preclude it from happening again.

Chopping at the ice, Max continued to ponder his actions with Hannah. He was not a man who merely took a woman for his own pleasure. But he had discovered that he was a man who still had a man's needs, and she was a very desirable woman. There had been a pent-up tension inside him that until Hannah had come into his life and home he had kept buried deep inside.

In an effort to alleviate the tension and his growing feelings from getting the best of him again and setting something into motion that could never be between them, Max sent the pick spiking into the ice.

The ice splintered.

Physical exertion and the blessed exhaustion that accompanied it was the best way to keep the body from controlling the mind.

Again Max swung the pick with a force meant to block out all other thought.

Lissa could tell the moment they returned from the Herrias that things had changed between her papa and Hannah. The air virtually crackled with tension. She tried to be patient while she answered questions about their trip, but all the while her mind burned with questions of her own.

"Papa, I missed you." She thrust herself into his arms.

"You go for only one night," Max said, and hugged the girl. She clung to him, which was out of character for the girl, who generally offered a quick hug or peck on the cheek. It warned him that his daughter was up to something.

The feel of the soft new fabric caused Lissa to pull back, a troubled question crossed her face. "Where did you get the new shirt?"

Lissa's eyes trailed to Hannah, accusation now mirrored in the girl's dark depths.

"Hannah makes it."

A big knowing grin on Petya's face, he said, "She learns fast, that one, eh?"

"Faster than we all thought," Lissa muttered.

"That is enough, young lady," Max interjected. "Remember that Hannah, she is here living with us to do a job."

"Yes, and from that shirt it is plain that she is doing one on you," Lissa snapped.

Max's reflexes were lightning-quick. He grabbed Lissa's arm and hauled her over to where Hannah stood, shocked by the girl's open animosity.

"Apologize for the rudeness you display. I remain quiet at Hannah's request. But no longer do I have you continue with such lack of manners. Your mama and I, we do not teach you such ways."

"My mama is dead," Lissa cried, yanked her arm from her papa's grip, and raced from the room.

Max started after her, but Petya dropped a staying hand on Max's arm. "Why not allow me, big brother? I think what she needs is a man of my vast experience to explain a few things to her, eh?" Petya then left Max and draped an arm around the other two children who were uneasily studying the floor. "You two are old enough to hear this I think." To Max, he said, "You will see to the horses, eh?"

For once Max gratefully deferred to his younger brother. Left alone with Hannah, he said, "Lissa, she does apologize."

Hannah had been too astounded by the girl's rude outburst in front of everyone to say anything until then. "Max, perhaps it would be best if Franc and I went and stayed with one of the other families in the valley, as your brother suggested."

Her words struck Max flat in the chest. Everything inside him shouted that he should let her go, get on with his life as he had planned before she had entered it. But a small nagging voice from inside his heart refused to listen to his head.

"While I take care of the animals, you start to ready supplies for Petya to take back to camp with him." He turned to go out, then stopped and said without facing Hannah, "We do not discuss your leaving," before he left the house to care for the animals that his brother had left unattended.

Confused by his response, Hannah stood at the window and watched Max's long, determined strides as he approached the horses. She could not help her attraction to the big man. His ways were as foreign as he and his animals were to her, yet the glimmer of something akin to love was not always so easily categorized and tucked into a nice neat little package.

And Max came as a package, as did she. They both carried responsibilities and pain from the past. Max had three children, two of whom might never accept her. Although Hannah believed that in time André may come around, Lissa was another matter. She was obstinate and steadfast in her dislike, and Hannah wondered if she would ever be able to win the girl over. Franc was not much better, although she was no longer quite so vocal in her disgust since Petya had arrived and captured her attention.

It was apparent that Max had not completely accepted his wife's death. And Hannah had not forgotten Emmett's ways. At the moment she refused to think what Max would do when he discovered the secrets she harbored concerning Emmett, Franc, and her motherly way.

In an effort to redirect her focus, Hannah began gathering the supplies she thought Petya might need for his return trip to the winter camp, until Panda Pie let out a squeak that drew Hannah's attention. She walked past the door leading to the parlor to retrieve her precious little pet. Petya was sitting on the sofa, an arm around each Garat child. Franc sat with her legs crossed on the floor in front of him. The children were listening so intently, their young faces so completely enrapt with what he was saying, Hannah stopped to lend an ear to the flamboyant young man.

"Lissa, your mama, she would not want this."

"How do you know?" she sniffled.

"This I know because not long before she went away, your mama, she made me promise that I would watch over you and your papa. I think that she knew she would not be here to watch you grow up and she did not want you children to be filled with sorrow. Your mama, she was full of life, and she told me that she wanted her children not to waste their lives. And she did not want your papa to go through life alone either."

"But we are here and you and Grandpapa. Papa is not alone."

"Lissa, your papa does indeed have you children and Grandpapa and me, but when you get older you will understand that a man he needs a special woman by his side as well."

"Papa has me."

Petya smiled at the young girl. "Ah, that he does. And he would not trade you for all the sheep in the world. But, my little princess, every man needs a special woman who is not a daughter."

The girl crossed her arms over her chest and thrust out her chin. "You do not have one of these *special* women at your side."

He let out a laugh, unperturbed, and ruffled her hair. "I am too young yet, like you. But I too will one day want a special woman at my side." He did not see Franc squirm as he continued. "And I hope that when that day comes, you will be happy for me, like I hope that when that day comes again for your papa that you will be happy for him."

André sat wide-eyed, wondering how long he was going to be able to keep the secret of a bride from Lissa, and not totally comprehending what the conversation was all about. If it had to do with girls, he was sure it would never concern him. Franc did not say a word, but merely rolled her eyes. Lissa remained sullen.

"You do not want your papa to be sad all his life, eh, princess?"

"I do not want Papa to be sad, but why does he have to like Franc's mama?" Lissa persisted.

"Men and women, they do not always choose who they like, Lissa. And when you are older you will come to understand this, eh?" He sent her a conspiratorial wink.

Lissa blushed red down to the roots of her dark hair and let out a girlish giggle. But inside she did not altogether believe everything her uncle said.

"Now, the sheep at winter camp, they are waiting for me."

"And Grandpapa too," André put in, finally able to contribute to the conversation.

"Yes, and your grandpapa too. I want your word that you children will not interfere between your papa and Hannah if they want to be special friends, eh?"

Hannah watched as Lissa and the other children reluctantly nodded their consent. And while Petya seemed quite satisfied with his efforts to smooth over the difficulties the children were having, Hannah did not miss Lissa crossing her fingers behind her back while she nodded her agreement.

Despite Petya's good intentions, and Max's remark that they must stand together where the children were concerned, Hannah knew that if the relationship between herself and the children was ever going to change, it was going to be up to her.

Eighteen

After standing in the background and listening while Lissa elicited a promise from Petya that he would return at the first opportunity, Hannah stepped away from the door just before he swept into the kitchen to say his good-byes.

"Hannah, alas, the time it has come that I must leave you," he said with a dramatic flourish, his face long, a hand over his heart. "You will try oh so hard not to miss me, eh?"

Hannah could not help herself, his antics made her chuckle. "It will be difficult, but I'll try."

"Will you miss me as much as you would if I were my big brother perhaps?"

Hannah immediately sobered, then attempted to shield her reaction from him. "Of course."

Petya let out a laugh to lighten the mood and enveloped Hannah in his arms. "Ah, but I wish I see you first. You are most special, Hannah." He held her from him and gazed down into her eyes. "My brother, he is lucky, eh?"

"I am here only to work for your brother's family," Hannah protested.

"You cannot fool Petya. I see how you have eyes only for Maximilian. And I watch my brother. He is Basque and they do not know how to easily show their feelings sometimes, my people."

"You are Basque,"

Petya shrugged. "But always there is the black sheep, yes? Let me tell you how to read my brother, it will be a good guide to his moods." Hannah cocked her head, her interest piqued. "If he is wearing his beret tipped back on his head, then he is a happy man and can be approached with demands. If he pulls it down far over his forehead, then his mood, it is not so good and you must be cautious. If he tips it to one side, then my brother, he is a man in a rakish humor, eh?" He winked and flashed his brows.

Hannah pursed her lips at the outrageous notion that Petya intoned so easily. But she quietly filed his information in the back of her mind.

"You try to be patient with my mule of a brother and it will reward you." He grinned with a nonchalant shrug. "And if not, remember, Petya is nearby, always ready and willing, eh?"

Before Hannah had the opportunity to deny any interest in either brother, Petya reached out, clamped his fingers around her arms, hauled her back against him, and placed a smacking kiss on her lips.

"You do not waste time, Petya," Max said, glowering at the pair.

Max had just finished with the animals, only to return to his house and find his brother kissing Hannah. It did not please him, to say the least, and a fit of jealousy rose in his gut.

Hannah struggled out of Petya's embrace. Unaffected, Petya flashed Max a knowing grin. "Be careful, my big Basque sibling, you let your feelings show." Then to Hannah, "I must leave now. Remember our conversation."

Petya said to Max, "Good-bye, big brother. Do not forget me and your papa again or to the ranch I return, eh?" With a wink and a flash of his brows he grabbed the bag of supplies Hannah had readied earlier. As a final gesture he flipped Max an irreverent salute and left the house.

Hannah watched the flamboyant young man depart from the ranch with a jaunty stride to his step, a whistle on his lips, and the bag slung over his left shoulder.

Max waited until Petya was out of sight before he twisted toward Hannah. "Petya, he likes the ladies and they like him."

At the jealousy in such a statement, Hannah swung around. Max was standing rigid, his arms straight at his sides. Feeling peevish from his remark, she snipped, "Yes, *he* certainly does have a way with the ladies."

Hannah was in no mood to practice Petya's suggestion of patience at the moment. Max had glared at her for sitting on his bed, then out of the blue he would not hear of it when she sugested that she and Franc go to live with one of he neighbors in the valley. Well, despite Petya's brotherly advice, she was getting sick and tired of being subservient to a man who discussed only what he wanted to discuss only when he wanted o discuss it. She had spent five years being a totally spiritless wife, and she was not going to accept that position ever again.

To her further chagrin, he added, "Petya, his reputation it is to not stay around once he makes a conquest, Hannah. He would hurt you."

"And I suppose you have not?" she shot back, mindless of the impact her words would have on him. "Perhaps that trait runs in your family."

Max's eyes sparked at the unexpected accusation. "My brother I am not."

"No? What would you call bedding me in the kitchen, then looking at me as if I had committed a heinous crime when I unwittingly followed you into your bedroom and sat on your sacred bed?"

"I lose my wife on that bed," he fired back. It was the first time he had spoken so openly to anyone about the loss he had held inside for so long, and he tensed.

"And that is why you bedded me in the kitchen, so it would not remind you of your deceased wife or so you would not desecrate the sacred shrine your bed has become."

"What makes you think you got the right to speak this way?" he spat out angrily.

"You gave me the right when you bedded me
and then would not hear of me leaving."

"One it is nothing to do with the other."

"Isn't it? Then why not just take Franc, and
me to your neighbor's, Max? You have slaked
your male needs. I'm not an experienced seam
stress, so it should be easy to cast us out
shouldn't it?" When he did not answer, but stood
before her silently seething, she hissed, "Well
shouldn't it?"

Max shoved his fingers through his hair in ut-
ter frustration. His Mary never fought with him
and this was a new and alien experience to have
his word questioned. But Hannah was not Mary
Mary was dead two years now. Hannah was very
much alive. But she was an American woman, so
unlike the women of his village, who were taught
to defer to their men as part of Basque patriarchal culture.

At the most inopportune moment the children
chose to make an entrance. They were standing
in the doorway with expectant faces. His gaze
swung from the children back to Hannah. Her
face was red with anger, and she was not simply
going to let it go this time. Well, neither was he.
They had a few things to straighten out between
them . . . now!

"You children, you go out to the yard and see
to the chores. Then pitch the horses their hay in
the barn until I call you."

"But I thought you saw to the horses while Un-

le Petya and us were talking, Papa?" André
uestioned, totally bemused by the day's events.

At the sound of his brother's name, Max glow-
red at his son. "Do not question me. Go."

"Yes, sir." André lowered his head as the other
hildren gathered their jackets and trudged from
he house. André stopped at the door and
·lanced back. "Sammy is playing on the rug with
iis toys."

Max nodded toward his son before the boy
losed the door behind him. Even the children
iad begun questioning his authority, Max
roused sourly.

"So, you take your anger out on your children
iow?" Hannah accused.

"If you got a complaint against me, fine. But
warn you, you do not dare to bring my children
nto this, Hannah."

"I was not the one who barked at them. Al-
hough from now on the children are going to
reat me with the respect I deserve!"

Max knew she was right about the children,
)ut he had no intention of admitting to any ac-
:usation or observation she made. He was getting
.oo angry, too angry even to trust himself to fin-
sh the argument they were having.

"I do not bark."

She balled her fists on her hips and thrust out
ier chin. "No? I'll have you know that you act
like an ancient caveman. All you haven't done is

beat on your chest and roar like some Neander thal.''

That was the final insult. He snapped. If sh thought he was a roaring *Neanderthal,* then h was going to be one. In a flash he swooped dow on her, scooped her up, and held her arms a her sides so she could not beat against his ches

"What're you doing?" she cried, experiencin a side of the man she had not seen before. Sh had accused him of being a caveman, but sh never truly expected him to act like one.

"I do not want to make you more of a story teller than you already are, so I show you first hand how a caveman he treats a woman."

With determined strides he stomped to hi bedroom door. He was determined to show he that he had not made his bedroom into some sor of shrine. His gaze caught the patchwork quil with its fine stitches detailing his past life, an the anger instantly drained from him. Every ma jor event of the family's life was woven into tha quilt. Every one, that is, except for the death o his wife. Slowly he set Hannah on her feet.

"You are right, Hannah," he said, his anger deflated, and turned to leave the house.

They had just had their first argument. Han nah wanted to cry out her frustration. She had run away from one man only to be brought to gether with another who was as elusive and dif ficult to understand as her own feelings.

The only thing that she knew for certain was

that she could not just let him walk out on her this time. She was in danger of falling in love with the stubborn, impossible Basque.

She rasped out, "Max?"

He took a deep breath, stopped, and pivoted around. His face was unreadable, set in impassable stone. "Yes?"

"There is no reason to fight."

"You are right. There is no reason," he answered in accord. "Now that we agree, our lives they will go back to normal, yes?"

But as he lay in his lonely bed late that night with his arms behind his head, unable to sleep, he knew their lives were anything but normal. He could not keep Hannah and her accusations about his bedroom being a sacred shrine from his mind.

No matter how hard he tried to block her out, he thought about Hannah now asleep in his kitchen. She was lying on the straw he had arranged. He wondered if her glorious long, wavy hair was fanned out across the pillow. The sensual consideration caused his fingers to sensitize, and he rubbed his thumbs along the insides of the rough tips, imagining the texture of the soft, silken threads, and the satiny smoothness of her naked flesh beneath his touch. In his mind's eye he experienced the flutter of her dark lashes when she closed her eyes and lifted her luscious full lips to his.

He could almost feel the curve at the small of

her back, visualize the white fullness of her breasts, taste the sweetness of those peaked centers, and inhale the spicy muskiness of her woman's scent when they had bedded.

Tension built inside of him like a coiled snake ready to strike until he sat up and mopped his drenched brow, panting at the uncensored ruminations. In the light of the moon he caught sight of the quilt that he had so carefully laid over a chair near where Samuel slept soundly.

He got up and ran his fingers over the coverlet. He could make out the events sewn into the fabric. Feelings warred inside him as they had for some time now—since Hannah's arrival. He thought about what the quilt represented. Maybe Hannah was right; it was a shrine to his past. He had been clinging to the memories, letting them rule his life.

On one hand were bittersweet reminiscences of a life that no longer existed, a life lost. On the other was Hannah. She was alive and warm and the present. And if he did not relent and finally tuck away the quilt and the memories it represented, he could never live in the present and he would never be able to look toward the future.

"It is time," he murmured softly to the treasured piece.

His resolve set, he carefully bundled the quilt into his arms and quietly climbed the ladder to the attic room where his children slept. Cautious not to awaken Lissa and André, he lifted the trunk lid housing his wife's cherished valuables that he was saving for his daughter and tenderly placed the quilt inside.

He stopped to tuck the blanket up around his daughter's neck. She was the image of her mother. He dropped a gentle kiss on the girl's forehead, then with his burdened heart lighter than it had been in years, he turned and went back down the ladder.

Climbing back into bed, Max closed his eyes. The argument he'd had with Hannah had finally compelled him to come face-to-face with himself. She had forced him to see himself as others had seen him.

With removal of the symbolic quilt, the constant painful reminder of his past life had been dislodged from the forefront of his mind. Finally he felt that he would be able to truly let go of Mary and allow her to rest in peace. And he could truly let go of the pain of the past.

In the morning he would remove the wreath of hair, the perfume bottles, and the sign signifying that the home was Mary's house. Then he would be ready to try to live in the present and look toward the future.

In his mind his future was entwined with one very obstinate American woman.

Nineteen

"What the hell is this supposed to mean?" Emmett roared, and slammed the heirloom brooch down on his desk in front of him.

The tall, lanky detective shifted from foot to foot in front of the huge mahogany desk, his hat in his hands. While Emmett Turner was paying top dollar, he was a bastard to work for, and the man silently wished to hell Turner had engaged another agency to locate his runaway wife.

"Well, speak up. Don't just stand there like a beaten-down dog with your cock hanging limp between your legs. Have you located her yet?"

"Well . . . no. But before you get upset, we have a pretty good lead, sir."

"Before I get upset? You haven't located her, but you have a pretty good lead," Emmett mimicked, screwing up his face into an ugly pink twist.

"Sir, we now know that she is nowhere in the city."

"I could have told you that, you imbecile. What the hell am I paying for? Incompetence?"

"We learned that she pawned the brooch and used the money to buy a ticket on a train heading west, sir," the man forged ahead despite the bile rising in the back of his throat at losing the toss of who had to break the news to Turner.

"Fine. She headed west," Emmett sneered, and reached for the bottle of fine imported Irish whiskey he kept in his desk drawer.

"And I'm heading down to the station as soon as I leave here to buy a ticket. I'll have my best tracker on the first train heading west in the morning. It shouldn't be very difficult to trace her."

A calculating glint sparked into Emmett's eyes. "No, not very difficult at all, since I am going to accompany him," he announced, and took a long, satisfying pull from the bottle.

"It will not be very difficult at all, since I am going to prepare the entire dinner myself," Hannah boasted.

October had slipped into November as the days passed with no more than a whisper. Snow lay piled high against the old battered fence surrounding the yard. Life for Hannah seemed to settle into a routine despite the children's continued mulish refusal to accept her. At least her relationship with Max had seemed to take on a new dimension. And she was learning to sew and cook and felt very domestic as Thanksgiving approached the isolated ranch.

"This special American day you say you observe, this Thanksgiving you speak about,"— Max looked skeptical—"why celebrate it?"

"It is a tradition where I come from. Each year we give thanks to God for our blessings during the year. . . ."

As Max listened to Hannah animatedly explain her American holiday, he could not help but silently think that this year he may have something to give thanks for, too.

"We give thanks with feasting and prayer. It was first a harvest festival for the plentiful crops and included clams, eel, ducks, turkeys, geese—"

"Geese we have."

"Yes, one very mean one. Anyway, our first president issued a proclamation naming a day in November as a day of national thanksgiving. The woman editor of *Godey's Lady's Book,* Sarah Josepha Hale, worked to promote the idea.

"Then President Abraham Lincoln proclaimed the last Thursday in November as a day to give thanks to our beneficent Father. Each year since then our American presidents have formally proclaimed that it should be celebrated." She hesitated a moment before adding, "At home we always celebrate it."

"Gol-ly, you shoulda been a little ol' schoolmarm," Franc scoffed. "Why, I bet you're just chock fulla learnin', ain't you?"

"Enough to teach you a thing or two," Hannah said with a new authority to her voice, causing Franc to defer without further argument.

Max cocked a brow at the woman who had emerged stronger from the argument they'd had weeks earlier. "A good idea maybe."

"What is?" Franc grumbled, wishing she had kept her thoughts to herself. She was not sure she cared much for the bossy way Hannah had begun treating her lately.

"After this American *Thanksgiving* Hannah speaks about, she maybe agrees to begin teaching all you children your lessons," Max announced.

"You and your big mouth," André shot at Franc. "Wait until Lissa hears what you have done."

Hannah watched André race toward the attic room with Franc hot on his heels before Hannah swung her attention back to Max, who was seated on the floor in front of the fire, playing with Sammy.

"I'm not a teacher," she said softly. Before she had gotten the courage to leave Emmett, she had merely been someone for Emmett to take his drunken rages out upon.

"You are not a seamstress or a cook either. But you teach yourself."

"With your help."

He gave her a gentle smile. "You do not give yourself enough credit, Hannah."

She swelled with pride at the praise he heaped

on her. It was such a change from when she had first arrived at the ranch. But it was part of the transformation she'd noticed in Max after the argument they'd had. Secretly, she admitted that this new side of Max was endearing him to her more each day. Too much perhaps.

"You know things about this country and its history. And you read and know your numbers, yes?"

"Yes."

"Then maybe you teach the children these things. And educate them about the history of this land. Come spring, I plan to send the children away to school, but perhaps with you here they do not need to go." Hannah watched him stop and take a breath as if another thought had just entered his mind. "And maybe you teach me better English too."

Hannah's heart nearly stopped at the implication. Was he hinting that he wanted her to stay?

Her hand ringed her belly which was swelling with each passing day, and her mind conjured up a picture of the woman Max did not know was coming to be his bride. Those thoughts in mind, she could not help from asking, "Am I still going to be here in the spring?"

"The snow, it blocks the pass into the spring," he answered evasively, unsure whether he was ready to put what he had been thinking and feeling into words.

"Then I suppose I could work with the children until then, and maybe help you with English."

Even as she spoke, Hannah felt a stab of mixed feelings at the response he had given. On the one hand was disappointment. The argument they'd had transformed their relationship. Max no longer mentioned his deceased wife, and the quilt had disappeared as had the many bottles adorning the dressing table and the wooden sign from above the door. He was more considerate and responsive, too. Yet he had not attempted to bed her again. Although at times she would catch him staring at her with what she could describe only as a look of raw hunger on his face.

On the other hand, her baby was due in spring and she had planned to be gone before she had to explain why she had not mentioned her pregnancy. But that was no longer possible, and Hannah found it weighing heavily on her mind as her waist thickened. Soon Max would guess, if she did not break down and tell him. Then what would she say? What would he do?

"Do you think you remain longer than spring, maybe?" he questioned, cutting into her troubled concerns.

"We can't continue to live together this way indefinitely," she responded softly, and held her gaze steady.

There was a time in her life that she would have lowered her eyes. But this was too important; she had to see his reaction. And she no longer was that timid woman, totally unsure of herself. "What would people think?"

"What other people, they think, is not of concern."

You make your bed, you lie in it. Her mother's now infamous words rang in her mind.

She raised her chin in a defiant gesture but did not trust herself to speak. She had no intention of living in sin until some Basque woman arrived unannounced from his village to claim title to his name.

"Maybe they think that you and I, we make a handsome pair with all these children, yes?"

Surprised and uncertain exactly what to make of his response, she continued to stare at Max. He was gazing deeply into her eyes, delving intently, as if he were waiting for a reply from her.

"Max, we are not a pair—"

"You are right, Hannah," he said with a mixture of disappointment and inner relief after blurting out what had been on his mind for some time. He did not blink, keeping an unreadable expression on his face.

There were things he had almost said, but now was not the best time. He could not put off taking the supplies to the winter camp, or shipping the lambs to market, and he did not want to say more until he had time to thoroughly think through the idea he had set forth. Being away would also allow him time to clear his head. Lately, when he was near Hannah day after day he had a hard time thinking about anything else but her.

"Outside, the sheep, they need my attention. I must go out into the yard now and see to them."

He turned to leave the house, then pivoted around. "As far as this Thanksgiving of yours, I think it is a good firsthand history lesson for the children, this American tradition. And you got time to prepare the entire dinner yourself, as you mention. While I take the supplies to the winter camp and ship the lambs, you prepare this feast, yes?"

"Yes."

Hannah was a little dismayed when Max handed Sammy over to her, put his beret on, and went out with his sheep. She had hoped he might remain and elaborate on his comment concerning them. But she had noticed him pull his beret down far over his forehead, closing himself to her. Remembering Petya's remarks about the telltale hat, Hannah had sagely swallowed any further questions.

She held Sammy to her. "I know your daddy is not comfortable talking about his feelings. But I had hoped that we would finally sit down and discuss what I think may be on both our minds."

"Mama, Mama," Sammy cooed, and ringed chubby arms around her neck.

Hannah hugged the little boy to her. She had grown very attached to the toddler. Secretly she acknowledged that she couldn't love him more even if he were her own, which was how she was coming to think of him.

Hannah was so wrapped up with Sammy, she did not see Lissa standing in the doorway of her father's bedroom.

Listening to Hannah and watching her hug her brother as if he were Hannah's own son made Lissa burn inside. Lissa already had been upset since her papa had stored her mama's things away. Now she was more upset. After André had told her what her papa had said about Hannah teaching them, Lissa had come down to plead with him to reconsider.

Overhearing Hannah startled Lissa, and she realized that she would have to do something pretty drastic soon or they would be in danger of that interloper moving into the house permanently!

"Hannah,"— Lissa strolled into the parlor as if she hadn't a care—"let me help you with Sam."

Hannah glanced up, expecting to see Lissa's tight expression, but to her pleased surprise the girl's innocent look momentarily disarmed Hannah. She had tried to be tolerant of the girl, since Hannah understood Lissa's pain. But Hannah was not going to allow herself to be lulled into letting her guard down around the girl.

"Thank you for offering to take Sammy," Hannah said, and handed the toddler over to his sister. "There are preparations I need to start making for our Thanksgiving celebration while your father is away shipping the lambs to market and delivering supplies to your uncle and grand-father."

"Thanksgiving?"

"A special American tradition I plan to teach you about."

And I plan to teach you about my own special Basque tradition. "Maybe I can help," Lissa offered as she took her little brother, who promptly began fussing to go back to Hannah. "Sammy, Hannah is busy, so you and I are going to play."

The toddler settled down and Hannah said, "That's very considerate of you, Lissa. I would appreciate the help planning the festivities. I want to make this a very special Thanksgiving to remember."

Lissa immediately brightened as an idea flashed into her mind, and she nodded her head. "Yes, I think that making this American Thanksgiving of yours a special day we will all remember would be a very good idea."

Twenty

His hands clamped around a steaming cup of coffee, Max sat before the flickering fire, staring intently at the dancing flames. His mind was so filled with thoughts of Hannah that he did not hear his father come and settle down beside him.

"Your mind, it weighs much on you, my son?"

From behind them, Petya chuckled as he walked from the shadows and took a place around the fire. "No doubt about one hundred thirty pounds, eh?"

Max shot his brother a frown cold enough to freeze the desert in summer, then turned back to his father. "I got much to sort out, yes."

"Not nearly as much as you will come spring," Petya supplied again.

"By spring I settle everything," Max snapped, his annoyance heightening that his brother would make such light. Max refocused his thoughts back to Hannah and what she had said to him before he'd left for camp. She would not continue to live under his roof indefinitely under their present arrangement, nor would he expect it or want such a covenant.

"Do not be so sure, big brother."

This time the eldest Garat sent his wayward son a silencing frown, which caused Petya to shrug his indifference and fall mute.

"Your brother, he does not know when his tongue, it runs away with his mouth."

Petya shook his head at his father's foolish old-world wisdom. The old man had advised Petya not to mention Uncle Laborde's efforts to locate a bride for Max. He did not want Max dissuaded from making up his own mind about the woman who had put the light back in Max's life, should he learn that a Basque woman from his own country may be on her way that very moment to become his wife. Although Bernard did feel that a Basque wife would be the best choice.

"I hope you know that which you do, Papa," Petya said.

"Is there something I should know?" Max questioned.

Bernard's expression did not waver. "I am no more than an old man from the mountains who comes to this country to help his son with the sheep. What it is I know?"

Max raised a brow at the sly old man. "I think maybe you know more than you are willing to say."

Bernard laughed at that, and raised a gnarled finger, shaking it at Max. "You are too smart for

me. I want a surprise for you, but the wool, it
cannot be pulled over your eyes, so I confess."

Petya straightened and crossed his arms over
his chest, amusedly waiting for the fireworks to
start when Max learned what his father had
planned.

"Petya, he goes to the Herrias to ask a favor
from them. The two older boys, Jean and
Étienne, they agree to watch over the sheep at
Christmas so you and the children are not
alone." A cunning smile on his face, the old man
said, "Petya and I, we spend Christmas at the
ranch with you."

Max nodded. But he now had another concern.
He did not like the idea of Petya being anywhere
near Hannah. And what of his papa? The old
man was notorious for his well-intentioned meddling!

"Maybe you should stop meddling," André
suggested when he heard what Lissa planned to
do to disrupt the celebration that Hannah was
planning.

"What do you mean?" she demanded. "You
want her for our mama?"

André shrugged. Then, with a mutinous stare,
he blurted out, "Hannah is not at all like what
you said. She is nice, Lissa."

"She is only pretending to be nice because she
is trying to get Papa to marry her."

"Lissa, Mama is not coming back," he said sadly. "You do want Papa to find a special woman, like Uncle Petya was talking about?"

Tears began to mist into Lissa's eyes, and she turned her head to keep her brother from seeing the salty drops as she wiped them. Her face was a study in determination when she swung back to glare at André. "Do not help. I do not care. But if you tell, I will never forgive you. Never. Before we go into the parlor and help Hannah like she said we had to, I want you to promise that you will not say anything."

André sighed. He didn't like everybody swearing him to secrecy. What if he slipped and said the wrong thing to the wrong person? He could really make a mess of everything. Secretly he hoped that no one else told him a secret.

But as André was in the attic room reluctantly promising not to tell about Lissa's latest planned mischief, Franc was sprawled in the parlor grudgingly promising Hannah that she would keep a civil tongue in her head from now on when Max was around.

"I'm glad that we finally have that settled," Hannah announced. "Now, I expect you to pitch in and help make this a memorable Thanksgiving."

"Me? Why me?" she whined.

"And henceforth there will be no more whining," Hannah directed, ignoring another round of Franc's continual questioning and complaining.

Franc let out a disgruntled snort and rolled her eyes. "I ain't told your secret about me not bein' your kid. How come you expect me to do work like some dumb slave around here?"

"Because in order to have everything ready by the time Max returns, I'm going to require your help, that's why. And you can start by going out to the root cellar and gathering an armful of carrots and potatoes."

Franc thrust out her chin. "And what're we goin' to eat for meat, another one of them dumb awful *blood* sausages?" She stuck her tongue out and pointed her finger down her throat to signify her distaste for the sauages.

At that moment Lissa and André joined Hannah and Franc. Looking angelic and purely innocent, Lissa looked to Franc and narrowed her eyes only slightly as Franc sucked on her finger with a guilty grin. "I doubt that Hannah would want to serve a traditional Basque dish for an American celebration." Then to Hannah she said, "André told me that geese were part of the first celebration, and Papa is aware of that. Why not serve that big fat goose that is always chasing you when you go out into the yard?"

André hung in the background, shaking his head in an effort to warn Hannah away from the mean goose without breaking his promise. But Hannah did not glance in his direction.

That big goose was meaner than a cattle rancher after the sheep had munched down the grass on the range!

Even as Hannah answered, "A goose is a good idea, Lissa, I'm glad you thought of it," she knew that this was going to be another test, another obstacle she had to overcome before she could reach the girl.

But Hannah had never killed anything in her entire life!

"Ma, I don't think no goose is such a good idea," Franc put in in an effort to protect Hannah without alienating Lissa. Lissa was up to something, and Franc had already had firsthand experience with that lowdown old goose. Even Panda Pie stayed clear of that devil demon disguised in white feathers.

"Maybe Franc is right," André added, and wrinkled his nose for effect. "It is greasy."

"Humph," Lissa snorted in dismissal. "Only if it is not cooked right. I am sure Hannah wants to keep this celebration au-au . . ." Her voice trailed off, unable to think of the proper word in English. She looked to Hannah.

"I believe the word is *authentic*," Hannah supplied.

Lissa raised her chin in triumph. "Yes, authentic. I know you want this dinner to be authentic." Lissa grabbed André's hand. "Come on, we will take Sammy out to play before it gets too cold."

Franc waited until she heard the kitchen door

slam before she bent toward Hannah. "Golly, *Ma*. You teached us a new word. But what does it mean?"

Hannah inwardly sighed. She did not have the slightest idea how to cook a goose, let alone prepare one and have it come out without being greasy.

"It means, Franc, that I just may be about to cook my own proverbial goose."

Preparations for the Thanksgiving celebration went forth smoothly. Hannah was delighted that none of the children was causing any problems. Each one had been recruited to take part in getting ready for the dinner, which Hannah planned to have become her first history lesson as well. Each child had been delegated a specific job. To Hannah's amazement, everyone was following her dictates without any bickering.

André seemed to take pleasure in fashioning the husked corn stalks into table decorations. And his efforts demonstrated his creative side to the sensitive youngster.

Franc gathered the vegetables, even whittling the potatoes into shapes of Indian heads, after Hannah had begun telling them about the first Thanksgiving. Hannah noted that it was the first time that Franc had taken any true interest in what she did, and Hannah smothered her with praise, which caused the girl to beam with pride.

Even Lissa seemed to become absorbed in the preparations despite herself. After several trials, Hannah learned how to fashion Pilgrim caps and had the girl collecting feathers for the Indian bonnets? It was Hannah's idea that they dress in period attire, and she spent hours detailing the event.

Everything was proceeding better than Hannah could have imagined until the actual day approached, and Max was due to return. Hannah knew he would be expecting a feast.

One way or another, Hannah was bound to give him one!

The table had been set, the children dressed in their costumes early, and everything was ready.

Everything . . . except the goose.

Max was due back by nightfall. The time had come. The day of reckoning for Hannah and the goose.

Hannah had blocked out the unpleasant thought that it was up to her to provide the meat. Instead, she had focused on the rest of the meal. She had even written a little skit for the children to perform for Max.

"Hannah," Lissa said, a huge hatchet in her hands. Hannah jumped at the sight of the weapon. "Here, I thought you might need this." Lissa thrust out her hand and gave over the sharp weapon. "André and I would go out with you, but since we are already dressed and you wanted us to practice our lines for the sketch, you know we cannot help."

"Just make sure that you all have your lines memorized before this evening. And keep an eye on Sammy while I'm busy."

Lissa smiled brightly. "You do not have to worry about Sammy. I will always take good care of *my* brother."

Hannah watched the girl flounce off in her Pilgrim outfit, and tried not to visualize her on the dunking stool, which would be a fine place for the angry young girl.

Hannah sighed and set the hatchet on the long table while she donned a jacket and a large work apron she had found hanging on a hook in the barn a few days before. It was bloodstained, and she had guessed it had been used on numerous occasions for the very purpose she was about to use it for.

She immediately felt like the butcher back in St. Louis, where she used to purchase the special cut steaks.

"Now is not the time to get cold feet," Hannah said to the huge hatchet as she picked it up and examined it.

Her stomach protesting the very thought of chopping off the goose's head, Hannah had to force each foot, one step at a time, in front of the other until she was standing before the pen that housed the vicious fowl.

Hannah carefully lifted the latch. The goose

seemed to sense her intentions. It honked at her, dropped its head, stretching its neck into an aggressive line, and appeared ready to charge her.

Hannah's heart rate increased and blood surged through her veins. Not about to let that feathered monster think it had bested her, Hannah raised the sharp-edged weapon, took two deep buoying breaths, and slowly slipped inside the pen.

Twenty-one

From the window of the kitchen, Franc snorted in disgust as she held back the curtain and watched Hannah's wretched efforts with the goose. Panda Pie was circling the pen, barking, but was careful to maintain her distance.

"I don't care what you say, Lissa. I ain't stayin' inside here. I'm goin' out there and make sure my ma ain't kilt by that feathered devil."

Her dark eyes flashing, Lissa grabbed Franc's arm. "No, you are not. You said your mama is as good as anybody's. So, let her prove it."

"And if she does?"

"I will never say another bad word about her again."

Franc pouted and sneaked another glance out the window. What she saw in the distance helped her to face Lissa and Andy square on. "Okay." Her confidence returned, she suggested, "But let's up the ante. If we eat goose for this dumb old Thanksgiving supper tonight, you eat crow." Franc dangled her fingers in challenge. "Ain't you willin' to shake on it, or you scared you'll lose?"

Lissa looked to André, who merely shook his head and walked away from the pair, muttering his disgust. Her brother didn't know anything. She was doing it only because she loved her papa.

Lissa took Franc's hand. "I accept. Only what are you going to do when there is no goose on the table?"

Franc narrowed her eyes, considered her best options for a moment, then proclaimed, "I'll guarantee that my ma and me're gone before that dumb old pass is cleared."

Lissa found it a curious comment, yet she was confident that Hannah would never be able to produce a cooked goose. She jabbed out her hand, but Franc had retrieved hers.

"What is the matter? Change your mind?"

"Hardly."

Lissa wrinkled her nose when Franc spit on her palm and spread the salvia around with her tongue.

"Well, what you waiting for? Spit in your hand so we can seal the deal."

Lissa stood there with a blank stare.

"Ain't you never learnt nothin'? If we mingle spit, there's no goin' back. It's official."

"I knew that," Lissa bluffed, and proceeded to follow Franc's lead.

The two girls sealed their bet, then on Franc's suggestion they trailed after André to rehearse their lines.

* * *

Hannah was panting as she scrambled from the pen. She was covered with mud from having to dive out of the way when the goose charged. And she had dropped the damned weapon.

"You are not going to win," she said to the big bird. She wiped her face, only to smudge the mud across her cheeks. Letting out a grunt of frustration, she garnered all her resolve and stumbled back into the pen.

The goose honked and charged.

There was no time for retreat. In an effort to protect herself, Hannah grabbed it by the neck.

A big mistake.

It hissed and threw her off, snapping at her and catching her arm with a good nip. Hannah let out a croak of pain and clambered into a far corner of the enclosure.

She was trapped!

From the murderous look in its beady eyes, Hannah could have sworn it was regrouping for its final assault.

She would never be able to climb over the fence before it reached her. The goose was between her and the gate, and it was in a ready position to charge.

She quickly skinned off her apron. Perhaps if she threw it over the goose's head she could confuse it long enough to reach the hatchet. The goose dropped its head even lower as she tossed the apron, sending it spinning onto its back.

With the honk of battle, the chase was on.

Hannah screamed and ran for her life.

"Hannah!" Max shouted, fear squeezing his heart that she was in imminent danger, as he whipped around the corner of the barn.

Seeing Hannah in jeopardy caused Max to lunge into the pen and grab the goose a second before it was about to chock up another bloody victory. With experienced efficiency he dispatched the creature, then swung to where Hannah had fallen into the middle of a mud puddle. She was sitting there, a monument to good intentions, poor choices, shaking her hands, and sobbing while her little dog whined and tried to climb into her lap to comfort her.

Worried that she had somehow been harmed, Max set the dog aside and pulled her to her feet. After a visual examination he discerned that she was unharmed except for a little nip on her arm and a lot of mud on her person.

"What is this you do?" he questioned. "That goose, it would hurt you or worse," He wiped the smudged mud from her cheeks.

"That damn goose," she swore, causing Max to force back a smile. Her courage impressed him. She was angry. Most city women would have dissolved in tears.

"I—I was just trying to prove that I could be a good ranch woman and serve goose for our

Thanksgiving celebration like they did for one of the first Thanksgivings." She sniffled back the urge to cry her frustration. "But I've never killed anything before in my life." She ran her hands down her filthy skirt. "And now everyone inside will know that you had to rescue me."

"This is what troubles you?" he questioned, again within a few minutes having to hide a smile. She was not upset over the incident as much as she was over her perceived failure. He found that incredulous and admirable.

"Yes."

"Then you worry no more. I help pluck the bird, and you cook it while I do not arrive until dinnertime, yes?"

"You mean you aren't going to tell the children the story of my dismal confrontation with the goose?"

"That is what I mean."

"Then, yes. Yes! You do not arrive until dinnertime. Yes!"

She ringed her arms around his neck and hugged him in her exuberance, getting mud down the front of his shirt and jacket. "Oh, dear." She tried to wipe the brown streaks when she realized with horror what she had done.

"I think you make it worse. You go get a clean shirt from the line maybe while I start plucking the bird."

Hannah pulled out of his embrace, then hesitated while he shrugged out of his sheepskin jacket and shirt. Overwhelmed with emotion, she moved closer to him. To demonstrate her gratitude, she cradled his face between her palms and kissed him.

It was meant to be a gentle kiss of thankfulness, but it swiftly transformed into much more when he slipped his arms around her waist and held her against his naked upper torso.

She leaned into him, remembering, welcoming, reveling in the feel, the taste, the texture of his mouth until her mind forced her to recall that they stood in plain view of the house.

Reluctantly, she pulled back. "Max, the children."

He ached to prolong the kiss, to expand it, to possess her again. But he nodded his understanding and dragged the goose out of sight of the house.

Hannah stood and watched him. Those strong, masculine hands had held her so gently, known her so intimately. Her vision shifted to his bronze back and a fantasy in which he took her to his own bed threatened to take hold of her until she realized it was cold. She had been so wrapped up in acquiring dinner, then experiencing and reveling in their shared kiss that the temperature had slipped her mind.

She rushed to the clothesline, grabbed a shirt, and returned to where Max was already bent over, jerking out handfuls of feathers. "Here. It's cold out here."

"Yes, that it is."

He rose and his washboard chest and stomach caused her breath to catch.

He was a gorgeous, beautiful man.

Outside and inside.

Her hands trembling to touch him, she forced herself to hold the shirt while he slipped his arms into the sleeves. She could feel his muscles flexing through the fabric, and her heart beat faster.

She was spending too much time thinking of him as a very desirable man with strong arms which could hold her in the circle of his embrace. Quickly, she shook her head and buttoned the shirtfront before she embarrassed herself. She retrieved his jacket and held it for him as well.

"I suppose you should leave now."

"As soon as I finish the plucking maybe." He bent down on one knee and returned to work.

"Max?"

He got back to his feet before her. "Yes?"

"Thank you," she said in a voice hoarse with emotion.

He nodded and caressed the softness of her cheek with the back of his hand. "We work good together you and me, I think."

"So do I." Hannah felt silken threads entwine around her heart and squeeze. She did not trust herself to say more. Rather, she stood mute until he returned to the task at hand, all the while instructing her on the fine art of cooking the goose. He finished the job in record time. They exchanged a brief farewell and he was gone.

Hannah leaned against the barn and stared after him until he was out of sight.

If only there were not so many obstacles, so many insurmountable secrets, she thought with regret and headed back to the carcass.

If only . . .

Lugging the cleaned bird into the kitchen, Hannah glanced up to see three astounded young faces staring at her, open-mouthed.

"You can close your mouths." Hannah wore a triumphant smile and she said, "All I have to do to finish the job now is to cook it."

Franc let out a howl of laughter in Lissa's direction. "I'd say that my ma's sure goin' to cook your goose."

Lissa glared at Franc, but her shoulders slumped and she sighed. To all present it was apparent that she was deflated.

All afternoon, as the fragrant, hearty aroma filled the house, Lissa remained quiet. Until she heard her papa enter the house she said very little.

"Papa, Papa, I missed you. Did you ship all the lambs?"

He hugged his children and told all about his trip before he questioned, "What is it you all wear?"

"Us Pilgrums and Inyuns," Sammy gurgled.

"So you are." He lifted the tot into his arms

and headed into the kitchen. At the sight of the long table decorated with corn husks, he grinned. "This is Thanksgiving, yes?"

"Yes." Hannah beamed at him as she set a long-feathered headdress on his head. "There. Now you look the part. And you've arrived at just the right time. I am about to put the food on the table. Shall we begin?"

The dinner went off without a hitch. The children presented their skit of the Pilgrims and Indians coming together to celebrate Thanksgiving, then everyone took a seat at the table. Max laughed out loud with pleasure at how much his children had learned by making the presentation. Hannah had demonstrated what a fine teacher she would make for the children, for not even Lissa could help showing her delight at having the largest part.

The goose was cooked to perfection. Much to Lissa's chagrin, everyone devoured the meal, even Sammy. When she opened her mouth to tattle that Hannah was slipping her little black dog bites under the table, Franc smirked and cocked a brow, which reminded Lissa of their deal.

Max polished off the last Indian-head potato that Franc had carved and pushed back from the table, rubbing his stomach.

"I think maybe you all outdo yourselves. I am not even the least bit hungry any longer."

Franc actually giggled girlishly. A first for the

usually sarcastic young girl. "Gol-ly, you sure ate enough."

"Hannah ate almost as much as you did, Papa," André joined in.

"Hannah has been eating a lot lately. So much that she is getting fat around the middle," Lissa remarked out of turn, causing all eyes to swing to Hannah.

"That is because of all the good food." Hannah forced a smile, got up, and busied herself clearing the dishes.

"It is time for you children to give Hannah a rest and clean up the kitchen. Then you go upstairs and do your lessons," Max advised. "Lissa, you put Samuel to bed on your way up, yes?"

"Yes, sir," a daunted Lissa answered. Her innocent comment had seemed to put a damper on the celebration, and she had not meant anything by it. It was just an observation. She gathered up the platter of bones but hesitated. "Hannah, I did not mean anything by it."

"I know, Lissa. You did a nice job with the preparations."

Lissa blushed with pleasure despite herself while Franc said, "What about me?"

"You all did a nice job. And because you all worked so hard and did so well with the skit, I'm going to clean the kitchen this evening," Hannah announced.

Not giving Hannah a chance to change her

mind, the children quickly disappeared, leaving Max alone in the kitchen with Hannah.

He swiveled around on the bench so he could study her as she put the water on to heat. Her movements were graceful and assured. He let his eyes rove from her head to toe twice, lingering at her breasts and waist. Max rubbed his jaw and considered her figure for a moment. Her middle had thickened and her breasts seemed more generous.

"Hannah, there is something maybe you got to tell me?"

At the soft probing tone to his voice, Hannah froze. Her hand stopped in midair and she closed her eyes, frantically trying to come up with a lighthearted response.

"Hannah?" Max prodded when she did not respond.

Moments passed.

Still she did not respond; she did not look at him.

"Hannah," he said softly, "why do you not tell me you are pregnant?"

Twenty-two

Hannah stood blankly staring out the window, not seeing the gentle flutter of snowflakes that had begun to fall. She was thinking that she could not continue to stand with her back to Max, although it was a mighty tempting thought at the moment. What was she going to say to him? How was she going to explain yet another of her secrets?

"Hannah?"

There was no escaping. She was trapped, just like she had been out in the pen earlier in the day, only the pen seemed preferable at the moment. Trapped with no way out. Slowly she pivoted around and raised her chin.

"Hannah, why do you not tell me you are expecting a child?"

"I—" Her voice failed.

"It is mine?"

The question nearly floored her. She had never considered that their one coupling could lead him to think he had fathered the child she was carrying. Her waist would not be thickening so soon.

For an instant she thought about letting him claim the child as his own. Her conscience would not allow it. And she realized that when the baby arrived he would know she had lied again.

Max got up and stood before her. With the crook of his finger he lifted her chin so he could gaze into her eyes. He saw much trouble, pain, and panic mirrored there. "If you fear that I do not know my duty, you do not got to worry."

The word *duty* did not alleviate her apprehension, nor did it disarm her fears.

Max waited.

Again nothing.

"Hannah, why do you not answer?"

Her lips trembling, she managed to say, "B-because the baby's n-not yours."

"Now I understand." Hearing from her own lips that she was indeed pregnant caused his nerves to tense. His wife had died in childbirth. It was a frightening memory, the terrifying vision embedded in his mind. Only his stoicism helped him to keep his expression unreadable.

"You do?"

"A woman who loses her husband, she must support her family how she can, yes?"

Hannah relaxed. The news had not seemed to have a negative effect on him. Then another thought hit her. He would no doubt no longer want under his roof a woman who was carrying another man's child.

"I suppose that now you will be sending Franc

and me to live with one of the other families in the valley until I have the baby in early spring."

"Hannah, you do not know much of the Basque tradition. Basque men, they are not like the men of your country. Children, no matter the circumstances, are welcome."

She wanted to scream what about the mothers as *no matter the circumstances* rang in her ears like distant wedding bells. The very idea of marriage was a sobering thought, but it began a germ of a thought whose seed had been planted in the inner recesses of her mind.

If only Max's Basque bride were not on her way by now. If only Hannah were a widow. She knew that his religion forbade divorce, and she had no doubt that Emmett had not wasted any time carrying through with his threat. She was a divorced woman now who had run away from her husband without informing him she was carrying his child. She wondered how Basque tradition dealt with all that.

"I see you continue to trouble over something. Somehow I can help?"

"N-no."

"It does not change the way I think of you, Hannah."

That declaration finally should have relieved Hannah's mind if it were not for Emmett's vow to find her. If there was one thing she had learned about Emmett during her five years of marriage, it was that he was true to his vows.

"Does it not please you?" Max questioned, re-directing Hannah's thoughts away from her con-tinuing complicated situation.

Hannah forced a smile. "It pleases me very much."

"It is a happy day with much to give thanks for, this Thanksgiving, yes?"

"Yes." She gave a halfhearted nod. "Happy Thanksgiving."

"Happy Thanksgiving, my ass," Emmett spat out at the painted woman saloon owner in the godforsaken dusty little town where he filled a barstool in the filthy bawdy saloon. Emmett wiped the glass with his shirtsleeve before he al-lowed the woman to pour his drink.

"Ain't clean enough for a fine gentleman such as yourself, huh?"

"Can't you get anyone to come in here and clean up this pigsty?" Emmett easily responded to the woman's sarcasm.

The woman puffed up with indignation. "I'll have you know I got my standards. I don't accept just any old slopbucket help. I turned down the last woman who wandered in here off the train pleading for a job 'cuz she was too old for my customers' tastes. What're your tastes, honey-buns?"

Emmett momentarily ignored the woman's blatant proposition. "You say a woman *wandered* in here looking for a job?"

"Yeah, so? She had just got off the train."

A spike of excitement pricked his chest. He pulled a small framed daguerreotype from his inside vest pocket. "Yeah, so is this her?"

The woman took the representation, studied it then gave the good-looking stranger a sly grin. "What's in it for me?"

Emmett could see the dollar signs dancing in the stupid bitch's eyes. Christ, he hated calculating women who weren't smart enough to hide what they had on their little female minds. His eyes shifted about the room. Other than one old passed-out drunk at a corner table, Emmett was the only one in the saloon.

With lightning-quick speed his hand shot out and grabbed the woman by her dyed red locks, yanking her head toward him until they were nose to nose.

"What's in it for you? Well, bitch, how does your life sound?"

Her eyes huge, she choked out, "Since you put it so eloquently, sure, it was her. And the name's Sugar Lee."

He released her and watched as she straightened the frizzy curls back into place, then, uneffected, came around the bar and perched on a stool next to him. She crossed her legs, giving him ample view of her charms.

"Anything else I can do for you, honeybuns?"

"You see where she went?" Emmett took the drink, in one gulp and let his fingers slowly slide up her inner thigh underneath her hiked skirt.

Undaunted by his rough treatment, she slipped off her shoe, propped her foot up on the stranger's stool, and toyed with his bulging crotch. "She got back on the train heading west. What's she to you?"

Emmett ignored her question, pushed her foot off the stool, and got up.

"You ain't leavin' yet, are ya?"

Again Emmett ignored her and sauntered from the saloon, past the only hotel in town, and headed toward the train station, whistling at his good fortune.

The detective was waiting at the station. "Mr. Turner, I'm glad you're here. I've got news—"

"Save it. I already know Hannah was in town and got back on the train. And as soon as the train arrives, we'll be on our way."

The detective took off his wide-brimmed hat and shoved his fingers through his hair. "That's what I been trying to tell you. The station master just received a telegram. Seems there's been a bad blizzard up ahead west which derailed the train and caused the collapse of a bridge."

Emmett's good mood ended as the eastern train arrived. He was still fuming over being stuck or returning east until repairs could be completed, when the largest middle-aged woman wearing a hideous plumed hat accentuating her reptilian features barreled off the train, nearly knocking him over.

She marched right past him without so much as an excuse me and right up to the station master standing nearby.

"I want you to check your records," Wilma Timm demanded. "I've been travelin' back and forth on this train, tryin' to locate my property and I urgently need to know if this is where a Hannah Turner purchased a ticket heading west on your train."

The detective and Emmett both perked up their ears.

The detective started for the woman, but Emmett grabbed his arm. "I'll take care of this. You'd only bungle it."

Emmett straightened his coat, painted a phony smile of sympathy on his face, and strolled over to the woman. Tipping his hat, he said, "Pardon the intrusion, my dear lady, but I could not but help overhear your conversation."

"So?"

Keeping up his act, he ignored her rudeness. "So, I believe I may be able to be of service to you."

Wilma Timm narrowed her eyes suspiciously. "You know of this Hannah Turner person?"

Emmett sent her his most dazzling smile. "You might say that."

* * *

"You might say that I was left with no choice," Hannah said in response to another of Bernard Garat's probing questions as to what she was doing at an isolated sheep ranch in her condition.

For three peaceful weeks after Thanksgiving the children had been on their best behavior. They worked hard at the lessons she presented, and even Max was beginning to master a few of her suggestions regarding his English. Christmas was approaching. They had been told that St. Nicholas came to the homes only of good boys and girls, so the children no longer staged any scenes where Hannah and Max were concerned. The threat of not receiving any gifts had even captured Franc's attention.

It was not until Max's father and brother had arrived to spend Christmas with the family that the strain returned. Petya never missed a chance to rile Max. The old man, who Max had instructed to speak only English around Hannah, was fiercely protective of his eldest son and had not missed the changes in Max's speech.

"So, Hannah, you sit at that machine. You do sew?" Bernard questioned, watching the robust young woman closely.

Hannah glanced up from the rose-checked gingham she was stitching. "I am learning."

Bernard looked askance at the young widow. He had not counted on this. Although he had previously encouraged his son, Basque custom did not smile on the remarriage of widows. The old man worried about his son, for even if Max had not admitted it yet Bernard could see and feel the tension between them when they were in the same room. And he had seen the light come back into his son's eyes, troubled though it may be at times.

"She learns fast, Papa," Max offered, coming into the room.

Hannah's eyes lit up and Bernard wondered what effect the bride he had secretly requested would have if and when she arrived. Hannah was not Basque, and did not know the Basque ways. And yet Bernard had found a soft spot in his heart for her.

"So early you are up, eh?" Petya said as he joined them, yawning.

"There is much to do on a ranch the day before Christmas, if you forget," Max shot back.

"How is it I am allowed to forget with you always reminding me?"

"I think it is the time to take the children out to cut a pine for the American celebration Hannah tells us about," Bernard suggested. He was growing tired of the constant bickering between his two sons. So unalike those two, but so close to his old heart.

"I go wake the children so we make an early start. It will take all day to find and cut the right tree." Petya winked at Hannah and sauntered off.

Hannah declined the invitation to accompany the tree-hunting party and prepared a picnic lunch. To her surprise, Franc even volunteered to carry the ax as they set out.

"What do you think got into Franc?" Hannah asked Max after the tribe had left.

He surprised her with "You do not celebrate Christmas?"

"Of course we do."

"I ask only because your Franc asks me if she is very very good if it will make a difference on Christmas morning."

"The last few years we haven't had much of a reason to celebrate. It has been difficult for Franc." It was true. "I guess being part of a happy family is a new experience for her."

"For you too a new experience, Hannah?" When she did not answer, he added, "Your marriage was not a happy one?"

His accurate observation startled Hannah. She did not think it was that obvious. "There were happy times at first, but Emmett was not a happy person. He expected perfection, so it made it difficult for him to take pleasure in the simple things of life."

"A man who is not satisfied with his lot in life cannot experience joy and often makes those who love him suffer for it."

Hannah nodded at the insight Max displayed. Although painful, she had answered his questions, which made her wonder about his marriage enough to ask, "And what about your marriage, was it happy?"

Had she asked such a question when she'd first arrived, he would have told her it was none of her damn business, but they had reached an understanding of sorts these past several weeks, and Max was no longer the angry shell of a man he had been since his wife's death.

"My marriage was good."

"You must have loved Mary very much," Hannah said in an empathetic voice.

"My family arranged my marriage, Hannah," he admitted. "Love I did not expect, but it grows from a strong bond of friendship that comes slowly with respect and regard. . . ."

Hannah listened to Max's story with fascination. He was loyal and steadfast, a man who made a commitment and honored it.

Max had made such an open, loving declaration that it caused Hannah to place a gentle, reassuring hand on his arm in understanding of the ordeal this man had suffered as he fought so valiantly to hold his family together.

"I would never marry again without love," Hannah said.

To her surprise, he covered her hand with his work-roughened one. "Love is that important to you?"

"I didn't think so once, but yes, now it is that important."

"I see" was all he said, and Hannah longed to ask why he had questioned her. She held her tongue as they gazed into each other's eyes for moments, for she had no right to hope, although if truth be known, she had begun to.

Unable to tolerate the burgeoning tension filling the room any longer, Hannah tried to retrieve her hand and rise, but he held tight.

"No. Do not go this time."

He was so near that she could feel his warm moist breath caress her neck, his eyes silently devour her lips, his fingers memorizing the contours of her hand, mesmerizing and heightening her senses until she leaned toward him and closed her eyes, longing, anticipating his kiss.

Although not normally controlled by his emotions, Max could no longer deny himself. He cupped his hand behind her head and joined their lips.

It was as if they had broken through a barrier with their conversation and sealed it with a kiss. Now they would be ready to take another step in the direction in which they quietly had been moving since she had settled in at the ranch.

But even as he deepened the kiss, there was one barrier which Hannah doubted could be surmounted—she was not a widow; Emmett was very much alive.

Twenty-three

Hannah's eager lips parted beneath Max's. She trembled in his embrace and reached up to entwine her fingers in the hair at the nape of his neck. He crushed her against his chest, his hungry mouth devouring hers.

He pulled back and backed away, gazing into her eyes. "Oh, God, Hannah, I cannot help myself no longer. Every day I watch you. At first I think I should send you away, but I cannot. So I try to ignore you. But you living under my roof makes me want you," he whispered.

"Oh, Max," she moaned, and reached up to bracket his face with her hands, rubbing her thumbs along the line of his jaw with great tenderness. For a man who did not discuss feelings readily, he had opened himself up more than she ever expected.

A moment later Hannah found herself sitting on his lap, being cradled against his chest. His chin rested against the top of her head.

"Tonight is Christmas Eve."

"Yes," she breathed. Her head against his chest, she could feel his heart racing.

The thought of Christmas caused Max to consider its meaning. It was a celebration of that most special birth, which refocused his thoughts on Hannah and the baby she was carrying. It made him tense. Hannah was due in early spring she'd said, around Easter—around the same time that he had lost another loved one.

"Max, is something wrong?"

The sound of Hannah's melodious voice brought Max back from his brooding. He gathered her in tighter against him. Realization hit him hard; a part of him longed to hold her like this forever.

He was holding her as if he were afraid he might lose her, and in response Hannah embraced him.

For the longest time they held each other without speaking. Finally, he said, "Sometimes I am afraid that I need more from you, Hannah."

She was not sure exactly what he meant, but whatever it was, she knew that she was willing to give it to him.

"Kiss me," she murmured.

He did not need further prompting. His lips crashed against hers in a melding, searing meeting of mouths, teeth, tongues.

His hands found the swell of her breasts. They filled his palms and he closed his fingers over the mounds, kneading the sensitive centers into puckered peaks.

A spear of wonder filled her at his urgent need. Yet despite the physical coupling which she now knew would come, she reached a supreme realization that it was more than that. She truly meant something to this man. Suddenly she wanted to offer him her body, her heart, her love.

She began kissing his face. His brows, his eyelids, the tip of his nose. She nibbled at his earlobes, moving down to his neck. Her exploration stopped there, and she sucked at the strong, thick column until a dark purple mark of her passion branded him.

The sight of the temporary label of her love brought her back to her senses. She tenderly touched the imperfect circle. "Oh, Max, what have I done? What will the children think if they see it?"

Max chuckled, his heart so full as he gazed into her eyes. "My children think maybe their papa makes love to Franc's mama, yes?"

"Max!" she squealed, and playfully swatted at his chest. But she did not miss his use of the word *love,* and it sent her heart spinning.

He grabbed her hand and brought it to his lips, immediately transforming the momentary frolicsome tone back to a more serious expression of his feelings. He sucked each slender finger and rubbed them against his cheek.

Hannah's desire grew until she could wait no longer. She slid from his lap and took his hand.

"Max," she begged. "I want to touch you . . . intimately."

She began to lead him toward her straw bed in the corner of the kitchen, but Max hesitated.

"Don't you want me?" she asked, concerned that she had been too bold.

"Yes, but—"

The *but* caused her to worry that she had been too eager. "Maybe I shouldn't have—"

"Maybe you should. Only . . ." His voice trailed off and he stared at the makeshift bed where the little black pup was perched in a sitting position, eagerly waving its paws in anticipation.

"Only?"

"Only maybe we get fleas this time."

She cocked her head. Then it suddenly dawned on her that he was making light, something he had been accused of being incapable of. It demonstrated to Hannah that there were many sides to this big, wonderful man.

"Well, I suppose we wouldn't want to get fleas. Perhaps we should forego *it* until the bed can be defleaed."

Max turned her to face him so he could gaze directly into her eyes. He saw perfection. Wonderful green eyes the color of the mountains in the old country in spring, and they drew him into their depths like the caress of a warm day.

"I do not want to *forego it,*" he murmured. "Come with me."

Hannah expected to follow him into the parlor, where they could bed before the roaring flames in the warm glow of the firelight.

He led her past the parlor and into the bedroom. His bedroom. Hannah feared that her legs were going to fail her, she was so surprised. Nearly two months earlier he had been horrified that she had sat on his bed. She marveled at how much had changed between them in that length of time.

He lifted her high into his arms, nibbling at her neck as he moved toward his bed.

Hannah held her breath, afraid to breathe for fear that he would again be reminded of what he had lost on that bed. Then he would turn around and walk from the room.

Her fears went unfounded.

Tenderly, he set her on the bed and lay down next to her.

"Max," she whispered, caressing his cheek. "Are you sure . . . in this room . . . in this bed?"

He leaned up on his elbow and gazed down at her. She not only was warm and loving, she was considerate of his feelings.

"Yes, Hannah" was all he said.

The moment had come once and for all for him to put those feelings about his bedroom aside. Hannah was alive lying beside him. She was the woman who filled his thoughts.

She was the woman he wanted.

With the utmost tenderness he kissed her while his fingers unbuttoned his white shirt that she continued to wear. Then his open mouth took possession of her breasts. She arched into him, anticipation sensitizing every nerve ending throughout her entire body.

"I need to touch you too," she moaned.

Their clothing seemed to melt away, and her hand closed around the center of his male power. He was hard and throbbed in her palm, causing her to become emboldened. She caressed all of him there, taking care to handle that most potent portion of him with gentle loving.

He groaned as his hands reacquainted him with the most intimate curves and valleys and crevices of her body.

Together they twisted and turned, sipped and tongued each other until they hovered near the pinnacle of their runaway rapture. Trembling with the urgency to consummate their desire, their bodies at last came together, united in a passion so powerful, so potent that explosion after uncontrollable explosion gripped them.

Hannah tautened against Max, crying out an incredible release and panting at the exertion as spasm after glorious spasm gripped her.

Max, too, experienced an orgasm so strong, so forceful that he stiffened and strained before collapsing, exhausted, on top of her.

Once his heart had finally slowed, Max moved

to Hannah's side. He stroked the drenched strands of hair back from off her face and held her naked body against his.

"I love you, Hannah." God help him, the words had tumbled out before Max could stop them, could stop and weigh their consequences.

He did love her.

But he was not prepared for the emotion that went with the declaration. A mighty fear gripped him. He could not tolerate the thought that she too could suffer complications in childbirth and possibly perish at the isolated ranch where there would be no help from a doctor if needed. He tried to swallow the lump of fear, but it stuck in his throat.

He left her side, walked to the window, and leaned against the frame, pulling back the curtains. He gazed out at the pristine winter. It was so untouched, so cold, so unforgiving.

Hannah wrapped a sheet around her shoulders and padded after him, not knowing what had made him leave the bed. She touched his shoulder.

She leaned against his back, circling him with her arms and laying her cheek on his shoulder blade. She gently kissed the bronze flesh.

"I love you, too, Max," she murmured.

For the longest time they stood there at the window, both full of fear.

For a man of great strength and endurance, Max was experiencing a kind of fear he had thought he had shut himself off from—the possibility of losing the one he loved. And it scared the hell out of him.

For Hannah the fear came from experiencing, for the first time, the kind of love she had never known existed, never thought possible. And the knowledge that her secrets could so easily destroy it.

Twenty-four

By the time the rest of the family had returned with a pinon pine almost too large to fit into the house, Hannah and Max had just finished wrapping the last of the gifts Hannah had been working on for the past several weeks.

Franc came up short when she caught sight of Hannah and Max. They were standing a mite too close for her comfort, and were a mite too cozy. But strangely, it did not rankle Franc down to the tips of her toenails as it once had, and her vision fell on the mound of presents.

Hannah noticed the girl's face undergo a complete transformation, and her eyes grew as large as sugar plums. Despite her usual dour demeanor, Franc was having a most difficult time containing her girlish excitement.

Hannah did not want to embarrass the girl by commenting on the sparkle she saw in her eyes, so Hannah walked past her to the pine and spread out her arms. "My, what a simply beautiful tree you men selected."

"They did not pick it, we did," the children chorused.

"Well, you all certainly did a fine job," she complimented them to a round of pleased childish giggles and shoving.

Even Lissa seemed elated despite herself, which gave Max cause for celebration. For two years his daughter had stayed in the attic room on Christmas, steadfastly refusing to come down regardless of his coaxing. But this year it would be different. And Max knew he had Hannah to thank for it.

This year there would be a big celebration like the family used to have. This year even Max felt like celebrating.

Bernard helped Samuel out of his heavy clothes and set the toddler on the rug before the fire. "My youngest grandchild, he pick these pinecones"— the old man removed a half dozen broken specimens from his bag—"to string on the tree."

"What a good idea, Sammy," Hannah remarked, and received a happy gurgle from the toddler. She grabbed a length of twine for ties and joined Sammy on the rug, crossing her legs beneath her skirt, to make him feel a part of the tree-trimming festivities.

While Hannah readied the pinecones, the older children cut shapes from the scraps of fabric Hannah had left over and fashioned bows. Petya and Bernard set up the tree, and Max brought

out a handful of candles so the tree would have
lights.

By the time they were finished decorating and
Max had lit the last candle, the tree was something to behold—a glowing labor of love.

To everyone's pleasure, Hannah began singing
Christmas carols and soon all joined in, the
Garats humming the tune. Then Max surprised
everyone by teaching Hannah and Franc a traditional Basque carol, which had originated from a
lovely poem about Mary and Joseph.

So emotionally touched by the sharing gesture,
Hannah was the first to take Franc's hand around
the tree. One by one they joined hands until the
last link, which would complete the circle, was
Hannah and Max.

The singing sounds faded, and all eyes fell on
them, waiting, watching.

Hannah shyly looked at Max's face before her
eyes dropped to his hand. It was a closed fist still
at his side. She took a deep breath and held it,
wondering if he would take her hand in front of
his family.

Lissa made a move as if she were going to elbow a place between them, but Franc held fast
to her hand and shot her a quelling glance, reminding her of their deal.

Hannah waited and watched. At last Max's fist
slowly opened and he offered his hand, palm up,
to Hannah.

In front of everyone he closed his fingers

around hers, taking her hand in a symbolic display of unity, which seemed to signify the emotional cementing of their earlier physical union.

"We make a good family, yes?" Max observed to Hannah's pleased surprise.

Petya grinned.

André's gaze shot from Lissa to Franc. The two girls stared at each other, but both remained quiet, bewilderment and disbelief on their young faces.

"We Basques always make a good close family." The old man nodded, but there was concern in his eyes as he stared at Max.

Hannah lowered her eyes. She had not missed the meaning of the eldest Garat's remark. It was apparent he liked her. He had been most cordial, even more than merely polite, but it was also apparent he had serious reservations.

"Basques and Americans. In this country they are the same," Max said in a voice that challenged the others to dispute him.

It was a break with the Basque tradition of maintaining a distinct separation between themselves and all others.

At that, Petya shook his head in agreement and sent Hannah another wink, while the old man merely raised a brow.

"Well," Hannah said in an effort to break the awkward moment, "shall we eat? The children should be in bed and asleep early tonight before

St. Nicholas flies over in his sleigh, or he might
be forced to skip this house."

Long after everyone had retired, Max was pol-
ishing off one of the last cookies left for St.
Nicholas, when he was joined in the parlor by
his father.

"You rebuild the fire now that the children are
asleep. You know to let a fire go out on Christmas Eve it is a sign that someone dies within a
year," Bernard mentioned, shaking his head in
concern as he took a seat.

Max waved off the old man's distress with "Su-
perstition."

Bernard rubbed his hands against the cold
night and held them out toward the flames. "You
begin to turn from the old ways." He shrugged
then. "You share St. Nicholas's cookies with your
old papa?"

"You do not wait up for a cookie," Max observed. He knew his interfering father too well
and had been expecting this conversation sooner
or later.

"No, I do not."

Max set another log on the fire and settled
onto the sofa next to the old man. "Do you plan
to say what is on your mind, or eat your cookie
and return to the bed we share?"

"This bed you speak of, you also share it with

Hannah. How long do you share your bed with this woman?"

Max opened his mouth to inform his father that it was none of his business, until Bernard raised a silencing hand. "Do not try to tell your papa that it is not true. I see how Hannah she turns the color of the grass in the morning. You have four brothers and seven sisters back in the old country; I know when a woman she is with child.

"This woman, she is not Basque. She is different from us. She and her child, this Franc, their ways they are not ours. You are Basque, and the Basque ways they will always be yours, my son. It flows in your blood. You will come back to the traditions of your people. Even though tonight you sound like your foolish brother Petya, this statement of yours that Basques, they are Americans."

"No. Tonight I sound like a man in love with a woman. And I always will sound so."

"Bah. You sound like a man whose brain it slips between his legs."

"Be very careful, old man," Max warned. "Your meddling is not wise this time."

Bernard ignored his son. "You speak of love. But love, it does not a good marriage make. You need a wife who shares your heritage and understands Basque traditions."

Max was coming close to losing his patience.

"What I need is Hannah and the child she carries."

The old man squinted his eyes. "I think there is something you keep from me, eh? Your Hannah, how long she is a widow?"

Hannah had volunteered little of her husband, but Max was not about to share that with his prying father. "Not long."

"She is not a widow long, and you do not say *our* child when you talk. I think that there is something you do not tell me."

"I tell you what is your business . . . more maybe."

"This baby she carries, it is not yours."

"When it is born it is mine. Do not forget Basque custom."

Bernard threw his hands up in the air. "Now, my son, he reminds *me* of what it means to be Basque." He considered the situation for a moment. Bernard liked Hannah and she had made his son happy. But Max knew so little of her and her people that it worried Bernard. Remarriage was frowned upon although not unheard of in his country. He had even secretly requested his brother send a bride to stop his son's grieving. But Bernard wanted Max to be sure of his decision, to know of this woman. And he wanted his son to make the best choice.

Bernard contemplated the possibility that a Basque bride was already on her way. A Basque woman would give a clear view of the differences.

She would offer Max a choice after he had the opportunity to see the two women together and measure their differences for himself. The woman, if she were indeed on her way, would not arrive until the spring thaw.

What the old man needed was time.

"I listen to you enough," Max said. "Christmas morning comes early. Good night, Papa."

"Wait, Maximilian. I am meddling old man. I agree. But I live for many years and it gives me the right, eh?"

Max stood and stared at his father, listening out of respect. But what he was hearing did not change his mind. The decision regarding his future with Hannah was between Hannah and him. It was theirs and theirs alone to make.

"I like your Hannah, and I will give my blessing but one condition—"

"No conditions."

"First you hear me before you answer. I ask only that you wait until spring to marry." Bernard noticed his son's eyes narrow ever so slightly. "I see by your face you do not discuss this marriage with your Hannah. It will not be so hard for you to grant your old papa this wish, yes?"

Max did not respond. He had not asked Hannah to marry him. But he would not tell his father that he could not bring himself to ask her because she was pregnant. It was not due to the child, however. He could not tolerate the pain of losing another wife in childbirth. He could not bring himself to tell anyone this—not even Hannah.

"The pass, it will not allow you to travel to a priest until spring."

"Why do you ask this of me if it is not possible now?" Max questioned, although he was secretly relieved.

"Only I want you to take the time to know this woman."

"I know all I need to know to make a decision."

"These feelings, then, they will not change?"

"No."

The old man stood up beside his son, reached over, and clapped a gnarled hand on Max's shoulder. "No difference it makes then if you wait until after the spring lambing. Petya and I, we go to bring the priest for you right after lambing if this is what you want, yes?"

"This talk makes no sense."

"You agree. There is nothing for you to lose."

Max slapped his father on the back, conceding that giving in to the old man would make little difference, and save him from being subjected to his meddling. And secretly, it would give Max time to attempt to sort out his own fears.

"Come, old man, we go to bed. You will sleep well tonight. I agree."

* * *

Christmas dawned to a white and frozen wonderland around the isolated ranch house. Breakfast was a big family affair at the long kitchen table near the fire in typical Basque tradition with lots of food served family style in heaping bowls and complemented with communal gaiety.

Once the meal was over, the Christmas joy of gift giving around the tree began. The fragrant aroma of pine filled the parlor as everyone filed into the room.

"Hurry up, where's my presents?" Franc questioned, digging through the wrapped gifts on her hands and knees.

"You act as if Christmas presents, they are something you never receive before, my little Franc," Bernard commented.

Franc sat back on her haunches. "I—"

"Franc is merely excited," Hannah offered, coming to the girl's defense. Hannah knew of Franc's sorry childhood, and Christmas no doubt had been a difficult time for her. While the past Christmases Hannah had spent with Emmett were filled with sheer opulence, there had been lacking the true spirit of the yule season.

"So am I," Max seconded, causing Franc to cock her head in his direction. He was covering for her, and it confused her. Nobody except Hannah had ever done that for her.

Max got down on his hands and knees near Franc and passed out the gifts, then sat back next to Hannah, his arm strung across the back of the sofa behind her, and watched with pure pleasure as the children tore into their bounty. Petya and Bernard had knitted everyone scarves from the sheep's wool caught on fences.

"Gol-ly, my very own whittling knife!" Franc exclaimed, and held it up for Hannah's inspection. Her eyes trailed to Max, and she briefly smiled at him before returning her attention to her treasured possession. "Now I can carve up all sorts of stuff instead of just some dumb old potatoes like I did for Thanksgiving."

André was elated over a sack of marbles, since Franc had won some of his best shooters. Sammy cuddled the stuffed animal that Hannah had sewn.

Lissa sat in a corner chair and quietly stared while the other children took great delight in their gifts until Max suggested, "Lissa, you do not open your presents maybe?"

"Go ahead, open them," Hannah urged, and leaned forward with anticipation.

Lissa looked to her grandpapa, who nodded his encouragement and grinned when she opened his scarf. Hesitantly then, she untied the lavender ribbon and folded back the wrapping of her last present left wrapped. Her breath caught when the gift was revealed, and her hand smoothed over it as if she were afraid touching it would make it disappear.

"What is it?" André and Franc echoed in unison.

Lissa climbed to her knees and held it up against her. "It is a beautiful new rose-colored dress," she announced, her voice catching with emotion.

"It looks like it's decorated in the same stuff as Hannah's ripped-up dress was made out of—" André elbowed Franc, cutting her off from further comment. She shot him daggers but said no more.

Lissa looked to Hannah and fought to blink back tears.

In order to save the girl from the misery threatening her, Hannah said, "Why, St. Nicholas even had it wrapped with hair ribbons to match. He has a pretty good idea what young ladies like."

"Yes, and so does Hannah," Max said under his breath so only Hannah could hear, remembering Hannah's comment about hair ribbons when she had discovered that her dress had been shredded.

"Why don't you go try it on?" Hannah urged. "I bet St. Nicholas got the size pretty close. If not, perhaps I can help to alter it."

Lissa closed her eyes tight as if she were groping for an appropriate response to express herself. As if one could not come to her, she bolted to her feet and fled into the bedroom.

"No doubt, Hannah, you give St. Nicholas some help this year, yes?" the old man observed.

Hannah merely smiled and handed Bernard and Petya their gifts. Inside, she knew that she had succeeded in making a chink in Lissa's armor. And as she watched Franc race into the kitchen, return with a piece of kindling, and request Max's advice on how to carve it, Hannah was sure that Max had done the same with Franc.

After Lissa had calmed enough to model her dress, and André and Franc grew tired of playing with their gifts, Sammy started to fuss, which caused Petya to say, "I think I put Sammy down for a nap. Papa, you can come sing one of your Basque folk songs. It will put him to sleep, eh?" The old man frowned but got to his feet. "And you children, it is time you do chores."

"It's Christmas," Franc wailed.

Petya smiled at Franc, causing her to blush. "Maybe so, but hungry animals, they must eat every day too . . . like you and me."

Hannah waited until everyone had left the room before she glanced at Max. "I think we made real headway with the children today, don't you?"

"Yes, Christmas is good for them this year." He gathered her hand into his and gazed into her eyes. "Thank you, Hannah."

She squeezed his hand in return. "Thank *you*. I know Franc was thrilled, even though she may not come right out and say it."

He nodded. "Yes, as is Lissa. Now I think it is time I give you your present."

Hannah waited, filled with excitement and curiosity, while Max bent down, snatched a gift wrapped in a sack from under the tree, and shyly handed it to her.

"Shall I guess?" she asked, and compressed it with her fingers. It was soft. She had half expected it to be one of the carvings Max was fond of making.

"Do you open it, or toy with it maybe?" he asked, intently watching her.

Hannah smiled at him, then tore into his offering. "Oh, Max," she said in a bare whisper, her gaze shooting to his.

It was the forbidden dress. The same long-sleeved, scoop-necked blue gingham dress that Max had threatened to rip from her after Lissa had maliciously offered it to her to wear when she'd first arrived.

"I hope you like it. I do—did"— he corrected himself—"not know what to give you."

Hannah was thankful that no one but Max was there to see the tears spill from her eyes as she was overcome with emotion. She wiped at the salty drops.

"Max, you didn't have to do this."

"I wanted to, Hannah."

"Thank you," she murmured, and gave him a kiss meant to convey her appreciation. She pulled back from him and said, "Your gift is the last one left under the tree."

She dragged it out from under the tree and placed it in his lap. "I hope you like it," she said when he unwrapped it. "I made you another shirt while you were outside working. I thought you could use another new one."

"He quickly slipped into it. "You learn fast. This one fits perfect, even the sleeves are the exact length." He brought his elbows together. This shirt was not tight in the shoulders. "I like it very much," he proclaimed.

Hannah smiled at Max and thought about her first attempt to sew him a shirt and the consequences when he had tried it on. They had been alone at the ranch. One thing led to another, and they bedded together for the first time.

Secretly, Hannah wished that they were once again alone at the ranch long enough to make more memories. During her reverie, her hand caressed the dress Max had given her, and her thoughts shifted.

It must have been very difficult for Max to finally let go of the ghosts that seeing her in that dress for the first time had brought back. But the gift signified that indeed he had been released from one more dark shadow that hung over him.

And in her heart at this first and very special Christmas together, Hannah silently wished that that were true for both of them.

Twenty-five

Once the holidays were over and they all had toasted to the new year as a time to begin afresh, Bernard and Petya said their good-byes and returned to the sheep to once again take over watch from the two eldest Herria boys.

The household settled into a routine. The children no longer seemed to dislike Hannah's presence, and Max continued to be attentive and even romantic in his own way.

While the children were outside with chores, Max would sneak into the house and steal a kiss. Or on occasion he would seek Hannah's advice with something outside, demonstrating his growing command of the English language; or call her out to look at something he had done, then gather her into his embrace and kiss her before he would turn her around and give her a gentle push back toward the house with a teasing pat to her bottom.

It was all very endearing and playful, and it was a time for sweethearts and sharing. Except that Hannah did not reciprocate with tales of her "deceased" husband when Max brought himself to share small tidbits of his past married life.

It was times such as those when Hannah was filled with regret that she had not come right out and told Max the truth about herself from the beginning. Now she feared that it was too late, and she longed to beg for forgiveness. But before forgiveness could come, if it could, came confession, and Hannah did not have the nerve to unburden herself, afraid of losing the small measure of happiness she had found with Max.

"You look sad lately," Max commented, coming in from the barn. "I think maybe you need the company of another woman sometimes, yes?" While he spoke he recalled the times when his wife had insisted that he hitch up the horses and drive her to the Herrias so she could have female companionship.

"I'm fine, truly." Hannah could not confide in him that it was confession weighing heavily on her shoulders that caused the sad expression of which he spoke.

"I promised you before your Thanksgiving to take you to visit the Herrias, and tomorrow we will go."

"What about all the snow?" she hedged.

"It is not so deep now. The wagon has no trouble. You worry too much, Hannah."

Hannah nodded, but in the back of her mind she could not help but wonder what it would be like meeting the Basque friends of Max's deceased wife after the children and Petya and Bernard had already visited them and undoubtedly told them about her.

The children were already piled into the wagon by the time Hannah left the house, carrying her umbrella, along with a ham and a string of onions in a basket for Mara Herria. She had slipped one of Petya's sheepskin jackets over her dress against the cold, but it did not keep Lissa from gasping when she caught sight of Hannah.

Unable to help herself, Lissa pointed a finger at Hannah as Max helped her up into the wagon. "That was the dress I handed you when you first arrived. It is my mama's dress" she cried.

"No longer, Lissa," Max said in answer to his daughter's hysterics. "Now the dress belongs to Hannah." Lissa opened her mouth to protest, but Max raised a silencing hand as he continued to calm the girl.

Hannah was only half listening to Max, while inside she silently wished she had another dress that still fit her, for the Herrias were bound to recognize the dress as well.

"We will hear no more of this, Lissa," Max finally proclaimed, and took Hannah's hand, which redirected her attention. "Now, Lissa, you go sit in the back of the wagon with André and Franc."

When Lissa climbed in the back and plopped

down between Franc and André, Franc could not but help notice the two bright red blotches spotting the older girl's cheeks.

The wagon jerked into motion and Lissa sat quietly, staring straight ahead of her.

"Don't let it bother you so much," Franc soothed, and despite herself reached out and patted Lissa's hand. "It ain't so bad no more, is it?"

Lissa did not trust herself to speak for fear of crying in front of Franc, and that Lissa would not do if she had to explode inside first. She merely shrugged.

"You can blubber if you got to. It might make you feel better. It ain't so bad with us here, is it? I mean, look at me," Franc forged ahead without giving Lissa an opportunity to respond. "I've learned to put up with your pa and uncle pretty good—I like your grandpapa."

Actually Franc secretly liked Petya too. He was handsome and paid attention to her even if he did tease her a lot. She didn't tell anyone, of course, but she had already decided that when she was growed she was going to marry Petya, that is if she ever decided to get married at all after she first saw the world.

"If I can learn to put up with your kin, you can try to learn to put up with my ma, can't you?" When Lissa still did not answer, Franc added, "She ain't so bad, is she? Look at the pretty dress she sewed for you."

"I know," Lissa croaked. "But—"

"But nothin'. If I can do it, so can you."

Although Hannah did not say anything, she had overheard the children. Her nerves were already on edge over this visit, hoping it would not cause Lissa to create another incident. They had reached a tenuous peace since Christmas, and Hannah was sure that she had begun reaching the girl with kindness. Maybe she had. At least Lissa hadn't outright refused Franc's suggestions. Hannah sighed and snapped open her umbrella.

They traveled for some time in silence, all of them lost in their own thoughts when the Herrias' ranch came into view. The weathered house sat on a lone rise and appeared to look as if it were leaning into the wind, which Hannah could have sworn that she heard moaning as they approached through the snow-topped sage.

Mara Herria, a big woman with an open face, was standing on the porch, wiping her hands on a fresh white apron as they drove into the yard.

"At last," Mara clasped her hands together. "Maximilian brings me company."

Max helped Hannah from the wagon box while the children leapt down and raced toward the four Herria children coming out of the barn.

"This is Hannah," Max offered to Mara and Josef, who had just joined his wife. He was a short, wiry man with a bushy mustache, sporting the traditional black beret. "Hannah, these are my good friends, Josef and Mara."

Hannah relaxed when she noticed the man's

beret tipped back on his head and thrust out her hand. "I am happy to meet you." Hannah offered the woman the basket she had brought. "I brought your family a ham and a string of onions."

Mara accepted the offering and immediately shooed the men off. "You men, you go make man talk and leave Hannah and me to get acquainted with each other," she said, and took Hannah into the house.

Hannah was surprised at the sparsely furnished parlor. Although it was devoid of the stitchery that adorned Max's home, it was tidy and welcoming.

"You have the look of surprise in your eyes. Most Basques do not have homes with so much finery like Max's house," Mara said. "Max is a man and would hardly miss such items."

"Your home is lovely," Hannah remarked, and immediately liked the woman, who was making an effort to help her feel at ease. Hannah did not have the domestic skills that were displayed in Max's home, and it was a relief to learn that her lack of skill would not appear to matter to Max.

"Let me take that jacket so you can stay awhile." Mara chuckled at her own humor.

Hannah took a deep breath and peeled off the sheepskin jacket. Mara's eyes widened when she caught sight of Hannah.

"You and I"—Mara hung the jacket on a hook

near the door—"I think we should go sit in the kitchen so we can visit." Hannah was thankful that the woman had not commented on her growing belly or the dress she wore as she followed her into the kitchen. It was a traditional Basque room decorated in touches of blue with a central open fireplace and long table.

"My family will enjoy the ham. No one cures a ham like the Garats." Mara set the basket down and motioned to the bench beside the table. "Sit down. A woman in your condition needs to take good care of herself. When are you due?"

"Spring." Hannah's hands suddenly were cold. She had hoped to escape the delicate subject, but she had not been so lucky. Hannah settled onto the bench. "Max tells me that you are the best cook in all of Nevada."

Mara gave a dismissive wave, poured two steaming cups of coffee, set one in front of Hannah, and sat down across from her. "Max is one of my favorites. If I were not married or had a daughter of marriageable age, he would have to watch out. Oh, but, from the looks of you and the dress you are wearing, I would say that he has been taken, yes?"

Hannah thought she had managed to redirect the conversation away from herself, but Mara seemed equally determined not to let the subject drop. Hannah raised her chin, wrapping her hands around the cup to warm them.

"Max gave me the dress since my dress was

ruined and I have been too busy sewing for the family to fashion another for myself."

"I hear how you sew, Hannah."

Hannah straightened her shoulders and decided to confront the subject of her dress and the baby she carried.

"What else have you heard, Mara?"

"Oh, dear, I am a fool." Mara reached across the table and covered Hannah's hand with her. "I do not mean to make you uncomfortable in my home. I only thought to make it easier for you to talk about it, that maybe you might need another woman to talk to, yes?"

The woman's genuine empathy caused Hannah's face to start to crumble. "Mara, I don't know what to do."

Mara moved around the table and ringed a comforting arm around Hannah's shoulders. "You do not have to worry, Max is an honorable man. He got you in a family way, he will marry you."

Hannah wiped at the pools of tears to pull herself together. "Oh, no, I mean the baby . . . I—"

"The baby is due in spring." Max finished Hannah's sentence as he entered the house. "The dress is Hannah's, Mara."

Hannah was surprised that Max cut her off from explaining about the baby. A thought that he planned to claim the baby as his own flickered through her mind. She immediately wondered if such thoughts were wishful thinking.

Mara smiled at the forceful protectiveness in Maximilian Garat's voice and moved to the fire. "Coffee?"

Hannah noticed how strained the conversation seemed to be after that, causing her to say, "Max, Mara was only offering a bit of advice."

He frowned. "Mara is always offering a bit of advice."

Josef ringed an arm around his wife's waist as she passed. "My Mara, she is always willing."

Max stared at Hannah, who blushed, while Mara lovingly slapped at Josef.

"Ignore Josef, he only means to make light."

The tension passed, and Hannah and Max relaxed as the topic of conversation changed to the price they expected to get for their wool come spring. Hannah listened, growing comfortable with the couple. Every once in awhile she'd ask a question or make a comment. Max or Josef always took the time to answer her and include her in the discussion. And they laughed companionably.

Hannah was helping Mara set the table, laughing over a comment that Mara was making about pregnant women and men's virtues, when the door slammed opened and the children scrabbled in.

Lissa's giggling abruptly stopped when she heard Mara's remark, and she took a good, long hard look at Hannah. Lissa immediately slapped her hands over her mouth, her eyes the size of fists as they flicked from Hannah to Max.

Suddenly shaking her head with realization, she cried out, "I thought you were just getting fat, but no, no, you are going to have a baby! How could you!" Then she ran from the house.

Franc and André stood like statues and stared in disbelief, until Franc broke the thick silence with "Gol-ly, is it true?"

"Yes," Hannah said softly.

Although Franc had an idea about what went on between a man and a woman, her mouth dropped open and a burning question popped into her young mind.

"How'd you go and manage to get yourself in a motherly way?"

Twenty-six

Lissa had pitched such a hissy fit, refusing even to listen to Hannah or Max, that Max finally accepted Mara's gracious offer to keep the children for a few weeks and try to talk some sense into the girl.

The return trip to the ranch was anything but the pleasant trip that Max and Hannah had envisioned. To Max, Hannah continued to seem sad. For all their gaiety, Mara and Josef had not cheered Hannah up. And now Max had another concern to add to the one over Hannah's pregnancy. Even if he could overcome his apprehension over her impending childbirth, he began to wonder if his eldest child would ever accept his remarriage.

Hannah stared out at the harsh, unforgiving landscape. Lissa belonged on this land. She was as unforgiving in her determination to defeat Hannah as the land was to defeat those who would deem to conquer it.

"Max?"

He turned thoughtful eyes to her. Her distress

was reflected in the drooping corners of her lips. "Do not let the girl trouble you. She will come around eventually."

"I thought so before today, but now I'm not so sure."

He did not answer, rather, he returned his gaze back to the west.

"How can you simply ignore this situation?" Hannah demanded, becoming agitated by his seeming lack of concern.

He pulled up on the reins. Setting them aside, he dropped his hands on her shoulders and leaned his head toward hers. "My people ignore what is not worth fighting about."

Hannah could not believe her ears. She pulled back, brushing his hands from her. Her voice rising in a rare outburst of temper, she snorted, "Are you saying that your daughter is not worth—"

He sighed. "No. I do not say that. What I say is that it is not for you and me to argue over. Lissa is Basque and knows that a decision she cannot change she will have to accept."

"I don't want her just to accept some decision as unchangeable, I want her to accept me. I want us to make our peace!"

"Then maybe this is something you must do."

Hannah threw up her hands. "What do you think I have been trying to do since I arrived?" she charged.

She had not sought his help with his daughter before, but now she was at a complete loss. "I've tried everything I can think of. I've been patient. I've been understanding. Lissa looked longingly at the skirt I made, so I sewed her a new dress. Nothing seems to work with the girl. I don't have any more ideas. Do you?"

He admired her efforts. "Maybe now you try the Basque way we just spoke of" was all he said.

Hannah nodded, mulling over their conversation. "The Basque way, huh?"

"Yes." Max picked up the reins and snapped them over the horses' rumps.

About two miles from the ranch the wind kicked up. Max spurred the horses onward, the wagon bumping along over the rough terrain.

Hannah grabbed at the edges of the wagon box to keep from bouncing out. "Is there a problem?"

"South wind." She cocked her head, and he elaborated. "When the south winds blow, it means that anything can happen."

Hannah felt the skin on her neck crawl and her hair stood on end at the ominous tone in his voice. "Is that Basque too?"

He nodded, but kept his eyes on the terrain, alert and scanning the horizon for anything that may be out of the usual.

The cold, crisp air suddenly felt thick and oppressive, and Hannah had a difficult time breathing as they neared the ranch. She had no idea what to expect. There were so many dangers out there, so far from civilization. And not knowing, trying to prepare herself for any possibility, made the tension nearly overwhelming.

Max drove right to the barn, bypassing the house, and stopped the wagon.

"Everything seems to be in order," Hannah commented, nervously looking over her shoulder. It was late afternoon and the shadows were lengthening, lending even the most harmless fence post a suddenly perilous cast.

Hannah jumped when all of a sudden an unearthly scream echoed throughout the yard.

She watched in terror when Max quickly slid a rifle out from under the seat and checked it for ammunition.

"What're you doing?" she croaked, placing a hand over her heart to keep it from pounding right through the wall of her chest.

"Stay here," he ordered, and jumped down.

Hannah wanted to question him, wanted to demand an explanation, but she remained in the wagon, clutching her umbrella with white knuckles. It was the only weapon she had, but there was no doubt in her mind that she'd use it if she were pressed into service.

At another unearthly scream, followed by the panicked bleating of the sheep, Max began to run.

Hannah remained rigid, rocking back and forth and humming to herself in an effort to keep at bay her distress as Max disappeared around the corner of the barn.

Time seemed to stand still as she waited. Not a bird, not even the sound of the moaning wind broke the deathly quiet that had suddenly fallen over the ranch. Hannah took a breath and held it, waiting for what she had no idea.

The sudden barking coupled with the ear-piercing screams of the children's cat and the frantic bleating of the corralled sheep broke the quiet and set Hannah into motion. Ignoring Max's order to remain in the wagon and her own safety, Hannah scrambled down, lifted her skirts, and ran, knowing only that she had to do something.

Panic met Hannah when she rounded the corner of the barn. Her Panda Pie and the children's cat were standing off a crouched mountain lion that Hannah could describe only as enormous and bloodthirsty.

"Oh, my God, my baby!" Hannah screamed.

Max had a bead on the mountain lion, but he spun around, fearing that something was wrong with Hannah and her unborn child. He had expected to see her doubled over in pain, or worse.

He had not expected to see her with that damned umbrella raised high over her head, marching toward the mountain lion with blood in her eyes.

"Hannah, no!" he yelled, afraid that the big cat would pounce on her, but she kept going.

Its muscles bunched and poised, the big cat moved to face her just as she crashed the umbrella down on its nose. It roared and swung out its huge paw, catching the umbrella's fancy cloth and shredding it as the cat ripped the handle from her.

Panda Pie barked and raced around the big cat. Furball arched and hissed from under the safety of the gate leading to the sheep, panicky and huddled in the far corner.

Unable to get a clear shot, Max dropped the rifle and ran past Hannah, tackling the animal.

"Run," Max yelled as he rolled in the snow with the cat.

But Hannah could not run. And she could not stand by and do nothing. She grabbed her shredded umbrella and jumped into the skirmish, striking the big cat with enough force to deter its attention long enough for Max to pull his knife from his boot.

"Dammit, get back!" Max hollered, tumbling on the ground with the cat.

Hannah backed up and fought to swallow her screams, hardly able to believe that she had been so bold. Panda Pie leapt into her arms, Furball skittered underneath her skirts, and she stood, frozen, watching in terror the life-and-death battle between man and beast.

The big cat gave a bloodcurdling roar. Abruptly the fray was over. Blood, bright red against the stark white of the snow, pooled around Max.

"No . . . no!" Hannah screeched in a keening wail. The big cat had killed Max.

She was still standing, unable to move, when she noticed the big cat move. She was about to make a break for the rifle to shoot the animal, when Max gave a shove and the big cat rolled to his side.

"My God, you're still alive!"

"You doubt that I would win maybe?"

"Don't make light of something so serious," she chided him.

He wiped the blood from his knife on his ruined shirt and stuffed it back into his boot before crawling to his feet. "My family say I do not make light. But you, Hannah, you accuse me of making light when you stand there, a haven to our pets."

She stood and glared at him, but she had not missed him using the word *our* about Panda Pie and Furball.

"You're hurt," she cried when she noticed the blood trickling down his arm and spotting the front of his shredded shirt. She placed Panda Pie on the ground, ripped a strip from her only petticoat, and hurried to his side.

"Now you notice," he said in an amused voice. "I fear that the shirt you sewed is ruined."

"The important thing is to make sure that you're not badly hurt." She wrapped the abrasions and tied the ends of the cloth. "Come into the house with me before you bleed to death."

"You begin to sound like a wife," he said before he gave consideration to the significance of his words.

Hannah grew quiet and ceased her ministrations, lowering her arms. She shifted feet. "Your wounds need to be cleansed to stave off the possibility of infection."

"They are no more than scratches. I will come after I check the sheep."

Feeling awkward and unsettled, she did not wait for him. Rather, she swung around and headed for the house.

All the while he examined the frightened sheep, speaking in a soft voice to calm them, he was troubled by the comment he had made to Hannah. He was a very deliberate man, one who lived by design. He was practical and clear-thinking, so he could not understand how such words could slip from his tongue. Unless he was thinking with the back of his mind . . .

One lamb had been injured. By the time he had cared for the frightened animal and strung the mountain lion's carcass to ready it to be skinned, Hannah was waiting for him with an array of bandages and a bowl of warm, soapy water.

"Take off your shirt," she directed, "and let me tend those wounds."

A stirring smile spread across his lips, to her chagrin.

"What're you smiling for? You nearly scared

me half to death. I thought that horrid animal had killed you."

"I smile maybe because I remember another time that you ordered me to take off my shirt," he said as he slowly, provocatively, stripped the bloodied shirt from his muscled torso.

Hannah felt the heat creep up her face. How well she recalled when she had told him to remove his shirt. Her mind replayed the breath of shoulders, the ripple of muscles, the trail of hair down to . . .

"You stare, Hannah. Maybe it is that you remember, too, yes?"

Brought back from her erotic reverie to the reality of the deep scratches scarring the naked flesh, bronze and taut, she breathed, "I remember."

He stroked her cheek with the back of his hand, which seemed to spur her into action. She hurriedly dipped a cloth into the bowl of soapy water, wrung it out, and began washing the abrasions on his chest. It was an incredibly sensuous experience, gliding the damp cloth over his hard, glistening flesh and caused a moistened heat to dew at the core of her woman's being.

"There is something most sensual about water, yes?"

Hannah watched the drops of liquid slide in rivulets, like caressing fingers, down his chest, disappearing inside the band at his waist.

She imagined her own fingers disappearing inside his trousers.

"Hannah, what goes through your mind?"

She looked up into his face. His expression was intent, silently beckoning. "Max, I . . ."

"Maybe my mind, too, thinks the same as yours, yes?"

"Yes," she said in a velvety whisper.

Max took the cloth from her hand and tossed it aside. With an easy fluid motion he turned her around and began working the buttons down her back.

"What about your wounds?"

"What wounds?"

"But—" She swung around and allowed the dress to drop down around her ankles.

Slowly, with expert fingers he slipped her chemise straps off her shoulders and let it join her dress. Then to her pleasured surprise he kneeled down, untied the string from her underdrawers, and skimmed them over the flair of her hips and along her thighs.

"You are a lovely woman, Hannah," he murmured.

Standing before him in the light of the day with no clothing to hide her nakedness, Hannah bit her lip and made a study of the ceiling.

Max noticed her anxious expression and got to his feet. Concern crossing his brow, he questioned, "There is a problem, yes?"

Hannah's gaze fell to his. This was an honest

man who expected honesty in return. She could no longer lie to him.

"M-my stomach. It is growing."

His hands caressed the swell of her abdomen. "You are beautiful, Hannah." He leaned over and kissed her belly before looking up at her again. "You carry inside you a most precious life. When you grow heavy with child, you become even more beautiful."

He lifted her from her feet, high into his embrace, and strode into the bedroom. Hannah clasped her arms around his neck, letting go of all anxiety over the shape of her body.

On his bed, Hannah watched as he divested himself of his clothing and joined her. Her body against his, Hannah could not help but savor how it was to lie next to this man. His body was hard, honed. He was tall and warm. So totally different. So totally, wonderfully untouched and untainted by the past. With his love he was nurturing and healing her scars, she thought, before the sensual magic took over her entire consciousness.

Maybe it was the danger, the death they had faced and beat. Maybe it was the way Max had used the word *our* when he referred to the pets. Maybe it was his reference to Hannah sounding like a wife. But the coupling that had begun slowly with great tenderness, touching, and caressing became a frenzy of mouths, hands, legs. Their bodies joined in wild abandon, unrestrained passions driving, spiraling until Hannah, then Max, shuddered with that supreme release.

Reveling in the sweet ecstasy of exhaustion, Hannah drifted off to sleep. She awoke when she felt Max rise from the bed, slip into his trousers, and silently creep to the back door.

Curious, Hannah leaned up on her elbow, only to hear Max softly calling Panda Pie and Furball into the house. She smiled, her heart overflowing, and settled back against the pillows; Max was making sure that her precious pet was in the house and out of danger's way.

Twenty-seven

The idyllic weeks in which Max and Hannah
had put their concerns in the back of their minds
and savored the adult sensual pleasures of the
body and mind came to an end with the return
of the children and the coming of spring. Hannah was encircled in Max's arms, snuggled before
the fire in the parlor, when they heard Josef's
shout.

Max rose and went to the window. "Josef and
Mara are bringing the children back."

"You've really missed them, haven't you?"

"It is time they are home."

"Yes," she said, and hoped that the time Lissa
had spent with Mara had made a difference.

"Next week, with spring coming soon, Petya
and my papa will bring the sheep from the winter
range and the work begins."

"André and Lissa help with the sheep?"

Max grinned. "I think maybe you miss the children, too, even though they can be trouble sometimes."

She nodded. Despite the problems she'd had

with the children, and her own burdens, Hannah had begun to think of them as a family. Even Franc, with her grumbling, had grown on Hannah, and she could not help herself thinking of Franc as her own. Although Hannah would not openly admit to looking forward to it, the return of the children gave her the opportunity to put into practice one of Max's Basque traditions.

Max helped Hannah to her feet, kissed the heels of her palms, and gazed into her eyes. "I will miss our time alone together. There is still much we have to talk about."

Hannah nodded and remained silent, the sentiment threatening to overwhelm her, while he led her out onto the porch to greet their neighbors. There was so much she had to tell him, but she had not been able to garner the courage to unburden herself.

Franc was the first to jump down and run up to Hannah. A sly grin to her face, Franc crinkled her nose and said in a singsong, knowing voice, "Since you didn't, Mara teached me exactly how women get in a motherly way."

Hannah fought to keep the blush from her cheeks and brushed the bangs back from Franc's eyes, hugging the little urchin.

Max chuckled despite himself. "Mara teaches you more than manners maybe."

Unaffected by Franc's bluntness, Mara joined them on the porch and handed over Samuel. Max hugged his little son, then went to greet the other children and help Josef see to the wagon and horses. Hannah was disappointed when André merely waved and skittered toward the barn, Lissa right behind him. She had secretly hoped that André would have stopped to see her first.

"Come on, Franc," André yelled, "we are going to see the mountain lion hide that Papa and Hannah killed."

Franc shot Hannah a questioning look, but did not remain to hear the story before she took off at a gallop behind the other children.

Hannah had just finished relaying the tale to Mara, when Josef handed Mara a wrapped package.

"Here is what you bring for Hannah," Josef said. "We stay only long enough for Max to show me this mountain lion he tells me about and saddle the horse. Then we must start back. There is much to do as spring comes."

Hannah accepted the *kaiku*, a wooden container used for milk, and studied it.

"The *kaiku* is your first house gift, eh?" Mara beamed.

"Ah . . . yes." Hannah admired the unusual diagonally carved piece with the asymmetrical appearance, wishing she had her own home in which to use the container.

"Josef cut it from a single tree trunk. The Basque kitchen is not complete without one, and I think you should have one of your own so you can use it to make special dishes for your man, eh?" Mara winked.

"Thank you," Hannah said shyly, unable to explain her relationship with Max, since she herself could not put a simple definition on it.

When Mara followed Hannah into the kitchen, her eyes caught on the straw bed and the small black dog curled into a ball, asleep there. Her eyes rounded and she swung out her hand. "What is this?"

You make your bed, you lie in it echoed with a warning ring in Hannah's mind. She took a deep breath to allay the case of nerves that her mother's favorite adage always elicited from her. "It is the bed I share with Franc and my pet."

Mara's hands dropped to her wide hips in surprise. Her brows rose and a mischievous grin settled on her lips. "If this is where you sleep, how did you get pregnant?"

"In the traditional manner."

Mara laughed, then grew serious. "Yet you sleep here?"

For some reason Hannah had not questioned Max when he had interceded when the topic of her unborn child's paternity arose. Max was nowhere in sight. Hannah was on her own.

"Max and I both have children."

"Ah, yes, now I understand." Mara nodded, obviously forming her own rationalization. Hannah was saved from a further barrage of questions, although she herself did not understand why Max had not merely allowed her to inform Mara that the child she carried was not his.

By the time the Herrias left and all the children were bedded down for the night, Hannah was determined to discover why Max had interceded at the Herrias when Mara had questioned Hannah's pregnancy. It had gnawed on her all evening, and she was curious why the Herrias had left their wagon and one of the horses.

Max was in the barn, supplying the wagon he would be driving out to meet his father and brother as they moved the sheep from winter camp. Hannah lit a lantern, slipped into the lambskin jacket, and crunched across the icy patches of snow.

After a few moments of small talk, Hannah could not put off what was on her mind any longer. "Max, can we talk?"

Noticing her stiff stance, Max jumped down from the wagon. "Something troubles you, Hannah?"

"When we were at the Herrias you stopped me from informing Mara that you are not the father of my baby. And today while Mara and I were in the kitchen she questioned the bed of straw in the corner." Hannah paused. "Max, I didn't tell her . . ." She let her voice trail off, hoping that Max would pick up the clue and explain his reasoning.

He pulled his beret down over his forehead, reminding Hannah of what Petya had told her.

It was not a question Max was happily going to answer.

He motioned to a stool. "Sit down, Hannah." He waited until she was settled, then began to pace back and forth in front of her. "There is no one simple explanation."

"Mara gave me a milk pitcher as a housewarming gift. She is under the impression that you and I . . . that we are going to . . ." The word *marry* stuck in her throat, for she had no right even to be thinking of such a topic, let alone broaching it with Max, until she was assured that she truly was indeed free. "What I mean is—"

"I know of what you speak." He stopped in front of her and rubbed the back of his neck. "There is no easy answer we can speak of now except maybe I sometimes think I am the papa."

The thought of Max wanting to be the father of her child was incredible. The thought of having Max's baby was more than incredible. She wanted lots of babies, but even if he asked her to marry him and she were free to accept, she should not even be thinking about another child now.

There were the other children to consider. Franc and Lissa desperately needed nurturing and guidance. André and Samuel were such good children, but they needed a mother's attention as well. And she would have the precious baby she now carried to mind.

"Hannah, the expression on your face looks

like you are far away," he said, crashing into her happily-ever-after fantasy.

"What? Oh, oh . . . that would be nice."

He sent her a lopsided grin. "The making of one is nice, yes?"

"Huh?"

"I think you have much on your mind. Do not worry about Mara. She is well-meaning and will take good care of you while I am away."

She crinkled her forehead, not believing what she was hearing. "What?"

"Mara, she will take good—"

Hannah's brows drew together. "I heard what you said."

"Why do you ask me to repeat myself?"

"Because I can't believe what I'm hearing, that's why."

"Hannah, I am a sheepherder. My papa and brother tend the flock, but now it is time for me to go to work."

"So that is why Josef left the wagon and horse? Am I the only one to be shipped to the Herrias in their wagon?" she grated out, reeling that he had just spent weeks devoting himself to her, and now she was to be sent away so easily.

Max pulled his beret ever farther down on his forehead. "You and your Franc."

"Oh? And what about Sammy and Lissa and André?"

"Hannah, you start to sound like a hysterical pregnant woman."

"I am a pregnant woman," she snapped before she recalled that that was his reason for sending her to the Herrias.

"And because you are a woman and carry a child you will go to the Herrias. Mara will care for you and help with the birth." *If Mara had been in attendance two years ago . . .* "You need help, yes?"

He had her there. She hadn't told him that she had never given birth to a child and had no idea what to expect. "Well, I suppose," she admitted grudgingly.

"André is old enough now to help with the sheepherding. Lissa comes along to care for Samuel. The Herrias' middle son is to take care of the ranch. In Basque culture, if one family has children enough to do work, they lend out their children to families who do not have enough."

Hannah raised her chin. "At the moment I'm not interested in your Basque culture. The baby isn't due for a while yet; Franc and I can go along and help too."

"You do not listen maybe when I speak," he said in exasperation. "We speak no more of this. You do not go."

To Hannah's total frustration, he put an end to the argument by turning on his heel and leaving her standing in the barn alone to stew. Well, she was not done with the topic yet! He was not simply going to have his patriarchal Basque way without a battle this time.

She did not want to go to the Herrias and be badgered with well-meaning questions she was not prepared to answer. And a part of her did not want to be away from Maximilian Garat.

She followed after him and argued her position. She did not know anything about driving a wagon, so he could not leave her. The stubborn man was not willing to make any concessions, and all she managed to accomplish, if she could call it that, was that now Lissa, driving the wagon, and Sammy, would be accompanying her and Franc to the Herrias.

"Why do I have to go back there? I just came from there. You said I could go with you this year," Lissa pleaded that evening while the family sat in front of the fire, engaging in their store of legend, telling folktales handed down from generation to generation.

"I do not think that is a Basque folktale, but maybe you start another one with this tale of woe you tell, Lissa, yes?"

"Papa," Lissa whined, "you promised."

Max's eyes flashed. "You know a Basque is as good as his word. I do not make such a promise."

Lissa hung her head. "I am sorry, Papa. But I know how to drive the wagon, and I can be of help with the shearing and lambing."

"And because you learn so well, you will drive Hannah and Franc to the Herrias."

* * *

Despite all the arguments Hannah presented, by the end of the week Max had not changed his mind. He had seen to all the arrangements for the ranch and family, stood unmovable against Hannah's last onslaught, and mounted the supply wagon.

Lissa came running out of the house, leaving the back door open in her haste to hand up to Max a basket filled with preserves and bread she had baked fresh. "They are Mama's preserves. I remember how Mama used to send you away with a basket."

Max's gaze lingered on Hannah before he thanked Lissa and tucked the basket behind the wagon box.

Hannah forced herself to disregard the girl's calculated cutting remarks as Lissa slyly grinned at Hannah before she twirled her skirt and returned to the house.

"Lissa, remember that Hannah is in charge now. You do what she tells you," Max ordered in a commanding voice.

Lissa's shoulders slumped and she pivoted around, saying, "Yes, sir" before she disappeared inside the house.

"You will do well," Max said to Hannah with a wink.

Hannah nodded, not trusting herself to speak as she stood in the warming sun, shading her eyes, and watched the wagon rock and sway until Max and André were out of sight.

Left with her determination to deal with Lissa according to Basque tradition, Hannah set out to continue to ignore the girl as much as was humanly possible.

At the dinner table Lissa grumbled, "My mama used to drive the supply wagon."

"Franc, please pass the potatoes," Hannah requested, and served Sammy a small helping. "Potatoes, Lissa?"

Lissa frowned and continued. "My mama knew how to fix Papa's favorite kind of potatoes."

"Tripotak, Lissa?" Hannah responded.

"My mama never hid in the kitchen while my papa made those Basque blood sausages."

"Carrots, Franc?"

"My mama gave birth to me under a wagon out on the range while she was helping my papa. She delivered me with only Papa's help."

That had pricked her interest, but Hannah said, "Franc, pass Lissa the bread."

Franc slid the plate of bread and shot Lissa a glowering frown, but Lissa ignored her and directed her attention toward Hannah.

"There is no butter on the table," Lissa complained. "I cannot eat bread without butter."

Hannah kept her voice even when she said, "It was your chore to set the table, and you know where it's kept."

Lissa snorted and swung from the table. Hannah had always bent over backward to make up to her, and this was a new experience for her.

She did not have her papa to turn to; André had told her outright that he liked Hannah and was not going to do anything to make her unhappy. Sammy continued to call Hannah Mama, and Franc was frowning at her.

Feeling outnumbered and out of sorts, Lissa tried to figure out what she could do about it. She grabbed a bowl, stomped to the space under the shelf where the big butter crock was kept, and kneeled down on the floor to slide it out.

She was met with distinct clattering sounds in rapid succession.

Lissa recoiled, kicking the butter crock over with her heel, and let out a terrified, blood-chilling scream.

Twenty-eight

"Snake!" Lissa screamed repeatedly, hysterically gasping for air as she cowered against the wall, cupping her ears.

While Franc grabbed Sammy and Panda Pie and ran from the kitchen, Hannah rushed to Lissa's side.

That's when Hannah saw it. A huge rattlesnake was tucked between the butter crock and the wall, shaking at least a dozen rattles in warning.

Her instincts taking over, Hannah shoved the girl aside and immediately flung open the door. She quickly scanned the kitchen. Sighting a broom propped in a corner, she grabbed it by the bristles. With her hands shaking and her heart pounding so she could hardly hear herself think, Hannah moved back to the snake, carefully slid the wooden handle underneath it, and scooped it up. It shook its rattles furiously. Fearing she might drop it, Hannah slowly inched to the door and flung it and the broom out. She slammed the door and leaned against it for a moment to catch her breath before going to Lissa.

"It's all right now, Lissa. The snake is gone. t's gone." Hannah pulled the hysterical girl into ᴇer embrace, and held her, stroking her hair in ᴎ effort to calm her.

Lissa could not be calmed. Her gasping con- inued and caused her to hiccup while she ᴏbbed. She pointed to the broken crock, where ᴛhe snake had been, uncontrollably shaking her ᴇead back and forth. "The devil has come after ᴎe. He is after me."

Hannah grabbed the girl by the shoulders and hook her in an effort to bring her back to her enses. "Lissa, the snake's not in the house any ᴏnger. It's gone. You're all right now."

"But he is after me."

"Not anymore."

Her eyes wide in childish innocence and disbe- ief, she clung to Hannah. "The devil thought he ᴎad me. And you got rid of it for me even after ᴛhe way I have treated you?"

"It was just a snake, and it's gone now," Han- ᴎah said, although it was *just* the largest snake ᴛhe had ever seen in her life.

"Oh, no, you did not kill it, did you?"

"I tossed it out the door."

"The door?" Lissa pulled back from Hannah ᴎnd stared at the door for the longest time.

"Yes."

Realization suddenly hit Lissa. "I left that door ᴏpen earlier when I rushed out to give Papa the

basket I had packed for him. It was the devi
and I let him in."

"It was not the devil, it was a snake. Now, wha
is all this talk about devils?" Hannah questione
the troubling girl.

Taking deep breaths in an effort to calm her
self after such a close scrape with Satan, Liss
said, "My people believe that snakes are linke
with the devil. We really don't like them an
never say we killed one—"

"Even when you do?"

"We *finish* a snake," Lissa explained shyly, stil
trembling.

Hannah nodded, finally understanding wha
Lissa was talking about. "You're still pretty shoo
up. Why don't you go to bed and get some sleep
I'll tuck Sammy in in a little while."

"Hannah, will y-you tuck m-me in too?"

"I'd be happy to." Hannah ringed an arn
around the girl and escorted her to the bedroom
She could hardly believe the breakthrough in he
relationship with Lissa.

Secretly Hannah wished that it would take onl
a snake to mend the problems she faced witl
Max.

Lissa got a nightgown, slipped into it, and
climbed into bed. Hannah drew the blanket up
around her neck and smoothed the stray hair
off her face. "Good night, Lissa." She leanec
over and dropped a kiss on Lissa's forehead be

ore she extinguished the lamp and turned to
eave.

"Hannah?"

Hannah stopped and pivoted around. Lissa was
eaning up on her elbow, an earnest expression
on her young face.

"I am sorry. Can you ever forgive me for the
way I treated you?"

"There's nothing to forgive. Sleep well."

The danger behind them, Hannah returned to
the kitchen, gathering Sammy and Franc and finished feeding them. Hannah sighed, and relaxed
enough to find humor in the incident as she
chuckled to herself. "Well, there's more than one
Basque tradition that'll conquer an obstinate
child."

Franc glanced up from her plate and wrinkled
her nose. "Huh?"

"I think this sausage is very mild." Hannah
took a bite, appreciating for the first time the
tripotak, the Basque blood sausage.

Franc just shook her head. "How can pig guts—"

"Kidneys."

This time Franc rolled her eyes. "Like I said,
how can pig guts taste anything but bad?"

"Do you think Papa would think I was bad?"
Lissa questioned Hannah.

Hannah did not want to put the girl in a position of taking any responsibility upon herself

for what Hannah planned to do. But Max ha
been gone several days and Hannah had no ir
tention of meekly going to the Herrias.

An idea came to Hannah. "Lissa, do you reca
the last thing your papa said to you before h
left for the range?"

Lissa thought for a moment, then her eyes wid
ened and her face lit up. "Papa said I should d
what you tell me to."

"And I'm telling you to take me to him."

"In the Herrias' wagon?"

"Unless you have another idea." Hanna
paused. "I don't think they'll mind. Josef left i
here, so he must not need it."

Franc sat quietly and listened to the exchange
She still had some lingering mixed feelings abou
this whole ranch life, although she had given u
actively opposing their stopover. And, of course
Petya was out on the range. Franc troubled ove
Hannah's decision. Hannah was starting to loo
like she swallowed one of those whole hams hang
ing from the kitchen ceiling. Golly, if Hannah
accidentally fell out of the wagon, she'd probabl
pop.

"Hannah, you ever fall outta a wagon?"

"No."

Franc mopped her brow in relief. "That sure'
good news."

Hannah looked at Franc askance, then let i
drop. There was no telling what Franc had or
her mind this time.

"Let's get the wagon loaded. We'll be leaving s soon as we're ready," Hannah announced.

Franc put provisions into the wagon while Lissa itched up the horse. Hannah bundled up ammy and gathered his favorite toys so he'd be ntertained once they reached their destination.

Hannah then slipped into the once-generous coop-necked blue gingham dress that Max had given her. Now it barely fit. She would need all he help she could get when Max saw her. She grabbed the lambskin jacket off the hook, took ammy by the hand, and closed the door behind her.

The girls and Panda Pie were already waiting n the wagon when Hannah handed Sammy up and climbed up behind him.

"Mama, Mama," he cooed, and tried to crawl nto her lap.

Hannah grinned at the persistent toddler and fluffed his dark hair. "Sammy, I don't have a lap right now. Here, you sit right beside me and I'll put my arm around you."

Lissa snapped the reins over the horse's rump and they were on their way. The wagon bumped and rocked over the desert as the sun rose high n the sky and the day warmed, signaling that spring was indeed on its way. The cactus flowers had begun to bloom on the barren landscape.

"Are you sure that this is such a good idea?" Lissa asked while they were stopped so that Sammy could relieve himself.

"I'm not," Franc put in, and stroked Panda Pi
behind the ears.

Hannah helped Sammy adjust his trouser
then looked up. "Franc, you are starting to soun
more and more like a mother."

Franc took one glance at Hannah's swellin
belly and said, "I ain't never goin' to be n
mother."

"I am, but not until I find a very wealthy ger
tleman who has a fine house in the big city,
Lissa chimed in. "When I grow up I am not go
ing to live on some isolated ranch surrounded b
sheep."

Hannah gave a bittersweet smile at Lissa'
grand design for herself. It sounded too muc
like Hannah's past life for comfort, and Hanna
made a mental note to talk to Lissa someda
about it. "Oh, I don't know. I think an isolate
sheep ranch is a very nice place to live."

"Only because Max is here," Franc observed.

Hannah smiled. "Well, Max does have some
thing to do with it."

Lissa took Sam and set him beside her. "Yo
really do love my papa, yes?"

It was a serious question, and Hannah gre
thoughtful. "Yes, Lissa, I love your papa."

"Are you going to get married?"

"He hasn't asked me."

"If he does?" Lissa pressed.

If only it were that simple. "There are certai
considerations that must be addressed first befor

our father and I could even begin to think about
marriage."

"Such as?"

"Don't you think we oughta get goin' before
we get stuck out here at night alone?" Franc suggested, uneasily looking around at the barren
landscape with a few flowers here and there.
"Who knows what's skulkin' around out here.
And I ain't got no intention of findin' out."

Hannah laughed and told Franc there was
nothing to worry about, but silently she did not
want to spend the night alone out in the desert
without protection either.

The hours passed without a hint of a herd of
anything except sagebrush. Hannah watched the
sun dip behind the mountains to the west and
began to question her judgment, as she had back
in St. Louis.

"If you hadn't been so incompetent, I'd be
back in St. Louis by now," Emmett sneered at the
detective. "But no, I've been forced to spend the
entire winter in this filthy hellhole calling itself
a town while I had to wait for some heathen Chi-
namen to relay train tracks because the damned
train quit running."

The detective stood before what had become
Turner's personal table in front of the window at
the only saloon in town. The man kept a straight
face, although he wasn't blind. He knew that

Turner had spent the winter in town because tha
redheaded whore who owned the saloon ha
obliged Turner's every perverted whim.

"Mr. Turner, you'll be happy to know that th
tracks're almost fixed and the train'll be runnin
again any day now. So we ought to be prepare
to leave when it gets here." His eyes slid to th
woman hovering at Turner's side like a vultur
"If you're ready, that is."

"If I'm ready?" Emmett barked, incredulou
"It is about damned time we got word on tha
train! Go tell that grotesque Timm bitch that I'r
paying to put up at that fleabag masqueradin
as a hotel to be ready. She and I will be on th
first train out of here. You are fired."

Sliding her long-nailed fingers over Emmett
chest and around his neck, Sugar Lee purre
"You're takin' me with you, ain't ya, honeybuns?

Emmett glanced up and noticed the detectiv
was still standing around like a statue, staring a
Sugar Lee. "What the hell are you standing ther
for? Get your damn ass moving before I get
gun and shoot it off."

Emmett waited until the detective had left be
fore he directed his full attention to the whore
A calculating frown on his handsome face, Em
mett clamped hurting fingers around Sugar Lee'
wrists and yanked them from around his neck.

He dug his nails into the soft skin at her pulse
"Now, what were you saying?"

Sugar Lee swallowed the urge to cry out i

pain. Rather, she smiled her most seductive smile and decided to brazen it out. Slowly licking her heavily painted lips while she stared down at the bulge in his crotch, she purred, "I said that it'd be a awful borin' trip without me."

Emmett grabbed a handful of hair and yanked until they were nose to nose. "What makes you think that I'm not done with you?"

Sugar Lee gulped back her fear, for she recognized his moods, and blurted out, " 'Cuz I got your kid growin' in my belly."

Twenty-nine

"We there yet?" Franc asked for the ninth time within less than twenty minutes as the sky darkened and the moon began its assent in the east, full and a ripe golden-orange.

Lissa sighed, scratched her head, and scanned the wide-open terrain. "If I figured right, we should have been there by now, since they are traveling in our direction."

Hannah cuddled a sleepy Sammy, who was sucking his thumb, into the crook of her arm and drew one of the blankets she had packed up around his neck. Panda Pie climbed into the toddler's lap and burrowed into the blanket.

"I'm sure it won't be long now," Hannah said with a certain bravado she did not at all feel. She could not allow the children to know that the desert, with its stark, haunting beauty, frightened her. "How many sheep are we looking for?"

"Papa keeps about two thousand ewes in his winter bands."

"There's only one me," Franc joked, dredging

up a remembered incident in an effort to keep from showing that she was scared.

Hannah smiled and Lissa groaned.

Hannah combed the land up ahead of them. How hard could two thousand sheep be to spot if they were indeed anywhere nearby?

Lissa suddenly bolted up in the wagon, sniffing the air.

"What is it?" Hannah asked, careful to keep from asking what was wrong.

"Do you smell it?" Lissa questioned.

Franc made a big production of sniffing. "Smell what?"

"Fire."

Hannah recalled the threatening fires they used to have in St. Louis and pulled her jacket closed around her neck.

"What's there to burn out here?" Franc questioned. "Cactus and sagebrush?"

"No, dummy," Lissa responded to Franc's usual sarcasm. "Papa told me that they build many small fires around the sheep at night to scare the coyotes away."

Relief flooded through Hannah. They were not lost. Then another emotion began to take hold.

Apprehension.

If they were close to reaching Max, then it also meant that she was very near to reaping Max's wrath for going against his specific instructions to go to the Herrias. Her pulse starting to increase, Hannah straightened her back, raised her chin, and gazed straight ahead, preparing herself for what she knew was coming.

"They come straight toward us, eh?" Petya laughed when he recognized the familiar silhouettes against a deep-wine-colored sky. "You teach your daughter well. Let me see, what is it you preach to me of orders, big brother?"

Max had sensed it before he even saw the wagon heading toward camp. Ignoring his brother's unrelenting ribbing, Max grunted, grabbed his rifle, and set out to meet them.

"Papa, maybe it is that Maximilian does not know ladies as well as he thinks, eh?" Petya called out for Max's ears.

Max was angry enough that he did not need or want to know any females at the moment. And from what he could see, that included his own daughter, who was driving, no less.

He marched up to the wagon.

"What are you doing here?" he demanded upon reaching them.

"We brought more supplies. Papa—"

"It's all right, Lissa," Hannah said in a soothing voice. Then to Max she said, "Do not blame Lissa. If you will recall, you left me in charge, and I directed her to bring us out here."

Max recalled all too well. He noted the transformation in his daughter's posture and the way she looked to Hannah, but he was much too angry to appreciate whatever had brought about the unexpected change.

"Get down from the wagon, Hannah."

"What?"

"Hannah, do not argue with me."

"Well, you'll have to help me. I'm not too agile these days," she said with the most endearing grin she could possibly muster in an effort to lighten his dark mood.

He did not so much as crack a smile. "Lissa, you and Franc take Samuel to camp . . . now."

He waited while the girls jumped down without an argument, took Samuel by the hand, and skittered toward camp, Panda Pie lopping along behind them.

"I thought you wanted me to get down?" she questioned when he hooked a boot heel onto the wagon wheel.

"No longer."

"Then what are you doing?" she forced herself to ask.

"I will unload the wagon, then I take you to the Herrias."

"No! I won't go."

The unexpected forcefulness of her refusal caused him to look up. He could almost admire her spirit if he weren't so angry with her. "The choice is not yours, Hannah."

Hannah crossed her arms over her chest and frantically tried to think of a plausible explana-

tion why she should not be taken to the Herrias
"I can be of help."

He did not even so much as look up from un
loading the wagon. Scratch that general argu
ment.

"What if I cook?"

"Not good enough."

"I'd offer to sew . . . if I had the machine. O
course, I don't suppose you need any clothing
mended out here."

"No."

"What if I gather more kindling to keep the
fires going? Surely, you can use more firewood.'

At least that got his attention.

He stopped what he was doing and glared a
her, causing the hair on the back of her neck to
stand on end, he was that incensed.

"You cannot touch your toes any longer. How
can you pick up firewood?"

She shrugged. "Very carefully?"

Max stared at her. He did not find humor in
her attempts at levity. She would be giving birth
soon, and he wanted her safe. He tossed the last
of the supplies to the ground and plunked down
next to her. "No more excuses."

"You aren't truly going to take me back in the
dark, are you?" No answer. "At least let me stay
the night."

A snap of the reins muted the sharp ring of
his no.

They had traveled no more than a half mile,

when three shots rang out, followed by the yelping howl of a hungry coyote pack.

The coyotes managed to accomplish what Hannah had failed to do. Max pulled up on the reins
and directed the wagon back toward camp.

"You won't be sorry," Hannah offered, although with the rocking of the wagon she wondered if she would be the one with regrets.

"I do not do this for you. The sheep need pro-
tecting."

But by the time they reached the camp, the
sheep were peacefully banded together in a circle.
Petya was leaning on his rifle, a wily grin on his
face. "What do I say? I miss Hannah, eh?"

"The coyotes?"

He gave a wolfish shrug. "At a distance they
howl. Papa's big white dog watches over the
sheep."

The girls and André, seated at the campfire,
hid smiles behind their palms while Bernard
slowly shook his head. "My sons, they forget the
welfare of the sheep to think of other things.
This is not good. Not good at all. Lambing, it
already begins. We need every hand not to lose
a one." Bernard's gaze shifted to Hannah. "The
girls, they say you come to help. So help."

"Hannah's baby comes soon," Max grated out.

"The way you drive, Maximilian, the baby, it
comes too soon. Your mama, she helps with the
sheep when out you come. Hannah, she is
strong."

What Max's father said was true, they did need all available hands to help with the lambing. Some of the ewes had already had a difficult time with giving birth, and it was getting late. His gaze went to Hannah. The baby was not due yet.

Against his better judgment, Max grated out, "Hannah watches Samuel. No more."

Feeling properly chastised by his father that he had lost sight of his responsibility to the animals and angry that Hannah had ignored his instructions, Max remained in camp only long enough to listen to his daughter tell about the snake Hannah had removed from his house, then stomped from the camp to add more wood to the fires and help with the lambing. But it was not due to his father's remarks that Hannah was still in camp or his admiration that she had dealt so ably with a snake, it was by virtue of the fact that come morning, they would no doubt desperately need the extra help that Lissa and Franc could provide.

"Come with me and sit by the fire, Hannah." Bernard ringed an arm around Hannah's shoulders and led her to the warmth of the flames. "My son, he worries too much. You lend extra hands with the lambing, yes?"

"Yes." Hannah nodded, but *you make your bed, you lie in it,* could not help but chime loud and clear in the back of her mind. Then, as Petya handed her a warming cup of coffee and she greeted André and listened to his youthful tales, she rationalized that what better experience for her own impending birthing than helping with the lambing while being able to remain close to Max.

That night Hannah was anything but close to Max. He did not return to camp. Rather, he remained out with the ewes to help with the birthing, and she was forced to bed down under the wagon with Lissa, Franc, and Panda Pie. The ground was cold and hard, and her back ached, not to mention that she could not find a comfortable position.

She had barely dropped off to sleep when morning dawned much too early in her sleepy mind. Sammy was the only one left with her and Panda Pie in camp. Hannah propped herself up on her elbow to marvel at the numbers of sheep. Then she saw the others in the distance, including Franc, already busy at work.

Once she had seen to Sammy and her needs, Hannah walked out to where some of the ewes had already been lambing for two days. She stood in awe, silently marveling at the miracle of birth.

For the longest time Hannah watched the parturient ewes. The others circulated among the sheep careful not to disturb them unless the lambs needed help.

"Over here, Max!" Franc shouted. "This one ain't breathin'. Quick! Hurry!"

Petya was nearby and came running with a large bucket, sloshing water as he ran. He lifted the lamb into the bucket and began scooping snow from the few patches left on the ground around the little critter. An instant later the lamb let out a loud plaintive bleat. Petya removed it from the bucket, dried it, and put it to its mother. "We do good, yes?"

"Yeah." Franc shuffled her foot. "Guess we make a pretty good team, huh."

Petya grinned and gave Franc a big hug, causing her to blush down to her little toes.

"Now you keep the droppers away from this baby and its mama, eh?"

Franc was at a loss. "Droppers?"

"Ewes which do not lamb yet. They want to be a mama so much that they sometimes try to steal babies from their mamas."

"Oh, yeah, sure, I can do that."

Hannah watched Franc make such an intent effort to protect that ewe and its baby that her heart swelled. Franc had come such a long way from the little scamp who had stolen her money. Hannah should thank Franc for that, since it had brought her together with Max, for if she'd had money she never would have been forced to resort to her scheme.

"Max!" Bernard bellowed. "This ewe, she needs your expert hands. Come."

Brought back from her private thoughts, Hannah hurried over to where Max was already preparing the laboring ewe. With an efficiency Hannah could describe only as amazing, Max reached into the birth canal and pulled the lamb out and downward.

"André, bring the warm water," Max hollered to his son. To Hannah, he said softly, "Hannah, I need a blanket."

She smiled at the big, muscular man cradling the infant lamb as if it were a human baby before she hurried to fetch a blanket. Max emitted an air of physical strength and prowess, yet he could be so tender and caring and gentle.

By the time Hannah returned with the covering, Max had immersed the lamb in the warm water up to its neck and was speaking softly to comfort it. He removed it and wrapped it in the blanket.

"Baby, baby," Sammy gurgled, and pointed at the lamb.

"Yes, like the baby in Hannah's tummy, Samuel," Max said, and glanced up at Hannah.

Sammy screwed up his pudgy little face in question. "Out?"

Max glanced at Hannah and at her belly. "Soon, son. Soon."

For five days the ewes' parturition kept everyone busy, and did not give Hannah a chance to ponder over Max's lingering anger over her presence. In his playful and teasing manner, Petya directed André and Franc's efforts with great success. Lissa took over Sammy's care so Hannah could help Max, while Bernard moved the rest of the band forward.

It was an exhausting five days, and shortly after most of the ewes had lambed and they had caught up with the rest of the band, everyone except Max and Bernard had fallen into bed exhausted right after dark.

Bernard was out on the night watch with the ewes while Max sat staring into the dying flames, when Hannah awoke and noticed he had not turned in yet. She stole from her bed and joined him, feeding the fire a handful of sage. It filled the cool night air with a spicy aroma and spicy thoughts.

"We haven't had a chance to talk," she said.

"No."

"You're magnificent with the ewes. I've never seen anything like it. Helping the animals give birth is an incredible experience."

"Do not think it is not work. You work very hard, Hannah."

"She works hard like the Basque wife, eh, big brother?" Petya cut in from his bedroll.

Max shot his brother a frown dark enough to freeze the night and rose, but his thinking already had been concentrated along that same vein. "We go to bed now maybe. The band must keep moving. It is time for shearing soon."

Hannah was disappointed that they had been interrupted. There were so many things left unsaid, and time was running out. The weather had turned warm, the snow in the pass would be melting, and Max's bride was probably on her way.

Max offered his hand when Hannah struggled to get to her feet. Silently his fingers lingered on hers. Rough against smooth. Warm against cool.

"Good night, Max," she said finally, and headed for bed.

"Hannah?"

She took a deep breath and swung around. "Yes?"

"Tomorrow you go to the Herrias."

Hannah did not respond, she could not, she was so disheartened. She had hoped that all her hard work would have made him realize that she could help, that he would want her at his side. He was still sending her away. She had waited too long to unburden her secrets, and now he was sending her away.

Hannah climbed into bed and shut her eyes, but she did not sleep.

About an hour after she had laid her head on the rolled blanket, she had the first contraction.

Thirty

Exhausted, Hannah had slept soundly after the pains ebbed, and she'd had time to think. The baby wasn't due for weeks. No doubt the pains were just twinges warning that her time was nearing.

Shortly after she and Max had waved good-bye to the others, who went on ahead with the sheep band, Hannah experienced another stronger spasm.

"I will take you to the Herrias as soon as I pack the wagon."

"I don't think so," she said, breathing hard.

Max swung on his heel, his brows drawing together in question at the unnatural expression on her face. "Hannah?"

"I'm glad you've had recent experience at delivering babies, because I think I am about to become a mother."

It was a curious comment, since she already had Franc. But when another pain caused Hannah to double over with a moan, her remark dropped from Max's mind and one of his biggest fears became reality.

Hannah was about to give birth out on the range, in the middle of nowhere with no one but him available should complications arise.

Max scooped Hannah into his arms and purposely strode to the wagon. "You must help me put you in the wagon bed."

"Help you?" she panted as the pains grew stronger. "I'm not sure I'm going to be able to help myself this time."

"Do not worry. Did I not help deliver over two hundred lambs maybe the last few days?"

She forced a smile while she half slid, half crawled until she was lying in the wagon bed. "If only I were a ewe."

"Hannah, I wish you are me."

"You're making light. But this time it's not particularly funny," she gasped as another spasm gripped her.

"Hannah"—he unfolded two blankets and positioned them around her—"I do not try to make light. I wish I could take the pain for you."

"Ohhhh," she moaned at the intensity of the pain. "Right now I wish you could too." She reached out to him, her fingers splayed. "Max?"

"Yes?"

"Hold my hand."

Max closed his big hand around her small one, which seemingly disappeared within his. She was so fragile, so vulnerable, so dependent. "Do not worry. I am here. Together you and I will birth a baby, yes?"

"But the baby's early. It isn't due yet."

"The baby does not have a calendar. Babies come when they are ready."

She nodded but did not speak. Max could see in her face that she was valiantly trying to hold another pain in before it finally let go of her and her breathing returned to normal.

"Hannah, I must go add wood to the fire to boil the water we need."

"No. Don't leave me."

"I will be nearby if you need me." He got out of the wagon and quickly set about readying everything he could think of that they might require.

"Max? I need you . . . now. Now!"

Max rushed to her side and took her hand, but he had never felt so utterly helpless, so utterly useless in his entire life. He could not even send someone for help.

All day bitter memories haunted him and fear circled him. He hovered over Hannah, mopping her brow, holding her hand, and loosening her clothes.

In an attempt to alleviate her own fears, she said, "Here I am, about to have a baby, and you are trying to separate me from my clothing."

Max forced a smile, although he did not feel like smiling. Rather, he considered making a deal with the devil himself if it would ensure Hannah a safe and healthy delivery. "I am keeping in practice for the future, yes?"

"Max, about the future. There're things I must tell you. I—"

A pain clasped her in its viselike grip with such overpowering intensity that she screamed. Not five minutes later, after one pain had hardly abated, another excruciating wave squeezed her.

"I think the baby comes soon maybe," Max said.

On the outside he appeared calm, efficiently seeing to Hannah's care with the skill of a doctor. On the inside he experienced every spasm right along with her.

All day and far into the night Hannah labored, but the baby's head still had not appeared. Hannah was exhausted and weak, drained from the exertion, her hair drenched.

"I don't think it wants to be born," she said in a small, fading voice, and tried to smile as the night sky began to give way to the dawn of another day.

"It is stubborn like its mama." He grinned at her, but secretly he worried.

"Max, I'm scared," she blurted out, unable to keep up a brave front any longer. "Something's wrong. It should've—"

In the next moment she screamed and pushed for all she was worth.

Nothing.

"It isn't coming."

Max then recognized the danger signals. It was the same for the ewes he had helped days before. The baby was breech. If he didn't do something, he could lose her.

At that moment Max realized that he never wanted to lose this woman.

He looked skyward, then squeezed his eyes shut, every muscle in his body tense, and he prayed for the first time since he had become a widower.

"Max, please!"

Her cries spurred him into action. If it were within his power, he would not fail her.

"Hannah, I must turn the baby inside you. Remember how I helped the ewes?"

"My God," she cried, and fought to keep from panicking.

"You are a woman about to hold a baby, but you must help me." He spoke softly, soothing words of encouragement while he washed his hands and kept repeating to himself that this was just like what he had been doing for years with the ewes. But in truth it wasn't. This was the woman he loved. He could not lose this woman.

His hands shaking, he fought to shut his ears to her screams as he managed to reach in and turn the baby. "Now you must push, Hannah. Push!"

Panting and gulping for air, Hannah struggled to follow Max's instructions.

"It comes!" he trumpeted at the first sign of the head.

Hannah was crying and laughing at the same time when Max finally placed her newborn infant son in her arms. She blinked back tears, gazing at the most perfect child in the world.

"He's so beautiful. Thank you, Max."

Max nodded and gave her a warm smile. "What will you call him?"

Hannah considered the baby for a moment before the perfect name came to her. "I think that I am going to name him Range for the place of his birth."

"Range," he tried the name out. "I think that it is most fitting."

"Hello, my little Range. Your mommy loves you very much." She glanced up at Max with tears in her eyes. "He is so perfect," she said before her lids grew heavy and she drifted off to an exhausted sleep, the baby in her arms.

"So is his mama," Max murmured, and went to perch on a nearby rock. He had just experienced, firsthand, the joy of birth with this woman he loved.

He had been forced to face his worst fear, and had overcome it. Mama and baby were doing well. Then it hit him. This time perhaps it was mere luck. Max gazed at his hands before he dropped his head into them. He could have lost Hannah too.

"But you did not lose her," a soft female voice said in a whisper.

Max's gaze shot up.

Before him stood the wavering, transparent manifestation of his deceased wife, dressed in her black burial attire.

"Mary?"

"You have the look of surprise. You forget that the spirits of our people return to those if a desire or vow, it is not fulfilled. Do you forget my desire for you, Maximilian?"

Max did not respond at first. He was depleted and hadn't slept for nearly forty-eight hours. He was merely imagining it; it was an illusion. "My mind plays tricks on me."

"No, it does not. So soon you forget my last wish, Maximilian. My desire for you that you do not live your life alone without again knowing love. Now I may go to my rest and leave you in peace, for you are no longer alone."

It was too fantastic. Max blinked and rubbed his eyes. But when he looked up again, the apparition was gone. His mind filled with a mixture of thoughts and feelings, his eyes trailed to Hannah. The baby had begun to stir.

Max went over and picked up the baby. He returned to the rock and held the small bundle to him. Against the odds, he had helped bring the tiny life into the world, and just now he had come to realize that it was time to accept and put behind him as final his past life.

He had faced and overcome his worst fears. And it was time to look toward the future and make a new life.

"Max?"

He strode over to Hannah and handed her the baby. "So, finally you awaken."

"Oh, Max, thank you."

"You do not need to thank me."

"I couldn't have done it alone. You should've been a doctor, you were so magnificent."

"A sheepherder is what I am and what makes me happy. Could it make you happy?"

Was he about to ask her to marry him?

"It could make me very happy," she said through trembling lips. She waited, almost afraid to breathe for fear that she was dreaming until the baby started to fuss and she set him to her breast. "I still can't believe I've actually become a mother."

Her comment shifted his thoughts and brought to mind a remark she had made the day before. He cocked his brow. "Hannah, what of Franc?"

She raised her eyes to his. The love in his face had been replaced by an intense stare she tried to define. The realization of what she'd unthinkingly blurted out and Max's response to it suddenly hit her.

She had been caught in another lie. He may have just been about to ask her to marry him, and she had been caught in another lie.

"Max . . . Franc . . . she—"

"Franc is not your daughter?"

Another moment of truth. But why now? She had not wanted him to discover another of her falsehoods like this. Not now.

"Hannah, you do not answer because maybe it is the truth, yes?"

All her joy of a moment ago, the overwhelming happiness that she had been responsible for creating this precious life, suddenly became muted and a dark veil dropped over her bliss.

With a defeated sigh of regret for all the lies she had been forced to tell, she answered, "Yes."

There was a troubled light that flickered into his eyes which stabbed at her heart. Maximilian Garat was everything that Emmett had not been, never could be. All the years she had been married to a man she did not love, she had told only one major lie—she glanced down at her precious baby—and now here she was, desperately in love with a man to whom she had been anything but honest.

Misgivings over how he would react circled around her like carrion eaters. "Max, I—"

"What other lies did you tell, Hannah?"

Thirty-one

You make your bed, you lie in it.

Hannah stared up at Max, her mind whirling. She had just been given one of life's greatest gifts, but she was about to lose another. Over and over in her mind she had attempted to formulate the best way to tell Max the truth. The Basques prized honesty, and the most expeditious time to be honest never seemed to have materialized. Now it was no longer her choice.

"How many other stories did you tell, Hannah?" he prodded when she did not immediately answer. "This time the whole truth, yes?"

You make your bed, you lie in it.

Her shoulders slumped and she looked away. She could not stand the thought of seeing disgust or disappointment or even hatred enter his eyes.

"I never meant to lie to you. Truly I didn't. It's just that shortly after I met Franc on the train she stole all my money and lost it. Then after Franc and I got off the train she stole that loaf of bread in the station because she was hungry. You caught her, and then we were standing on the train platform and the sewing machine was accidentally unloaded—"

"The sewing machine does not belong to you? You took this machine?"

"I didn't mean to take it," she cried, her voice catching. "I had no money, I was pregnant, and had nowhere to go. I tried to obtain gainful employment, but no one would hire me."

"You did not write those letters to me?"

She closed her eyes and took a breath before she forced herself to look at him. "No. But I never meant to deceive you. One thing just seemed to lead to another, and the next thing I knew I was at your ranch and Franc was my daughter."

"And your son's papa?"

"Range's father?" she repeated, frantically trying to forestall the inevitable. Max would never understand about Emmett.

"You did marry him?"

"Y-yes."

There was something about her answer that made Max suspicious. A part of him did not want to know. Another part of him, the traditional Basque that severely condemned adultery, made him ask, "You are a widow, Hannah?"

"I . . ." Her voice quivered and failed her. She could not force the words from her lips that would destroy her life.

Her mother's voice screamed *You make your bed, you lie in it* in her ears.

"Did you divorce him, Hannah?"

She slapped fingers to her mouth to hold back a sob.

"Hannah, you did not divorce this man?"

She hung her head. "N-no."

"You are a married woman with a husband?" he questioned, incredulous.

"Yes—no. I mean, I—I don't have a husband, but I—I didn't divorce him. There wasn't time." At his disbelieving expression, she blurted out, "I ran away." He spun away from her, and she cried out, "Max, please, listen. Please. You must."

When he kept going, Hannah knew she had to do something, and fast, before she totally lost this man.

"Max, the doctor had just told me I was pregnant, and my husband tried to strike me the night I ran. I had nowhere to go, so I just ran. He yelled that he would divorce me. He has always carried out his threats. Whether in the eyes of the law or Lord, my marriage was over." Speaking out loud of that night brought back all the terrifying images she had lived with, and she began sobbing uncontrollably despite a vow not to.

Max, too, was reeling. He was furious enough to use his bare hands to kill the man who would do such a thing to Hannah. And he was furious with Hannah for not telling him the truth. And as a Basque whose people believed in the holy sanctity of marriage, he needed time to think, time to consider and sort out everything that she had just told him.

His feelings tied in knots, Max stopped, pivoted around, and returned to her. He dropped a comforting hand on her shoulder. "Hannah, there is more?"

She shook her head, determined to calm down for the baby's sake. She lifted her eyes to him. "No. Isn't that enough?"

What she longed to ask was what her confession meant to them. What she said more calmly was "You know everything now. I never meant to deceive you. Never. Max, I'm sorry."

"I know, Hannah."

"Can you ever forgive me? At least yell or scream at me, but talk it over with me."

"I think today we do not talk any more of this. Today you are a mother. You need to care for your son."

He had not totally spurned her, and there was no disgust in his face. A glimmer of hope which refused to relinquish its light flickered in the corner of her heavy heart. "And tomorrow?"

"Tomorrow we go to the shearing. I must help my family."

Hannah weakly nodded. But inside she questioned whether she would be given a second chance or whether he could ever forgive her.

They drove into the shearing camp and everyone crowded around Hannah to fuss over the new baby. Max hovered nearby like the proud papa, and Hannah thought that perhaps he could forgive and forget. In front of the others, he treated her as if nothing had happened, but there was a part of him that had withdrawn from her. A part of him that was no longer available to her, that she could no longer reach. Keeping up a brave front, Hannah remained in her comfortable bed in the wagon, lying on a sheep fleece, while Max set to work.

Hannah sat, propped up in the wagon, nursing Range, and watched Max work with a vengeance, sharpening his hand shears on the hootenanny, dragging the sheep between his knees, and separating them from their fleeces in under five minutes.

"One would think you work off frustrations the way you toil, my son," Bernard observed while he handed a fleece Max had clipped over to André to be sorted, scoured, washed, and dried.

"I work to finish a job."

Bernard stared at his son in question but held his tongue as Max drove everyone in camp to finish the shearing in record time. The old man was so concerned about his son that he made the decision to visit the Herrias and enlist the aid of their sons to herd the sheep as they moved them up the mountain to summer camp so he could return to the ranch and be of help to his son if he should need it.

The children had begged to remain out on the range with the sheep for a few more weeks, so

Hannah and Max returned to the ranch in silence. Hannah had waited for Max to broach the subject she knew was on his mind as well as hers, but Max kept his silence until they neared the ranch house.

"Hannah, I think about these things you did for days. I mull them over and over in my mind. I try to make excuses for these things you did. But I do not know if I can."

Trepidation tore at her heart. Her lies had created a schism in their relationship that could not be mended. He was going to send her away. She attempted to resign herself to her fate.

As if fate had stepped in to deal Hannah another blow, when they drove into the yard the couple Hannah recognized as the contract station owner and his wife were just leaving.

They exchanged pleasantries and Max listened while Pierre explained that they'd had time to be away from the station restaurant, since the train had not been running. Max invited the couple to remain and visit, but they awkwardly explained that the train would be back on schedule soon and they had to get back.

Almost as if on cue, a pretty, dark-haired woman with an hour-glass figure and china-white skin stepped from the house.

"Max, we brought Monique out just as soon as we knew the pass was open," Pierre said while his wife's curious eyes sifted between Hannah and Monique. When Hannah shifted in her seat,

Marie noticed the baby in her arms. Marie's troubled gaze shot to Max in question.

"I don't rightly understand. I see one man before me, two women, and one baby," Marie said in true confusion. "I just don't understand this at all. Did you send for both of them?"

Pierre immediately pulled Marie close to him, cutting off further comment. "I think my friend does not need our help." Then to Max he said, "We must leave now." A grin slipped by Pierre despite his efforts to hide what he knew was Max's predicament. "You will invite us to your wedding when and if you decide who it is you will marry, yes?"

"Hannah, your baby—" Marie began.

"Not now, Marie," Pierre warned, quickly said farewell, and spurred his horse toward the south.

From Max's expression, Hannah did not think that he was expecting Monique's arrival. The children had indeed heeded Petya's advice to hold their tongues about the Basque bride.

"Maximilian, I shall be inside the house when you have seen to the animals." Monique's eyes lowered shyly for a moment before she raised them to Max, ignoring Hannah. "I have had a hot meal ready each day I have been here in preparation for your return, although I have been here only two days." Her dark eyes were bright with guileless innocence. "Your uncle Laborde said I should like America and already I do. Maximilian, I will try to make a good wife."

Max's jaw tightened and Hannah noticed his knuckles stand up white where he gripped the reins. "So, Monique, you come here to be a wife."

"Your wife, Maximilian." She smiled sweetly, ignoring his astonished expression. "I am eager to show you how good I cook and sew."

"We do not talk of this now," Max said.

"Of course." Monique's eyes shifted to Hannah.

"Now I put the horses in the barn," Max said. "Hannah, you must rest."

"Hannah, is it? Allow me to help you with your baby." Monique settled adoring eyes on Max before she said, "I love babies," not bothering to question Hannah further.

Hannah reluctantly handed Range to Monique and climbed from the wagon. But she did not follow Monique into the house. Rather, Hannah stood on the porch and stared after Max.

Hannah closed her eyes and leaned against the porch railing. She smoothed her mussed hair back, thinking of Monique's perfection. This had to be the worst time possible for the perfectly coiffed woman to arrive and announce not only that her presence was sanctioned by Max's family, but that she could cook and sew as well. Now all Hannah needed to hear was that the woman was an expert at churning butter and spinning wool into yarn.

At the supper table less than a hour later,

Monique set her fork down and smiled, wide-eyed, at Max. "I noticed the butter crock was broken, so at first light tomorrow I plan to churn fresh butter. I do hope you will not be upset with me, but while I was washing your socks I noticed that they were worn. If that was a fleece I saw in the back of your wagon, I will spin yarn so I can knit you new socks."

Hannah felt suddenly ill. Monique was the picture of domestic efficiency, everything Hannah was not. But the final straw came when Monique examined Hannah's *kaiku* and announced her intention to replace it with her own.

Hannah excused herself, checked on Range, who had been put down in Sammy's bed, and went out onto the porch. She gazed up at the darkening sky. The stars were just beginning to dot the sky with twinkling diamonds, but she did not take delight in nature's beauty.

Max had not attempted to so much as try to discourage the woman, nor had he questioned her about her presence or her announcement that she was there to be his bride. Maybe he had known about the woman all along after all, or perhaps he was so bitter, he was distancing himself and his life from hers.

Hannah was thinking about Marie and Pierre's hasty departure, when Max joined her on the porch. "You are still a new mother. You need your rest. You use the bed in the bedroom tonight."

"And I suppose you should be with Monique."

"He is," Monique said from behind him, glided to his side, and linked her arm with his.

Hannah's gaze shot to Max, but he had turned away from her and was facing Monique. At a loss of how to reach Max, Hannah went inside and slipped into bed.

She tried to ignore his scent that clung to the pillow and the bittersweet memories that lay next to her, where Max had lain.

She struggled to block out thoughts of Max with Monique. But tears welled in her eyes and she hid her face in her pillow to muffle the sounds of her weeping, even as those prophesizing words *you make your bed, you lie in it* assaulted her.

Thirty-two

Max only half listened to Monique prattle on about all she wanted to do to his house to make it a real home, the clothes she planned stitch, the blood sausages and cheese she would make, the children she would give him.

All the things she said did no more than bring to mind visions of Hannah and how she had valiantly grappled with the sewing machine to turn out that hideous outfit for Samuel, stayed in the kitchen while he had made sausage, and cried out his name while he helped deliver her baby.

Finally, he could stand no more of Monique's uninvited plans.

"Monique," he interrupted. "Do not make plans. I am not looking for a wife. How is it that my uncle sends you here to me?"

Her face lost its glow of adoration and her jaw thrust out. "Your own papa wrote to your Uncle Laborde. Arrangements were made and agreed upon. My family is paying your family a very handsome dowry. Your Uncle Laborde has assured everyone that you are a man of tradition and honor and will respect the contract our families made on our behalf."

Max watched the sweetness and light return to her face as if she had iron control over her smile. "My family and I expect that regardless of the circumstances, whether you were aware of your papa's request or not, you will honor this arrangement. Good night, Maximilian."

Max had anything but a good night. He settled on the bed of straw in the kitchen while the two women claimed the beds. But he did not sleep. For two years he had lived without a woman, and now two women slept under his roof.

Monique was bedded down in Lissa's bed and Hannah lay between his sheets. One fully intended to become his bride according to tradition and honor. The other had lied and broken all the rules and tenets by which he had lived his life, the one he should scorn and send away.

But Hannah was the one he could not banish from his mind.

"You must banish Hannah from your mind, Bernard insisted to his son.

"I think you meddle too much this time, old man."

"I do no more than any papa who loves his son does. And you do no more than your Basque heritage expects."

"Enough," Max spat out, and turned away

from his father to chopping wood for the kitchen fire. He was too angry at his father for doing such a thing as sending for a bride without consulting him to speak of it further without losing his temper.

"Max—"

"I hear no more! Go back to the sheep before you are no longer welcome in my house."

Bernard sighed at his son's virulent refusal not only to discuss Monique, but the demands that he leave. He wanted only his son's happiness. Now his own flesh and blood refused to talk to him and did not want him near.

He ran gnarled fingers through his white hair and trudged back to the house to prepare to leave, mulling and troubling over everything that had happened since his arrival.

Bernard had waited until the Herria boys had arrived on the range, then hurried back to the ranch. He had walked up to the house to find Hannah and a picture-perfect, dark-haired woman on the porch. Hannah was quietly watching while the woman worked a distaff to make yarn.

Bernard knew instantly that the unknown woman was sent by his brother, and he could not believe the luck that such a gorgeous woman was attaching the tuffs to the distaff, drawing them from the rod, and forming them into a string by twisting them with expert fingers. She would make Max the perfect wife.

"Hello, Hannah. Who do we have here?" Bernard questioned the two women.

"Monique Lhande, sir. My papa is Arnaud Lhande and owns many sheep." She gave him a dazzling smile. "And you must be Mr. Garat. Your brother, Laborde, tells the whole village all about you."

Bernard vaguely recalled the Lhandes and their many strong sons, but he did not remember the woman. But of course he had been away for over two years. "I know of your family and your brothers."

She shyly smiled. "This union between Maximilian and me will be good for both our families."

It was then that Bernard caught sight of Hannah's sadness. He liked Hannah. But Monique was Basque and it was tradition to continue the pure Basque bloodlines. After a few more minutes of conversation, Bernard was under Monique's spell and went in search of his son to accept the accolades he expected would greet him.

But now, as he trudged the last few steps to the kitchen door, Bernard considered the anger in his son's heart when he had attempted to discuss Monique. It left Bernard disheartened and questioning what he thought would bring happiness back into his son's heavy spirit.

* * *

Hannah's spirit ebbed with the heaviness which weighed it down, and it seemed to have a pronounced effect on her baby. Range did not sleep well and he fussed, often refusing her milk and her efforts to comfort him. But then, she could not expect her child to be happy and well adjusted if his mother was so miserable.

For nearly two weeks Max refused her attempts to speak to him alone, although she had noted his beret pulled low over his forehead. He was polite, and even attentive to Range, but there was a coldness about him, a distance that continued to leave her in tears each night while Monique regally sat in the parlor with Max.

But what Hannah did not know in her bed of misery was that Max did not sit enjoying Monique's company night after night. He also slept in a bed of misery. Although Monique put up a brave front, she was anything but happy either. Yet unlike Hannah and Maximilian, she had no intention of continuing to sleep in a bed of misery.

Monique had eyes. She could see the pair sneak looks at the other when no one was thought to see. Well, whatever the feelings they had for each other did not matter to Monique. She intended to do whatever it took to tie Maximilian to her. He and his family owed it to her, and she would not be forced to return to her village in the old country in shame, as she had left.

"Maximilian," she whispered, and kneeled

down next to his bed, placing a feathery touch on his bare shoulder. He was so strong, his muscles so tense. "Maximilian, are you awake?"

Max had been staring at the ceiling for another night, and now he turned his head to face the woman. "What is it you need, Monique?"

"Maximilian, I come to you to ask that very same question."

"Go to bed, Monique." In the bright moonlight he could see the flimsy nightgown she wore, which was meant to destroy a man's resistance. Not one of her charms was hidden from his eyes. Any normal man would have trouble ignoring her luscious body, which beckoned him. Although there was no denying her beauty, her blatant offering only annoyed Max, and secretly he thought how he much preferred the curves of Hannah's body.

"I told you to go to bed," he repeated more forcefully when she made no move to leave.

"I plan to," she murmured, and reached out to stroke his stubbled cheek.

He grabbed her wrist. "You come here without my consent. I did not encourage you."

She would not be put off easily. "You are a man with a man's needs. I am the woman who will meet those needs in our marriage bed. I want you to know the very good care I will take of you, Maximilian. You will want for nothing . . . nothing."

She leaned forward before he could stop her

nd brushed her heavy breasts against his chest
ust as Hannah, who could not tolerate another
night of silently suffering, entered the room.

Almost simultaneously as Hannah gasped in
horror, Max shoved Monique back.

"Hannah," he called out. But she had already
urned and fled.

Max turned furious eyes on Monique, who sat
n a heap, straightening her hair back into place.
"Monique, go to bed!"

"What is the matter? She knows that you and
 are going to be wed. I have told her," she said
ndignantly.

Max had been fighting an inner battle between
his beliefs and heritage and his love for Hannah
and what she had done. But seeing Hannah's immense hurt and suffering was too much for him.

He grabbed Monique by the shoulders. "You
listen to me. I did not encourage you."

"You did not discourage me either," she cried.

"I told you not to make plans. You did not
listen when I told you. I am respectful to you,
nothing more, until I arrange for you to return
o your home."

"I made plans!"

"I am sorry you did not listen."

"Well, I am listening now," she practically
creamed at him.

"Monique, I told you I did not ask for a wife.
This my papa did on his own—"

"But you are a widower with children. You

need a wife. You are Basque and I am Basque. Hannah is an outsider, an interloper. She—"

"No more! She is the woman I love! And if we mend our problems, she is the woman I will marry," he roared. "Now, leave my sight."

Monique shot to her feet, ignoring the fact that she stood before him without covering herself. She wanted him to see exactly what he was so foolish to be giving up. "Your papa will not stand for this!"

"My papa interferes no more in my life. Go before I am not responsible for what I do to you."

Her face flaming with hatred, Monique jutted out her chin. "When you come to your senses, you will not marry a woman like her. And when you crawl back to me, you will have much to atone for."

He got to his feet in a threatening manner and she screamed and ran off.

Once he was left alone in the kitchen, Max sank back onto the bed and dropped his head in his hands. For the first time in weeks he realized that he had finally come to his senses. He loved Hannah with all his heart, and although he was a very deliberate man, it had taken another woman to make him realize that Hannah mattered more to him than anything she had done in the past.

His mind made up, Max decided not to wait until morning to go to Hannah. He got to his

feet and padded through the parlor to his bedroom door.

But when he entered the room he did not find
Hannah.

Monique was alone in the dimly lit room, sit-
ing on his bed, waiting for him with a smug grin
on her face.

Thirty-three

"She and that baby of hers are gone," Monique said smugly of Hannah.

"What did you say to Hannah?" Max demanded, fighting to keep himself from strangling the complacent look from Monique's face.

"You can quit glaring at me like that. I did not do or say anything to your precious Hannah. I ran in here after you were so mean to me, and she was already gone."

She gave him a superior, self-satisfied smile. "I merely waited here on your bed to see the expression on your face. I must say it is most gratifying," she called to his back as he rushed from the house.

Max ran through the night and into the barn. There was nowhere else for Hannah to go, and as he searched the stalls, he expected to find her.

Only the family goat kept in the stable as a Basque preservative against evil spirits stamped the ground in acknowledgment of his presence.

Hannah was nowhere to be found.

He quickly saddled one of the horses while he

frantically tried to figure out where she would go in her state of mind.

Visions of her threatening to walk back to the train station in her lavender satin slippers if he did not allow her little dog to remain at her side rose before him. Panda Pie had remained with Franc at camp. He figured that she would not leave without her dog.

Max lit out from the ranch as if a *sorginak*, a witch, were chasing him. He kept watching for her as he rode, but by the time he rode into camp, Hannah was still missing.

"Do you run from female trouble back at your ranch, big brother?" Petya chuckled. He was privy to the would-be bride residing at the ranch, although his papa had clamped his lips together and would say no more than that.

"Hannah, she is here?"

The urgent tone in Max's voice caused Petya to lose his smile. "Hannah?"

"If she is here and you do not tell me, I—"

Concern replaced Petya's flamboyance. "She is not here. Why is it you ask?"

"Hannah is missing. I must find her." Max swung his horse around, but Petya grabbed the reins.

"Wait, Max. I come with you."

Not more than ten minutes later, the two men rode from the camp. Max had quietly explained things to his father so as not to disturb the children, and told the old man to keep a watch for Hannah in case she showed up at camp.

Bernard watched his sons' backs, despairing his meddling. He crossed himself and swore on the holy crucifix around his neck that if Hannah and her baby were found safe, he would welcome her with open arms and then return to the old country to face the wrath of Monique's family. And he wound never again interfere in his sons' lives

Max and Petya had not gone far when Max reined in his horse and suggested that they split up. "We cover more ground that way."

"Max, is there anywhere else you think that Hannah may go?"

Max thought to mention her threat to walk to the train since the pass was clear now. But then a more likely place came to him. "The Herrias There is nowhere else she goes at this hour."

"What do we sit here for, eh? We meet back at the ranch." Petya set his heel to his animal Max was not far behind for long. Shortly, he took the lead before Petya veered off toward the south and Max drove his horse west through the night fearing the worst could come to Hannah before he located her.

And fearing the worst—that she would refuse to return to the ranch with him—when he did finally find her.

Exhausted and nearing dawn, Max sighted her nearing the Herrias house.

He shouted, "Hannah?"

Hannah swung around and waited. Max reached her and jumped from his horse. He immediately stripped off his jacket and put it over her shoulders. "Hannah, you are shivering."

"I bundled Range up in my jacket when it started to get cold."

"You teach him to appreciate young a sheep's coat, yes?" he said rather than chastising her for foolishly taking her baby and running from a safe house.

She stared up at his face, which was illuminated by the graying sky. "Are you making light, Maximilian Garat?"

He gave her a half-smile. "Do I make light?"

He thought his remark would ease the tension between them so they could try to work out their problems without the incident with Monique that precipitated Hannah's flight standing in their way.

It was not to be.

"Max, why did you follow me?"

Her tone was accusatory rather than filled with relief that he had spent the night frantically searching over half the desert for her. "Give Range to me and climb up on the horse. I will hand him up to you, and I take you back to the ranch."

"No. I won't go back there."

His lips tightened. "I will take you to the Herias, then."

She lifted her chin ever so slightly which warned Max that he was not going to like what

she had to say. "What makes you think I'm going
to go anywhere with you?"

"I will not leave you out here."

"You do not have any say in it," she shot back.
"Why don't you go back to your mail-order bride
who's waiting for you dressed in . . . in practically nothing! It must have pained you"—she
briefly glanced at the potent male portion of
him—"to leave her when you two were so . . . so
occupied. I'm surprised you even knew I was
gone."

"You are jealous."

"I am not! You've made it plain by your actions
that you could not accept what I did." She knew
she was sounding affronted, but she did not care.
"Your precious Monique is Basque, which should
fill *your man's needs*"—she mimicked Monique's
sugary pronunciation—"as well as any other needs
you may have."

"I have no needs for Monique. I already told
her so when she came to me in bed with an invitation," he said evenly, trying to keep his temper in check under her refusal to be reasonable.
"Now, get on the horse."

"You don't listen, do you? I'm not going anywhere with you."

Her words brought to mind what he had accused Monique of earlier that night. "I listen,
Hannah. I listen to your lies. But I am only human. I am just a man. Do you expect me only
to ignore what you did without searching my

eart when I finally hear the truth of these
hings? I cannot make excuses for you."

"You what?" she shot back, a gate to her heart
napping shut under the weight of judgment. She
vas exhausted from waiting for him to forgive
er, and she was no longer going to prostrate
erself because of what she'd had to do to sur-
ive.

"You can't make excuses for me? Well, I'll have
ou know I don't need anyone to make excuses
or me. I should have been honest with you. Yes.
should have told you. Yes. I shouldn't have lied.
But I had no other choice at the time. And if I
vere in that same position again, I'd do it all
ver if I had to protect my child." She stood in
ront of him, trembling, glaring at him, challeng-
ng him to argue against motherhood and the in-
redible overwhelming sacrifices sometimes
equired of a mother.

"Hannah, come back to the ranch with me,"
he said softly, the anger having left him at the
udden realization of how his own family had
een shattered by the lengths his deceased wife,
. mother, had gone to birth her child. "We can-
ot settle this out here."

Her shoulders slumped then. "Max, we cannot
ettle this back at your ranch either. I did what
had to do at the time."

At that she started to walk around him toward
he Herrias.

"My God, Hannah," he said, and threw his

arms around her and the baby. "I try to tell yo
I love you. I cannot make excuses, but I work t
understand and accept. Do not go from me, Han
nah."

His open acknowledgement of love and willing
ness to try to understand and accept caused th
gate to reopen in her heart. She leaned into him
"Oh, Max . . . Max . . . I was so afraid . . . s
afraid you could never forgive me," she cried a
last.

At that Max did something he had not don
since he was a child: He too broke down and
sobbed.

"I forgive you, Hannah. Do you forgive me?"
She pulled back and stroked his face. "Max
your culture? Your heritage? Your family? I am
not Basque."

"Basque and American are the same, do you
remember when I said this, yes?" She nodded
She did indeed remember their first Christmas
"We will begin an American Basque family, and
we will leave our children a heritage to be proud
of, yes?" Again she nodded. "We live in the pres
ent and look forward maybe to the future, no
longer will we look at the past, yes?" Another
nod. "Then we decide maybe that we marry
yes?"

This time she did not nod. She looked away
causing Max to lift her chin so he could gaze
into her troubled eyes.

"Hannah?" Tears swelled in her eyes, making

them as green as the valley floor near his boyhood village on a misty spring morning. "This
does not make you happy?"

"Oh, Max, it would make me happier than anything in the world, except . . ."

"Except?"

"I can't plan to marry until I am sure I am
free to be your wife in every sense of the word."

"You say you will marry me if you are free?"
he questioned, needing to hear her voice the
words.

"Oh, yes, Max. Yes."

"Then we return to the ranch and I will go to
visit a Basque friend who practices the law. He
will make sure you are a free woman and will
take care of everything maybe, yes?"

"But what of your church?"

"The priest is a practical man."

She smiled at him, praying it was true.

He hugged her and the baby before his lips
found hers in a kiss meant to seal a pledge, a
kiss that promised a future filled with love and
devotion, and nights full of passion.

When the baby began to fuss, they finally came
up for air, and he suggested, "We go home now,
yes?"

"Yes."

By the time they returned to the ranch,
Monique was dressed and sitting in the parlor.

...nnah took Range into the bedroom to care for ...im and rest after the exhausting night, giving Max time to face Monique.

"We will take you to the train when you are ready," Max announced.

"Just like that? You simply expect me to disappear now that you return with that woman and her baby? You need time, Maximilian. Last night we were upset and said things. In time you will realize that I will make the best wife for you."

"I listen to no more of this," Max stated flatly, clenching his fists.

"What is it you listen to no more of, big brother?" Petya questioned as he walked through the kitchen to the parlor. He caught sight of Monique and came up short.

Monique's mouth tightened, her lips flattened into a thin, straight line, and her jaw jutted out.

Petya ignored her and asked Max, "You are here, so you find Hannah and the baby, eh?"

"They are well and are resting."

"Thank God for that." It was then that Petya swung his attention to Monique. The devil's curious gleam flickered into his eyes. "Do not tell me that you are the bride-to-be that Papa tells me he must face the family over?"

"And what if I am?"

"What is this all about?" Max questioned, not comprehending the strange exchange. "Petya, you know this woman?"

Petya looked to Monique. "Do you tell my brother or do I?"

"I—" Monique began.

"I come as soon as the Herria boys, they agree to stay longer at camp to watch over the children and sheep," Bernard said, rushing into the parlor. "Hannah, she is found?"

"She rests in the bedroom."

"Her baby?"

"Sleeping."

"Thank the Lord," Bernard said, relieved. Then he observed Monique's stiff, angry stance, Petya's smirk, and the impatient questioning filling Max's face.

"What goes on here?"

Thirty-four

"What goes on here between Petya and Monique, this is what I, too, wait to hear," Max said to his father.

All eyes turned to Monique. "It is all nothing but a pack of lies," she hissed, and crossed her arms over her chest. "Well, do not continue to stare at me."

"Monique"—Petya gave a guilty shrug—"is the reason I found it necessary to depart our village with such haste, if you know what it is I mean." He winked.

"Damn you, Petya Garat, why did you have to be here?" Monique sneered. "No one knew where you went."

Bernard raised his brows. "She is the one you—"

"Yes," Monique practically screamed. "I am the one he"— she pointed an accusing finger at Petya—"deflowered on my very own wedding day after you had already left for America!"

The shocked expressions on the other's faces did not faze Petya. He grinned and flashed his brows. "Do not look at me with such judgment.

I do not have to force this woman." Then Monique he said, "You make me tell them. You were not the innocent bride, if I remember our time together right, eh?"

"I do not understand why Laborde sends you here if this is what happens in my village," Bernard said to Monique.

"Laborde did not send you maybe?" Max stepped forward and questioned, suspicious of the woman's motives.

Monique dropped balled fists on her hips. There was no use trying to brazen it out any longer. "All right, no, Laborde did not send me. And Petya was not the first. But Petya destroyed my life, and when my family heard that Laborde was searching for a bride for Maximilian, they sent me."

"Revenge," Bernard mouthed.

"Your family, Bernard, owes me for what Petya did. Maximilian must marry me and restore my good name."

"What about me?" Petya asked, feigning pique. "You do not ask me to be the sacrificial lamb on the altar of matrimony?"

"Be quiet for once, Petya," Max grated. "We must figure this out."

"There is nothing to figure out," Bernard stated flatly, reclaiming the position he had vacated as the *etcheko jauna,* the eldest and patriarchal head of his family. "Monique does not marry either of my sons." To Monique he said with

.hority, "I am responsible for you coming here, ɔ I take you back to your village, where you belong."

"No, I do not belong there, and you will not take me back. I am in America, and I will not return to that small-minded village."

"Then you do what other Basque girls do if you want to remain. I take you to town and help you become a *domestique.*"

"I will not clean other people's dirt!"

"You do or you return to the old country."

Monique sank down on the sofa sullen and quiet, subdued and resolved to remaining in America and working for a living until she found another man.

Hannah could not stand to wait in the bedroom any longer. She crossed into the parlor, Max opened his arms, and she walked into them.

Bernard clasped his hands together. "Hannah, do you forgive a foolish old man?"

"There's nothing to forgive," she reached out and squeezed his hand.

"Thank you. And to show how I make a mistake right, when I take Monique to town, I bring back the priest so he ties the two of you together, yes?"

Hannah's smile became forced and her gaze shot up to Max's.

"What is this?" Bernard questioned, confused by Hannah's response to news he thought she would welcome. "My son, he does not ask you to marry him?" To Max he said, "Why do you wait?"

Max opened his mouth to warn the old man against meddling again, but Hannah placed a staying hand on his chest. "It's all right, Max." To Bernard she said, "Max has asked me to marry him, and we will be wed."

"In our own time, old man," Max added, and silently dared his father to continue to meddle.

Bernard held up his hands. "I learn my lesson. I do not push." He shrugged, unable to help himself. "But I do not want this woman to change her mind when she realizes the ogre my son is."

Hannah laughed at his joke, but inside she could not keep the concern from her mind. While she was certain that Emmett had followed through with his threat to divorce her shortly after she'd left him, she did not know what his reactions would be when Max had a lawyer contact him.

"I told you, as soon as my lawyer contacts me and sends the papers for you to attest to Hannah's thievery, you will have your money. Until then, if you want to collect so much as a flat dime, you will get on that train with me," Emmett spat out to the huge woman. Secretly he'd like nothing more at the moment than to leave bitch penniless on the platform where she .ood.

Wilma Timm glared at the man, then barreled onto the train in a huff. If that Hannah Turner person hadn't stolen her sewing machine, she never would have joined forces with that black-hearted devil, Emmett Turner. She knew a shifty, no-good ladies' man when she saw one. She plopped down next to an open window and stared out. What she saw and heard only served to confirm her disgust with the man.

"Emmett, ain't ya gonna take me along?" Sugar Lee begged Emmett, grabbing at the fine fabric of the lapel on his coat. "Please, please, I got your kid growin' in my belly."

He peeled her fingers from his clothing. "I already told you it isn't mine. So do not try to put responsibility for your stupidity on me. You'll not get a cent out of me. You're nothing but a cheap whore that I and many others before me used because there was no other whore in town."

"But I ain't been with nobody else since I started beddin' with you."

He threw back his head and laughed a hideous cackle. "You do not have a leg to stand on, and unless you can prove it, get out of my sight, because the very sight of you makes me sick." He shoved her from him with such force that she nearly tumbled backward. Without so much as a glance to see if she had fallen, he boarded the train.

Desperate to hold onto him, she cried to his back, "I got a paper you don't remember signing that says I ain't no cheap whore."

Standing just inside the train car, Emmett pivoted around and glared hatred at Sugar Lee. You'll need more than some *forged* paper."

Emmett left the whore where she stood and took a place across from Wilma Timm. "I should have private accommodations instead of being forced to sit here surrounded by such rabble," he grumbled.

Wilma Timm was neither impressed nor cowed by the man. "I ain't got no love for whores. But you should've done right by that little gal if she's carryin' your babe."

Emmett subconsciously rubbed his vest pocket, determined to make Hannah pay for putting him through such inconvenience. "Now, now, Wilma, how could I take Sugar Lee with me when you know that I am married to Hannah?"

"I'd still like to know for myself if you're really married to that woman who stole my sewing machine. Why was she as jumpy as a jackrabbit, and why'd she tell me she didn't have no man and didn't want one?"

Emmett balled his fists. He needed a drink to help him finish what Hannah started. He hated it when anyone questioned his word, and particularly when it was a woman. Fighting to keep his temper under control until he took proper care of his wife, he said, "I suppose you will just have

o remain in my company until we catch up with
her then, won't you?"

"You should remain in Hannah's company,"
Bernard instructed Max. "Petya and I, we do
these errands for you that you say you must take
care of in town."

"Petya went to bring the children home. Hannah needs help around the house while I take
care of business."

"What business errands can they be that I cannot handle them while I am in town settling
Monique at one of the Basque hotels? Or am I
too old for you to trust your papa to take care
of these tasks of yours?"

"Some things a man must take care of for himself," Max answered.

Bernard returned his son's conspiratorial smile,
although he did not understand what things Max
spoke of. Rather, he figured that it must be
something to do with love and hopefully a priest.

"You should not leave Hannah all alone out
here," Bernard lectured.

Hannah had insisted that Max accompany Bernard to town and talk to the lawyer, or Max
would not leave her alone.

"Bernard, you worry too much," Hannah said
coming out to the yard to be near to Max. "Furthermore, I will not be all alone. I have the baby
and Max agreed to go only if he stopped at the

Herrias on the way and had one of the younger children come over and care for the animals. Knowing Mara, she'll come running the moment he hears about the baby. So don't fret about me, Bernard."

Bernard sighed in defeat. "You get much rest for a few days while we are all away from the ranch. I go now to collect Monique and hurry-up Petya so you two say good-bye in private, yes?"

"Yes," they chorused.

They waited until Bernard had disappeared inside the house before Max took Hannah into his arms. "Papa is right. I do not like to leave you alone. It is not good."

Hannah cradled Max's face between her hands and gazed into his eyes. "Max, we've talked about this. You must go. I'll be fine." She smiled. "And just so you won't have to worry about me, I promise to bar the door and not let any strangers inside."

Thirty-five

Hannah lay in bed, nuzzling her face agains
Max's pillow, reveling in his male scent, and star
ing out the bedroom window at the incredibl
blue sky that greeted the morning. She stretched
and listened to a bird sing outside the window
Max had been gone nearly a week and would
return shortly. Finally all would be right with he
world.

Range began to fuss, and Hannah got out o:
bed to see to him. She picked him up and ruffled
the downy black hair on his head.

She cooed, "Range, with all that dark hair,
do believe you are going to grow up to look jus
like your daddy."

"My, my, I must say that is simply impossible
Hannah, since his daddy has blond hair."

At the frighteningly familiar deep voice, Han
nah swung around to come face-to-face with Em
mett.

"W-what . . . h-how . . . w-when . . ." Fea:
closed her throat and cut off her breath.

Emmett leaned against the doorjamb and

rossed his ankles. "Still the frightened little hurch mouse, my dear?"

Hannah gathered Range in closer against her hest and tilted her chin. "Get out!"

"Is that any way to treat the father of your aby?" A frown drew a line between his brows. Now, what is this about the baby's daddy having ark hair? I do believe you neglected to answer he."

"I do not consider you the father."

A vicious smile grew on his lips, and his eyes olled up and down her body.

Hannah put Range back in his bed and swung round to face Emmett. "The least you can do wait in the parlor while I dress."

His eyes slid over her again. "Why? I've seen ou naked before." He reached out and fingered he collar on her nightgown, only to have her ecoil from him.

Emmett smiled. He could feel her fright; the ir was charged with it. It was almost as good as ex or a drink. "You look wonderful, Hannah. "his broken-down ranch must agree with you." Iis face turned ugly. "You didn't think I was go-ng to let you go so easily, did you?"

Hannah grabbed one of Max's shirts and abbed her arms into it. "How did you find me?"

"I told him, you thief!" Wilma Timm stepped rom behind Emmett. Range gurgled and Vilma's eyes went to where the baby kicked his rms and legs. "You not only stole my sewing machine, you stole my livelihood and the man had all picked out."

"You told Emmett where I got off the train What're you doing here with him?" Hannah asked.

"I not only told him, I showed him and got directions from those dining station owners. He' goin' to pay me the money I lost because of you," she spat out, then asked, "Whose baby is it?"

"Mine," they both said.

"Range is mine," Hannah repeated.

Wilma's gazed settled on Emmett. "You go and get this one pregnant too?"

"Shut up and go out and get me a bottle Then you can wait in the buggy if you want you money. You have witnessed all you need to attes to Hannah's character as well as her thievery." Emmett waited while a grumbling Wilma Timm pounded from the house, returned with his whis key, and left before he smirked at Hannah.

He uncorked the bottle and took a long swig "You should not have run away from me. You know I could not let you get away with that. Now unless you do exactly as I instruct, I'll have tha bitch, Wilma Timm, on the witness stand to tes tify that you are a thief, living here with som unknown man, and therefore an unfit mother to raise *our* son."

"What do you want from me?" Hannah cried determined not to lose her dignity and beg while she watched Emmett guzzle the whiskey.

"You will return to St. Louis with me and be the dutiful wife until such time as I determine to divorce you in front of the entire town."

"You came after me so you can save face?"

He ignored her remark and continued with his litany. "Then you can come back here and live with your sand and sagebrush rancher, raise jackrabbits, and breed like them for all I care."

"You mean all this, the reason you followed me, is your bruised pride?"

He upended the bottle again and wiped his mouth with the back of his hand. This time he did not ignore her. "No one leaves Emmett Turner unless I say so. No one. I made you and I'll break you."

"I am not so sure of that," Max growled from the doorway behind the man Hannah had run from. "I see now why you ran and did what you did, Hannah. This man did not harm you or Range?"

"We're all right," Hannah supplied.

"Whoever you are and wherever you came from, you are interfering between a man and his wife," Emmett snarled, a slur evident in his voice.

Max disregarded the man and asked Hannah, "You are sure you are all right?"

"I'm fine now that you're here," she said to Max, although her voice quivered.

Max moved to Hannah's side and placed a protective arm around her shoulders. "You entered

my home without my permission, so you bette
leave now."

"My God, who does this foreigner think he'
talking to?" Emmett sneered, trying to focus hi
bleary eyes.

"An intruder."

"I'll have you know, immigrant, I am thi
woman's"—he waved a hand to indicate Hannah-
"husband. What do you think of that?"

"I think maybe we go outside and leave Han
nah to dress while we settle this, yes?"

Beginning to sway, Emmett snarled, "I'm nc
going anywhere unless—"

Max's reactions were lightning-quick. H
twisted Turner's arm behind his back an
marched a yelping, whimpering Turner from th
house none too gently.

Hannah hurriedly tossed on her blue ginghar
dress and ran from the house in time to se
Max's big fist connect with Emmett's pretty face
Emmett screamed and landed in a heap on th
ground, crying and cradling his face.

"I'll have you jailed for this. The law is on m
side!"

"I do not think so. While I was in town m
friend checked and you filed papers to dissolv
your marriage and deny your fatherhood of Han
nah's baby."

"You mean I am divorced?" Hannah askec
and held her breath.

"Since last fall."

"And Emmett has no legal right to Range?"

"His papers say he is not the papa. My lawyer friend says that he did this because he does not want the child to have his money. He says that as long as you do not want to say this man is the papa, he is not the papa." Then to Turner he added, "I think you better leave my land before I shoot you for trespassing maybe."

Emmett was seething to think that some foreigner sheep rancher would be smart enough to check on Hannah's legal status. Well, he wasn't done with her yet! Emmett's need for revenge was twisting in his gut when an idea came to him.

"You are still a thief and I have a witness to prove it. I'll see you in jail, Hannah, before I allow you to remain here."

"You have no witness," Max answered.

"That's where you're wrong, immigrant. Wilma Timm will testify that Hannah stole her sewing machine."

Wilma Timm had been sitting in the buggy, listening to the exchange until she had an opportunity to put in her two cents worth. "There ain't no thievin' to testify about. A little bit ago the rancher bought my machine, and paid a fair price for it too," she said smugly, getting down from the buggy.

Hannah swung her attention to Max. "You paid her for the machine?"

"What do I say, I have come to like the clothes you make."

Hannah threw her arms around his neck and hugged him. "You are making light."

"Wait just a damned minute," Emmett sniveled. "Where the hell does that leave me?"

"I brought the answer to that for you," Max said, and called, "You can come out now."

Emmett was horrified and his eyes rounded when he saw who the foreigner had hailed. Sugar Lee and two monsters of men on either side of her approached him.

"This is your legal husband, yes?"

"Yeah, and I got the papers to prove it," Sugar Lee said, and threw her arms around Emmett's neck. "I told you about the paper I got, remember, honeybuns, when you married me that night? You was drinkin' a lot that night though. But I was so thrilled to be Mrs. Sugar Lee Turner that I wired my brothers. They came into town on the same train you left on. Wasn't it just plumb luck that we was able to get on the next train? Now, Emmett darlin', I want you to meet my two brothers Bubba Joe and Billy Ray. They're gonna be livin' with us from now on."

Emmett gulped, and his gaze went to the two bruisers with their huge arms crossed over huge chests, glaring at him, and he reluctantly and meekly nodded his consent. With that pair present, he had no other choice.

"Oh, and honeybuns, since I got your kid growin' in my belly, we ain't gonna drink no more." She smiled sweetly at Max. "I sure am

glad we ran into each other in town at that la
yer's office. Why, I might never of found my hon
eybuns otherwise. Much obliged to ya."

Then she took Emmett by the ear and led him
toward the rented buggy. "It's time for us all to
go home to St. Louis and get all settled in that
big mansion house of yours. Emmett's sorry if
he inconvenienced you fine folks any, ain't ya,
Emmett?"

Emmett humbly nodded, for the first time discovering what it meant to be forced to endure
humiliation.

"Wait!" Wilma Timm hollered. "You mind
givin' me a ride back to the train station?"

"We don't mind none at all, huh, honeybuns?"

Hannah stood and watched in astonishment
while Emmett meekly sat between Sugar Lee's
brothers and Sugar Lee drove from the ranch.

"I think Sugar Lee's brothers will keep him in
line maybe, yes?"

Hannah nodded. "Max, does all this mean I
was free from Emmett before I met you? And
Emmett is married to that woman, who is going
to have his baby?"

"That is what it all means."

"Emmett never wanted children."

"His loss. Soon we will receive the papers from
St. Louis. My papa waits in town for them to arrive and then he will bring the priest, we will
marry and file papers of our own to make Range
ours, yes?"

Oh, yes!" She threw herself into his arms and kissed him with such force that she nearly knocked him off his feet.

When they came up for air, he panted, "I think you nearly . . . how do you say it . . . sweep me off my feet."

"Swept."

"Ah, yes, you nearly *swept* me off my feet."

She tenderly touched his lips with her fingertips, her love for this man threatening to overwhelm her.

An unanswered question came to her. "But how did you know about Wilma Timm?"

"You told me about the sewing machine, and when I arrived at the ranch I saw the same woman here sitting in the buggy that I saw at the dining station on my way back from town. I talked to her, yes?"

"You know, my mother always said, you make your bed, you lie in it. To my way of thinking, I can no longer argue with my mother. I have been making your bed for months, and for the rest of my life I plan to lie in it . . . with you."

Max whisked her into the warm strength of his arms. "We do not argue with your mama."

They laughed until Hannah grew serious and pulled back. "Despite everything, I'd like to think now that my mother meant well. And I think I will write to her and tell her about Range and us."

"It is a good idea to forgive and forget."

As the implications and reality of the event that had occurred began to sink in, tears of relief and joy threatened Hannah until she blinked and looked away to wipe them. It was then that she noticed Petya and the children running toward them.

"Hannah, Hannah! We saw that mean old lizard woman in that buggy with those people. She didn't hurt you none, did she?" Franc cried, coming to a halt in front of Hannah, Panda Pie right behind her.

Hannah picked up Panda Pie and ringed an arm around Franc's shoulders. "Everything is absolutely perfect now."

After Hannah had fed the hungry family, and put Sammy down for a nap on the big bed next to Range, Hannah and Max told of their plans and explained what had happened, in terms the children could understand, and answered all their questions and concerns.

"You children, it is time you go help your uncle with chores now," Max announced when there was a lull in the conversation.

Lissa and André got up and preceded Petya through the kitchen. Petya stopped and said, "Franc, my little kid, you do not join us and leave them to be alone, eh?"

"I'll be there in a minute," Franc answered, and lingered in the parlor on the rug, scratching Panda Pie behind the ears until the door closed behind the others.

"Is there something you want to say, Franc?" Hannah asked, noticing Franc's fidgeting.

"Guess I'll be leavin' the ranch now."

Hannah's gentle smile turned to dismay, and Max raised a staying hand when Franc labored to her feet. "Franc, while I was in town talking to the lawyer about papers to adopt Range, I also am talking about papers for you, too, if you want."

"Do I ever!" she squealed, her eyes wide with uncontrollable delight, while Hannah gasped in disbelieving joy and threw her arms around Max's neck.

"Oh, Max," Hannah murmured, choked up with great happiness.

Franc's eager gaze shifted between Hannah and Max. "You mean I'm really gonna be your kid?"

"I think you are already our kid, but maybe we make it legal, yes?"

"Yes! Yes! Yes! Gol-ly, wait till I tell the others," Franc exclaimed, then raced from the house screaming.

"Oh, Max, I love you. How can I ever repay you?" Hannah asked, nearly overcome with emotion.

He pulled her into his lap. "When you heal from the baby, I think I know a proper way maybe."

"No maybe about it."

SURRENDER TO THE SPLENDOR OF THE ROMANCES OF F. ROSANNE BITTNER!

CARESS   (3791, $5.99/$6.99)

COMANCHE SUNSET   (3568, $4.99/$5.99)

HEARTS SURRENDER   (2945, $4.50/$5.50)

LAWLESS LOVE   (3877, $4.50/$5.50)

PRAIRIE EMBRACE   (3160, $4.50/$5.50)

RAPTURE'S GOLD   (3879, $4.50/$5.50)

SHAMELESS   (4056, $5.99/$6.99)

Available wherever paperbacks are sold, or order direct from the Publisher. Send cover price plus 50¢ per copy for mailing and handling to Penguin USA, P.O. Box 999, c/o Dept. 17109, Bergenfield, NJ 07621. Residents of New York and Tennessee must include sales tax. DO NOT SEND CASH.